Praise for
Sisters of the Sari

"This compelling debut novel is a cross-cultural story of unlikely friendships, forbidden love, and families lost and found. *Sisters of the Sari* is armchair traveling at its best. It's a story I'll always remember."

—Laura Fitzgerald, national bestselling author of *Veil of Roses* and *Dreaming in English*

"A vivid portrayal of a woman's personal journey to redefine herself and make a difference in the complex, foreign culture of urban south India."

—Anjali Banerjee, author of *Haunting Jasmine*

"A captivating tale of one woman's quest to improve the life of another . . . and discovering herself along the way. A delightful debut that's a colorful portrait of southern India, painted with both touching emotion and wry humor."

—Shobhan Bantwal, author of *The Unexpected Son*

Sisters *of* the Sari

Brenda L. Baker

NAL Accent
Published by New American Library, a division of
Penguin Group (USA) Inc., 375 Hudson Street,
New York, New York 10014, USA
Penguin Group (Canada), 90 Eglinton Avenue East, Suite 700, Toronto,
Ontario M4P 2Y3, Canada (a division of Pearson Penguin Canada Inc.)
Penguin Books Ltd., 80 Strand, London WC2R 0RL, England
Penguin Ireland, 25 St. Stephen's Green, Dublin 2,
Ireland (a division of Penguin Books Ltd.)
Penguin Group (Australia), 250 Camberwell Road, Camberwell, Victoria 3124,
Australia (a division of Pearson Australia Group Pty. Ltd.)
Penguin Books India Pvt. Ltd., 11 Community Centre, Panchsheel Park,
New Delhi - 110 017, India
Penguin Group (NZ), 67 Apollo Drive, Rosedale, Auckland 0632,
New Zealand (a division of Pearson New Zealand Ltd.)
Penguin Books (South Africa) (Pty.) Ltd., 24 Sturdee Avenue,
Rosebank, Johannesburg 2196, South Africa

Penguin Books Ltd., Registered Offices:
80 Strand, London WC2R 0RL, England

First published by NAL Accent, an imprint of New American Library,
a division of Penguin Group (USA) Inc.

First Printing, June 2011
10 9 8 7 6 5 4 3 2 1

LIBRARY OF CONGRESS CATALOGING-IN-PUBLICATION DATA:

Baker, Brenda L.
Sisters of the Sari/Brenda L. Baker.
p. cm.
ISBN 978-0-451-23321-9
1. Women executives—Fiction. 2. Americans—India—Fiction. 3. Female friendship—Fiction. 4. Self-realization in women—Fiction. I. Title.
PS3602.A5848S57 2011
813'.6—dc22 2011003184

Set in Garamond
Designed by Ginger Legato

Printed in the United States of America

This novel is dedicated to

Shanty, whose dignity and integrity in the face of adversity inspired it

Lalitha, whose generous spirit gave it a home to grow in

Sisters *of* the Sari

Pondy Bizarre

YOU KNOW THAT LITTLE VOICE—the one that whispers, "Don't go down there!" when you hear a spooky noise in the basement? Does yours work? Mine seems to be broken. Oh, I get warnings—they're just so damn cryptic. Take India, for example.

It was four a.m. I'd been standing by the baggage carousel in the Chennai airport for two hours and had just learned that my suitcase was circling a carousel in Beijing. I heard my little voice. Now, if it had said something like, "Flee—before you lose half your life savings and two-thirds of a major muscle group!" I'd have been on the next plane to anywhere in a heartbeat. But it said, and I quote, "Well, this sucks." What kind of a dire warning is that?

Three hours later I stood in the bathroom of my hotel suite sponging cheese sauce, courtesy of turbulence over the Atlantic, off my sweat suit. I had a decision to make: crash or go shopping. On the crash side there was exhaustion, jet lag and the general grumpiness that follows loss of luggage. On the shopping side there was the ninety-degree temperature, the ninety-five percent humidity and the fact that my wardrobe for the foreseeable future consisted of one rancid sweat suit. I decided to go shopping.

When I chose India for my vacation, I had no desire to shuffle around the well-worn tourist trails of the Taj Mahal and Red Fort with thousands of other camera-clicking tourists. To ensure a less commercialized holiday experience, I chose to visit the southern tip of the subcontinent, where tourism had yet to become a major industry and I had a better chance at an authentic Indian experience. So for my first foray into what I hoped would be the "real" India, I asked the clerk at the front desk where she bought her clothes. She recommended Pondy Bazaar.

As my car and driver weren't due to arrive until later in the afternoon, she walked me to the entrance of the hotel and pointed out a cluster of bright yellow vehicles parked just outside the hotel gates. They looked like a failed mating between the front end of a motorcycle and the back end of a minivan, with one wheel at the front, two wheels at the back and no doors or windows. She told me they were called autos and advised me not to pay more than seventy rupees each way. This was just pure sadism. The price may have been seventy rupees for a cute young Indian desk clerk in a tight pink sari, but the going rate for an old tourist in a gamy sweat suit was two hundred rupees.

I climbed into the first auto in front of the gate, feeling cheated but too disoriented to haggle. There were no seat belts or handholds. I was forced to clutch the metal bars forming the back of the driver's seat as he careened off into oncoming traffic, dodging livestock, buses and pedestrians with millimeters to spare, while I bounced around on the hard bench in the back of the vehicle, wondering, in the intervals between trying to prevent my breakfast from joining the cheese sauce, how a country could claim to drive on the left if direction of travel in all lanes appeared to be optional.

Five minutes and ten cc of adrenaline after leaving the hotel, we stopped in front of a large granite building. I paid the driver and staggered up the steps. A uniformed doorman ushered me into the blissfully air-conditioned store, where a charming young man added new dimensions to the term "excess baggage" by attempting to sell me a five-hundred-pound bronze statue of the god Shiva, half an acre of silk rug and a nearly life-sized teak elephant before admitting that this was not actually Pondy Bazaar. I was in the Government Craft Store. I may have said some uncomplimentary things about his mother before stomping out to say something much stronger to the auto driver, who, of course, was long gone.

One hour, two autos, three hundred rupees and a quart of adrenaline later, I finally made it to Pondy Bazaar, a kilometer-long stretch of clothing stores and street vendors. At noon on Saturday it was a heaving mass of bargain-hunting Indian families. I struggled through the crowds, looking for something even remotely wearable. Indian fashion seemed to rely heavily on sequins, beads and ornate embroidery, none of which enhance the mature female form. Eventually I found a black T-shirt sedately declaring WHOSE YO MOMA across the chest in hot pink. Not exactly my style, but by then I'd figured out there wasn't going to be anything more appealing at Pondy Bazaar and decided to buy it.

I reached into my front pocket for money. My hand poked back out through the neat little slit razored by the thief who had removed my wallet. About thirty seconds after that, I slipped in a cowpat and fell heavily on my right hip.

I'd like to think that under normal circumstances the good citizens of Chennai would have flocked to my aid. But let's be realistic here; there are no circumstances involving theft and cow dung that fall remotely within the bounds of normal. By now the combination of adrenaline and jet lag had raised my mood meter to the spontaneous-combustion mark. I yelled out a few tension-relieving scatological opinions on Indian bovine hygiene. The good citizens of Chennai backed cautiously away from me. I had personal space again for the first time since getting out of the auto.

I closed my mouth and limped off, intending to put considerable distance between myself and anyone who may have witnessed my little temper tantrum before I asked for help. My hip hurt. Cow dung squelched its way deeper into my shoe with every step. I'd been walking for about twenty minutes when I heard a high-pitched voice call out, "Madam! Madam! You problem?"

I looked up. My first sight of Santoshi was through tears. I hadn't realized I was crying.

No Good Deed Goes Unpunished

❁ ❁ ❁ ❁ ❁

AFTER SIX HOURS OF SWEEPING hospital rooms and scouring pots, Santoshi's back hurt more than usual. She had not eaten since the previous day and it was a long walk back to the shelter. The warden saved no food for latecomers. She hurried through the crowds of Saturday shoppers in T. Nagar.

She spotted the white tourist the instant she rounded the corner of Rangoli Street. White people were a common sight in Chennai nowadays but not in the parts Santoshi inhabited. After a short inner battle between curiosity and hunger, she slowed down to get a better look. She saw a stocky older woman with short gray hair wearing a dark blue sweater and pants. Santoshi did not approve of women displaying their bottoms in men's clothes. The woman walked stiffly, head down, hands fisted, arms slightly bent at the elbows. She favored her right foot. Perhaps she was in pain. Everyone knew white people were rich and generous. This one might need help, might give her a reward. Putting aside her hunger, Santoshi crossed the street.

"Madam!" she called out. "Madam! You problem?"

The woman stopped and lifted her head. Her face was streaked with tears. Santoshi could see they were not from pain. This woman was angry.

"Madam," Santoshi repeated, "you problem? Foot bad?"

The small muscles under the woman's eyes relaxed slightly. She took a deep breath to suppress the tears. "My wallet was stolen," she said. "I need to find my hotel. I don't know where I am."

Santoshi did not understand most of what the woman said. She did recognize the words "hotel" and "where" and responded to the easiest word first. "Madam, this T. Nagar district," she said, then moved on to the more difficult task of forming a question. "Name hotel, madam?"

"Taj something. I don't remember." The woman's face brightened. "Wait! I have the key!" She reached into the pocket of her sweater and pulled out not a key, but a small plastic rectangle. "Here, this hotel."

Santoshi had never learned to read English, but she recognized the hotel's pink palm tree logo printed on the plastic. "Madam, very far, madam. Take auto."

"My wallet was stolen."

"No understand, madam."

The woman raised her voice and spoke each word individually. "I. Have. No. Money."

No money. Santoshi sighed. Although her hope of reward had evaporated and her conversational ability was strained to the limit, she could not just walk away from the situation. She thought. An auto to the hotel would cost at least fifty rupees, much more money than she had. She could walk the distance easily, but this overweight, overdressed foreigner with a bad foot would never manage it. It would have to be the bus.

"Madam take bus. Six rupees. I give."

The woman squinted, as though she had never heard of such a thing. "The bus?"

"Yes, madam."

"What bus?"

Describing in English how to take the number 59A bus from T. Nagar to the Thousand Lights district defeated Santoshi's linguistic skills. "Madam ask."

"Ask who?"

"Persons, madam."

"I'm asking you."

Obedience to authority fell somewhere between breathing and eating in Santoshi's survival strategy. With her limited understanding she heard an order in the woman's words. She resigned herself to the loss of half a day's wages and a long, hungry afternoon on the bus. Maybe the gods would remember this day. "Madam, come. I take madam."

The woman wiped her eyes and then her face with the sleeve of her sweater, straightened her shoulders and said, "Okay. Thank you. Thank you very much."

Santoshi led the way along the main road to the bus stand. They made slow progress because the white woman, instead of walking on the road like a normal person, insisted on using the sidewalk. Santoshi did her best to steer her limping charge around the piles of garbage and the carefully piled offerings of the fruit vendors. As they threaded their way through a cluster of parked motorcycles, Santoshi tried her English again.

"Country, madam?"

"I'm from Canada. Where are you from?"

"Madam?"

The woman put her palm on her chest. "Canada. My country." Then she extended her hand toward Santoshi, palm up. "Your country?"

Santoshi looked sharply up at the woman's face. Was this woman stupid or crazy? The woman raised her eyebrows and smiled. She'd made a joke! For the first time Santoshi saw a real person beneath the swollen eyes and sweat-soaked hair. She smiled back. "India, madam."

Santoshi stepped over a sleeping dog and tried again. "Husband, madam?"

"Not anymore," the white woman replied, studying the dog's scabbed back as she skirted around it. "I'm divorced. Do you have a husband?"

"Madam?"

The woman palmed her chest and held out her hand again. "No husband. You husband?"

"No, madam. Sorry, madam."

Edging gingerly around a cow browsing through the garbage, the white woman contributed her own question to the conversation. "What is your name?"

"Santoshi, madam. You good name, madam?"

"Kiria."

Neither woman could pronounce the other's name. They walked in silence until they came to a pile of sand blocking the sidewalk in front of a construction site. Santoshi stepped into the road to walk around the sand. She looked back and saw that Kiria intended to walk between the sand and the building.

"Madam! No!" she called out. But it was too late.

Kiria, focused on watching where she placed her feet in the slippery sand, did not see the man urinating against the wall behind it until she bumped into him. They stared at each other, mouths and eyes wide with shock, for the few seconds it took Santoshi to scramble around the sand pile. She grabbed Kiria's arm and pulled her into the road.

"He peed on me! Did you see that? You incontinent degenerate!" Kiria called back over her shoulder.

But at least she was willing to walk on the road now. She limped along, grumbling and holding the fabric of her pants away from her legs. When they finally reached the bus stop, Santoshi, exhausted from steering her unwelcome charge through traffic, prayed for the bus to come soon.

The Mirror

❁ ❁ ❁ ❁ ❁

DO YOU BELIEVE IN GOOD LUCK? I don't. I believe in hard work, smart choices and captaining my own destiny. Bad luck, on the other hand, does exist. It's the blind hand of chaos that reaches out now and again and whaps you on the back of the head. I call it the Slapstick Force.

If I'd been running my own rescue, I'd have sent myself a handsome, debonair businessman in an air-conditioned limousine to ply me with champagne and regale me with amusing anecdotes of Chennai's glitterati while his chauffeur drove us back to the hotel. The Slapstick Force sent me a scrawny old midget with bus fare.

I'm one of the shortest people I know and the top of Santoshi's head barely reached my shoulder. She was not exactly skeletal, but she had so little body fat I could see the muscles and tendons clearly under her skin. Her cheeks sucked inward where her teeth should have been, accenting high cheekbones and large, jet-black eyes. She wore a frayed sari in a peculiar gray-green that could not have been the original color. I estimated her to be in her sixties or at least a very well-used late fifties. At first I thought she was a beggar, but it soon became apparent she was my only hope of getting back to the hotel.

Santoshi and I made a few abortive attempts to communicate as she led me to the bus stop. She had a limited vocabulary, zero acquaintance with grammar and an excessive attachment to the word "madam." Perhaps we'd have done better if I'd tried harder, but with a liberal application of urine—don't ask—supplementing cheese sauce and dung, my sartorial crisis had reached epic proportions. I was far too preoccupied to devote full attention to her limited English.

By the time we arrived at the bus stop, I'd recovered from my little episode at Pondy Bazaar enough to notice things like hunger, thirst and the alarming edema ballooning my hands and feet. The bus stop was a long concrete shelter with every square inch of shade occupied by waiting passengers. We stood in the sun.

When I wasn't watching my extremities swell, I found myself wondering where the bus fare would come from. Santoshi carried no purse or bag. Was she going to pull the fare out of her bra? Actually, she had a much better hiding place. As we waited for the bus, she untucked the tail end of her sari from her waist, untied the knot in the end of the fabric, pulled out two ten-rupee bills and a small coin, knotted one ten-rupee bill back into the end of her sari and tucked the knot back in at her waist. If I'd had such a neat hiding place . . . Well, no point in what-ifs.

Now, here's some advice if you ever want to take a city bus in India—don't even think about it. The bus that finally came was packed, sardines-in-a-tin packed, resulting in some unavoidable familiarity with my fellow travelers. When a particularly good pothole created a bowling-pin effect among the standing passengers, I learned more about one poor young man's anatomy than either of us really wanted me to know. Hopefully, his reproductive abilities were not permanently impaired.

Bouncing around on the bus, wrapped in my own misery, I still managed to reflect that our fare had cost Santoshi over half the money in her sari. Judging by her appearance, it was difficult to imagine she had a stash of cash at home, if she even had a home. I would return to an air-conditioned hotel room complete with a shower, a TV and room service. What would she go back to? Looking down at Santoshi's neatly parted, heavily oiled hair, I realized that although I was half a foot taller, nearly three times heavier and immeasurably richer, there was no contest as to who was the bigger person. Somehow, I felt that I had incurred a debt far greater than a few rupees' bus fare.

Santoshi couldn't tell me where she lived, but the very polite young man whose armpit was hosting my ear offered translation services, and an older woman seated by my hip wrote down the address on a corner ripped from her newspaper. As we pulled up in front of the hotel, I promised Santoshi that I'd pay her back before squeezing my way off the bus.

Inside the hotel, I stopped hopefully at the front desk to inquire if my suitcase had turned up. Little Miss Pink Sari regretfully informed me it had not. I was seriously considering spending my vacation sitting naked in my hotel room when Little Miss Pink Sari, probably tipped off by my lack of shopping bags and the eau de barnyard wafting up from my right shoe, asked if I'd like the hotel to buy some clothes and put them on my bill. She'd been wildly unsuccessful at giving shopping advice the first time around, but everyone deserves a second chance, right? And seriously, how could she do any worse than I had?

The next morning, I stood in front of the full-length mirror in my room vowing never, never, never to accept fashion assistance from an Indian hotel desk clerk ever again. Some responsibility for my resemblance to a dump truck on its way to a party could be laid at my door. My size fours went to Goodwill decades ago. But by far the bulk of the effect was created by the humongous harem pants and shapeless dress of the outfit, called a churidar, that had been delivered to my room the previous evening. An avalanche of appliquéd crystals adorning the front did nothing to minimize the ensemble's proportions, nor did the two yards of matching shawl, called a dupatta. According to the label, I had a size small. Small what? Pregnant elephant?

Sincerely regretting the lapse in judgment that had allowed the desk clerk yet another outlet for her sadistic sense of humor, I donned my sunglasses to avoid blinding myself and sparkled my way down to the hotel lobby. Little Miss Pink Sari gave me a delighted smile and came around the counter to adjust the dupatta so that the ends trailed down my back. Apparently, I'd been wearing it backward.

My driver was waiting for me in the lobby, a short, wiry man with an enormous and constant smile. His name, most appropriately, was Joy and he had been ripped off by the same English school as Santoshi. We spent a few hours at Western Union sorting out the cash crisis and then I gave him the piece of newsprint with Santoshi's address.

Joy did his level best to talk me out of the excursion, even going so far as to rope in a few bystanders to dissuade me. Madam could be robbed. Madam could get dirty. Hey, déjà vu. I asked if Madam could get killed. No, Madam could not get killed. I foolishly told Joy that I could handle anything else and he reluctantly gave in.

Santoshi lived in Vyasarpadi, an area of Chennai definitely not on the tourist map. Cement-block buildings crowded right up to the edge of the road, which we shared with motorcycles and flat wooden wagons drawn by plodding white bullocks with long, gaudily painted horns. Half-naked children and tired women squatted in dark doorways, pointing at the car and exclaiming when they saw me. There were almost no street signs, but fortunately, the male reluctance to ask directions is only a Western phenomenon. Joy eventually found the place by dint of stopping every hundred feet or so and conducting extended arm-waving and hand-pointing sessions with auto drivers and shopkeepers.

Now I'm going to describe this building to you because I want you to understand the lengths I was willing to go to pay Santoshi back. It was single storied, square and flat roofed. Blotches of black mold obscured the original pale blue paint. Iron bars covered the windows, and a locked iron gate protected the doorway. To add to the overall curb appeal, it stood beside the Otteri Nullah river, which, like every other river in the city, was basically an open sewer. Mold had also colonized the unpainted concrete walls inside, where the heat absorbed by the flat roof raised the temperature to just below broiling. The stench of baby shit, urine and human sweat overpowered the miasma from the river.

In assuring me that Madam would not be killed, Joy had obviously overlooked the very real possibilities of heatstroke and asphyxiation.

Amusing the Gods

MARY ELIZABETH SAT IN THE warden's room waiting for Banu to come in. Like most of the rooms Mary Elizabeth worked in, this one was shabby and grimy. Priya, the warden, lacked the character to motivate herself and her charges to improve their surroundings. The single window looked out over the street, where a jasmine seller was setting out her evening wares. The scent of romance wafted into the room. Mary Elizabeth's father liked jasmine. She decided to buy some after the interview on her way home as a little celebration. Today was a good-news day, a rarity in Mary Elizabeth's line of work. She had purposefully left this interview for the end of the day, keeping it fresh to tell her father when she got home.

"Good evening, madam." A scarred woman in a faded cotton nightdress entered the room.

"Good evening, Banu," Mary Elizabeth greeted her client. "Come. Sit. I have good news."

Banu sat on the edge of the empty chair. "Tell me, madam."

"I have found a surgeon who can fix your fingers."

"I will use my hands again?"

"He says he must see them first, but, probably, yes. There is nothing wrong with the bones and muscles. The skin can be cut, made loose."

"And the rest of me, madam?" Banu raised her eyes hopefully.

Banu's flesh, from her jaw to her pubic area and from her fingertips to her elbows, was a gnarled mass of burnt tissue. When her sister-in-law poured cooking oil on her and shoved her into the gas flame of the cooker, Banu had been wearing a cheap nylon sari. The pleats at her waist had melted and clung to her hands as she pulled the burning fabric away from her body, searing away the flesh, leaving behind useless, contracted claws. Her belly, chest, neck and lower jaw were less damaged. She had no ears.

Mary Elizabeth did not allow her expression to reflect her thoughts. "No," she said levelly. "I am sorry, Banu. That is a much more difficult operation. I have not found a doctor who will do it yet."

Banu looked down at the twisted remains of her hands. "Better that I die."

"What kind of talk is that? God spared your life. Who are you to talk disrespectfully of God's wishes?"

Banu struggled to be silent. Her anger won out. "The gods, madam," Banu hissed in a low voice, "married me to a weak, stupid man. The gods ruined my father and he could not pay the full dowry. The gods gave my husband's mother and sister a great anger toward me. The gods, madam, spared my life only to laugh at my future suffering. Why should I entertain them?"

In twenty-five years of social work Mary Elizabeth had handled countless situations like this one. She knew exactly what to say. "You are angry now, but you will not be angry forever, Banu. Wait. Accept the operation on your hands. When you can use your hands again, then you will feel hope again. I have seen this before. Trust me."

There was a rise in the noise level from the street. The two women looked out the window and saw a plump white woman getting out of the backseat of a white Ambassador car with an *!ncredible !ndia* logo on the side. She had short gray hair and wore a beautiful pink churidar. One end of her chiffon dupatta caught in the car door as she closed it. She stood, hands on hips, looking at the building, then walked toward the gate. The dupatta slid off her shoulders and fell to the ground beside the car, where the driver, apparently knowing this would happen, was already in position to pick it up.

Mary Elizabeth rose and walked to the front door to greet the unexpected visitor. The door was open for breeze, but the iron gate was locked. She spoke through the bars. "Can I help you, madam?" As an Anglo Indian educated in English, Mary Elizabeth was justifiably proud of her English skills.

"I hope so. My name is Kiria Langdon and I'm looking for a woman named Santoshi." Unlike Mary Elizabeth, Kiria had no experience of hiding her reaction to disfigurement. Her eyes widened in shock as Banu moved up behind Mary Elizabeth's shoulder.

"Go to warden and get the key," Mary Elizabeth said to Banu in Tamil. Then she turned to Kiria and switched back to English. "I sent Banu for the gate key. My name is Mary Elizabeth. I am the social worker here. Why do you want to see Santoshi?"

"She helped me yesterday. I want to pay her back."

"Oh, are you the lady from Pondy Bazaar? Santoshi told us about you. An unpleasant experience."

"Well, it would have been a lot worse without Santoshi. What is this place?"

"This is the Radhakrishna Short Stay Home for Women."

Priya came trotting up to the gate. Normally she would have handed the key to one of the inmates and stayed watching her favorite afternoon soap opera, but the novelty of a white visitor was far more exciting than any television program. She smiled broadly as she reached her arm through the bars and inserted a key into the sturdy padlock hanging on the outside of the gate.

"Who is this?" she asked Mary Elizabeth.

"This is the woman Santoshi helped yesterday. She has come to see Santoshi."

Priya flung open the gate. She stepped back, pressed her palms together in front of her chest and said, *"Vanakam."*

"Welcome," Mary Elizabeth translated, gesturing Kiria into the shelter.

Mary Elizabeth knew perfectly well that the shelter was not an ideal place to host a tourist. She looked around at the unpainted concrete walls, the women sleeping on the grimy floors, the half-naked children, and knew she could be in trouble for this if the white woman was a journalist. But the money was important to Santoshi. Mary Elizabeth put aside concern for herself and led the white woman into the main room of the shelter. "Get our visitor a chair. Turn off the television," she ordered Priya. "Santoshi, where are you?"

Santoshi came forward from the clump of staring women. "Welcome, madam."

"Hello, Santoshi." Kiria tried to hide her disgust at the conditions in the shelter with a weak smile. "I've come to pay you back."

"She is here to return your money," Mary Elizabeth translated.

Santoshi's eyes flicked to Priya, who had not entirely believed the story of helping a crying white woman. A shelter inmate placed one of the office chairs beside Kiria.

"Please sit," Mary Elizabeth said.

Kiria looked dubiously at the chair's frayed cane seat and dark, sticky arms. "It's okay. I've only got a minute."

Mary Elizabeth suppressed a smile. This white woman had no control over her facial expressions at all.

Kiria turned to Mary Elizabeth. "Would you tell Santoshi that I was very disoriented yesterday and I'm sorry I didn't thank her properly. I'm very grateful for her help. I'd like to give her a reward."

Mary Elizabeth translated for Santoshi.

Everyone in the room except Kiria knew what would happen to money so publicly announced. Most of the women looked down at the floor. Priya kept her face steady; only the reflexive curl of her fingers betrayed her. Mary Elizabeth and Santoshi showed no sign of their thoughts.

"My duty, madam," Santoshi said solemnly.

Unnoticed by any of the adults, a toddler had crept up to Kiria's side. Fascinated by the white skin, the child reached out and gently touched Kiria's hand. Kiria flicked her wrist, hitting the girl hard on the side of the head.

"Oh my God! I'm sorry. I'm so sorry. I thought it was a fly." Kiria squatted down and reached out. Her loud voice and strange words terrified the girl, who ran back into the crowd of women.

"It was an accident," Mary Elizabeth said to the toddler in Tamil. "She thought you were a fly. Come here, Meeta. Show this woman you forgive her."

Meeta peered out from behind her mother's sari. Her mother grabbed her by the arm, pulling her forward and shaking her.

"Go," her mother scolded. "Don't be rude."

Meeta stubbornly held her ground.

Her mother slapped her sharply on the back. "Go."

Kiria held out both hands and started backing toward the door. "No, it's okay. Don't hit her." She bumped into the unwanted chair, lost her balance and fell on one knee. Her left hand landed in the puddle of warm urine deposited by Meeta in the excitement of her stealthy approach a few minutes before.

"Bring water," Mary Elizabeth ordered as she helped Kiria to her feet. "I am so sorry. Are you hurt?"

Kiria rotated her wrist and flexed her knee. "No, I'm fine." She smiled widely. "This time yesterday I was in much worse shape."

Santoshi handed a plastic beaker of water to Mary Elizabeth, then held a basin under Kiria's hands. Mary Elizabeth slowly poured the water for Kiria to wash in. "You mean that your wallet was stolen?"

"Actually, I meant the cow dung. Thank you." Kiria shook water from her fingers, looked around for something to dry her hands, then wiped them on the knees of her pants. She reached under the skirt of her churidar and pulled a money belt from around her waist. "Santoshi taught me this." She held up the belt. "I saw she keeps her money in her sari, so I bought this today." She extracted a small red envelope from a zippered pocket and held it out to Santoshi. "Here is the bus fare, Santoshi. And a reward. You really did save me. Thank you. Thank you very much."

Santoshi placed the basin on the floor and took the envelope in both hands. "Thank you, madam," she said, resisting the urge to open the envelope and see her reward.

"Well, I should be going." Kiria hooked the money belt back around her waist and turned to Mary Elizabeth. "If you are going anywhere, can I give you a lift?"

"This was my last visit for today. I am going home now."

"Well, come with me. I'd like to ask you something."

Mary Elizabeth thought about the two-hour bus trip from the shelter to her father's house and decided she could endure a few questions for the convenience of riding home in a car.

Santoshi's Story

MARY ELIZABETH INSTRUCTED KIRIA'S DRIVER on how to get to her house, then leaned back against the fresh white cotton of the Ambassador's rear seat cover. She tilted her head back and closed her eyes. This kind of luxury was rare in her world.

On the other side of the seat, Kiria turned her body so that she was facing the social worker and asked bluntly, "What's the deal with the reward?"

"I do not know."

"You know more than I do."

Mary Elizabeth kept her eyes closed and remained silent in an attempt to discourage further conversation.

"I'll tell you what I think," Kiria persisted. "I think the warden is taking her cut right about now. Am I warm?"

Mary Elizabeth felt a flicker of admiration at Kiria's perception. "It is possible."

Kiria leaned forward. "Joy, turn the car around."

"No!" Opening her eyes, Mary Elizabeth sat up and laid a hand on Kiria's arm. "You cannot help Santoshi this way."

Joy glanced back at Kiria in the rearview mirror. She gestured him to continue driving in the direction they were going, then focused her attention back on Mary Elizabeth.

"Explain it to me," Kiria said.

Mary Elizabeth never avoided the truth, and she was annoyed by Kiria's rude behavior. "Wardens are not well paid and it is a difficult job. Most wardens are not much better off than the women they supervise. Priya is not as greedy as some. She is too lazy to be cruel. And she likes her food. Her charges are well fed."

"But she's stealing."

"Is she? Priya knows she cannot take her cut if the women do not work, and she knows enough not to take too much. The women like this shelter. Priya takes care of them. She finds them jobs. She keeps them healthy. Do you not pay for such services in your world?"

Kiria had no answer. She turned away to stare out her window as the car passed through the slums. Perhaps Mary Elizabeth was right, but it still felt wrong.

Joy looked at his new client's profile in the rearview mirror. He hadn't understood all of the exchange, but he knew Madam was upset. It wasn't hard to figure out why. What did she think she was going to find in a slum? He almost felt sorry for her, but she was just another rich white tourist. She'd sit in the back of the air-conditioned car all day and walk into the hotel every night like she owned it. She'd never know where he slept at night, or what he had to eat, or if he had enough money to raise the family that he wouldn't see until the end of the tourist season. Joy had been a driver for fifteen years. On the whole he liked driving the white tourists. They gave bigger tips. But they weren't real people to him.

After a time, Kiria turned back to Mary Elizabeth. "Tell me about Santoshi."

"What do you want to know?"

"Why is she in the home?"

"For safety. A woman on the street does not fare well without a family to protect her. She does not earn enough money to afford a decent place to live. The best she could hope for is to share a room in a slum with four or five other women. Those rooms are easy to lose if someone else can pay more money. And she certainly could not afford the good food she is getting in the shelter."

"How did she get there?"

Mary Elizabeth's dark, almond eyes focused on Kiria's face. "Are you sure you want to know this?"

Kiria stared back steadily. "Yes, I'm sure."

Never taking her eyes from Kiria's, Mary Elizabeth began, "Santoshi was born in a farming village, just outside Madurai. She is the middle of three sisters. Her family was very poor. She believes that when she was seven years old, her parents gave her to a man who said he would take her to an orphanage."

"What do you believe?"

"If they were as poor as Santoshi remembers, it's possible she was sold. We do not know. She will not tell us the name of her village."

"Why not?"

"She says she does not want to bring shame to her family. The man took her to Madurai and he definitely sold her to another man who ran a children's begging ring. She begged for him until she was fifteen."

"So she didn't go to school? She's illiterate?"

"No. She has taught herself to read. She is very intelligent. Very good with numbers too."

"And her English?"

"She speaks English?" Mary Elizabeth asked with genuine surprise.

"I wouldn't go that far. So what happened then?"

"When she was fifteen, her owner took her on the bus to Chennai and left her in the station. She does not know why. The police picked her up for sleeping in the station and brought her to a women's shelter."

"And she's been in the shelter ever since?"

"Well, not the same one. These are short-stay homes. I have to move her every two or three years. But once they are in the system, if they are careful, they can live out their lives in the shelters."

"So Santoshi has been moving from shelter to shelter for what? Thirty years?"

"How old do you think she is?"

"Fifty-five? Sixty?"

"She will be thirty next month."

Up to this point in the discussion Kiria had seemed to be handling the story well. But at the last statement her eyes widened and her head jerked back. "What happened to her teeth?"

Mary Elizabeth had to fight not to smile. Americans were obsessed by teeth. "As a child she was only fed when she earned money. She was not a good beggar in the beginning. Her permanent teeth grew in while she was learning. We had the last ones removed two years ago to stop the infections."

Kiria had had enough. She broke eye contact and turned her head away to stare out the window again. Mary Elizabeth tipped her head back and closed her eyes. As he drove, Joy kept glancing back in the rearview mirror at the two women. He felt something had just happened between them. Something beneath all the words he hadn't understood. He didn't know what, but he was starting to think this tour could be very different from the others.

When Joy pulled the car up outside the gates of a small house, Kiria reached out and took Mary Elizabeth's hand. "Thank you. You didn't have to tell me all that."

Mary Elizabeth finally let her smile out. "Not many people would have asked. Thank you for bringing me home."

Mary Elizabeth paused for a moment when she entered the house, resting her back against the closed front door. Telling Santoshi's story had depressed her. She wasn't sure why she had done it. Perhaps because underneath all that loud American bluntness, she liked Kiria.

The day nurse came into the hall from the kitchen. "He was good today."

"Good," Mary Elizabeth replied. "Can you come tomorrow, Selvi?"

"Yes, of course. I made some tomato chutney and the chapati dough is ready."

"You are so good to us."

"The professor was good to me once. See you tomorrow."

After Selvi left, Mary Elizabeth checked her hair in the dusty hall mirror and minutely adjusted the folds of her sari before going into her father's room. "Papa," she said from the doorway. "Selvi tells me you had a good day today."

The professor shut the book on his lap with trembling hands. His sunken eyes brightened at the sight of his beloved daughter. "Yes, I feel good today. How was your day?"

Mary Elizabeth crossed the room and leaned over to place a kiss on her father's desiccated cheek. "The most amazing thing happened, Papa." She knelt by his knees and told him the story of the white tourist.

The Reluctant Tourist

ARE YOU THE KIND OF tourist who gets your travel jollies by ticking off every attraction listed in the guidebook? Go to India. It's a ticker's nirvana. Aside from the normal complement of museums and monuments, India is the birthplace of three major religions and hosts at least a dozen more, giving it one of the highest concentrations of religious architecture per square inch in the world.

Personally, I'm more of a seen-one-temple-seen-'em-all kind of tourist. The architecture of the older temples was impressive: tall, skinny pyramids, elaborately carved from top to bottom with scantily clad gods and goddesses in stylized postures. But I soon became bored of following droning guides around the temple grounds as they recited the names and histories of the gods whose statues we passed.

I also grew quite annoyed with the persistent beggars who accosted me every time I stepped out of the car. Having heard Santoshi's story from Mary Elizabeth, I could not bring myself to support a profession that encouraged slavery. The beggars, in turn, could not bring themselves to believe a white tourist was not a fountain of wealth. They followed me, the bolder ones tugging at my clothes, right up to the temple gates, frequently waiting there to pounce on me when I emerged after the tour. Eventually, the hassle of getting out of the car by far exceeded the rewards of temple viewing, and my trip devolved into tedious drives from one hotel to the next.

It wasn't all dull, though. The long periods of boredom were, as the saying goes, punctuated by moments of sheer terror, mostly due to road conditions. Lack of lane etiquette, exciting in the city, where the roads were reasonable and speeds never exceeded what could be expected of an arthritic snail, became population control on country roads. Frustrated Formula One truck drivers played chicken around gargantuan potholes. Troops of monkeys augmented the normal bovine traffic hazards. Overturned buses and hay wagons seemed to lie around every corner.

Partly from boredom, but mostly because my physical safety depended on Joy's reflexes, I developed an unhealthy fascination with his mental and physical condition. Detailed interrogations about his off-duty activities turned up the facts that Joy slept in the backseat of the car and frequently skipped meals. He sent every rupee saved by not eating or renting hotel rooms back to his family, who lived in an agricultural village just outside Thanjavur. The backseat sleeping seemed harmless, as long as he got enough of it, but low blood sugar was a suicidal risk given the nature of his work. I ended up buying his food.

In the intervals between shrieking out traffic warnings and insisting Joy stop for coffee, I found my thoughts straying back to that dismal shelter in Chennai and Santoshi's life.

Before we go any further, let's get something straight here. I'm not a bleeding heart. I have been called a "sadistic slave driver" (personal assistant), a "ball-breaking bitch" (ex-boyfriend) and "a hard-hitting CEO aggressively leading NOVIO into the twenty-first century of video gaming" (*Forbes* magazine and my personal favorite), but no one has ever accused me of being softhearted. I don't do pity. Which made my growing obsession with Santoshi freakishly perplexing.

How could a woman smart enough to teach herself to read be stuck in such a pit of an existence? What was wrong with her? Didn't she have dreams, hopes? Was she truly content to be sleeping on a concrete floor beside an open sewer and lining the knot in some corrupt warden's sari?

I didn't know and I got tired of waiting to become roadkill. I decided to go back to Chennai and solve the Santoshi mystery. The polite young man from Maharaja Tours had strong objections to canceling the rest of my itinerary. It took me half a dozen phone calls, the last three made after midnight to hike up the harassment factor, before we negotiated a settlement. I agreed to keep Joy and the car, easily the most expensive items on my vacation bill, and he grudgingly agreed to cancel the remaining hotel reservations and book me back into the Taj in Chennai.

On the way back we made one overnight stop in Thanjavur. Joy rarely got to see his family during the tourist season and since it didn't matter how we got back to Chennai as long as we did it safely, I decided he might as well drop by to check up on them. Joy was so pleased by this that he invited me to meet them. I almost refused, terrified his living conditions would be worse than Santoshi's. But rural poverty is a gentler poverty. Joy's house was small, unfurnished and as clean as anyplace with dirt floors and palm-leaf walls could be, which is not very. Joy borrowed a plastic lawn chair from a neighbor for me to sit on. While his children climbed on my lap and fanned me with an old calendar, Joy's mother, wife and sisters prepared me an elaborate meal in two tin pots over a twig fire under extremely dubious hygienic conditions. I ate it anyway. It was the best meal of my entire vacation.

I had Joy take me directly to Mary Elizabeth's house when we got back to Chennai.

Safe Sex

ON HER LAST DAY IN India, Kiria sat on a white plastic lawn chair under a banner proclaiming STOP AIDS NOW in Tamil and English, watching Mary Elizabeth deftly demonstrate condom usage. Sunlight flooded the empty lot in the heart of the slum, driving out all hints of shade. Sweat trickled down Kiria's body under her churidar, and the skin of her feet stretched uncomfortably over swollen ankles.

Women of all ages sat or squatted on the ground around Mary Elizabeth. Most of them wore gaudy saris, wrapped short to facilitate chores. Some of the younger women wore brightly patterned churidars. Children ran around the edges of the group or dozed on their mothers' laps. Sunlight flashed blindingly off gold earrings, necklaces and nose studs. Silver rings circled the women's toes, and their wrists clattered with bangles. After two weeks of following Mary Elizabeth through her working days, Kiria was no longer shocked by the amount of gold and silver worn in the slums and shelters. She knew now that only the most destitute of women wore no jewelry. This was an upscale slum, one where the houses had cement walls and tin roofs. Most of the jewelry here would be gold plate, and some of it would even be real.

The women giggled as Mary Elizabeth stretched the condom over her fist and along her arm. She said something that made the women laugh outright. Pulling the latex off her arm, she picked up a pitcher and poured water into the condom until it became as long and round as a large zucchini. Her next comment had the women shrieking hysterically and leaning against one another for support.

When the demonstration was over, it was Kiria's turn to join in. She pulled two boxes of condoms out from under her chair and joined Mary Elizabeth.

"What did you say at the end?" Kiria asked, handing one of the boxes to Mary Elizabeth.

"I said that they need not fear the condom breaking, no matter how large their husband is or how plentiful his seed."

Kiria chuckled. She dug a handful of condoms out of the box and started handing them out to the women who clustered around her. One of the women, her face liberally dusted with turmeric powder, and a bright streak of vermilion painted up the center part of her hair, took the condoms but remained standing in front of Kiria and asked a question. Mary Elizabeth replied. The woman said something else, pointing to a thin old man in stained khaki shorts standing hesitantly at the edge of the crowd.

"She asked if you were married." Mary Elizabeth's long eyes were bright with amusement as she translated, but her expression remained solemn. "I told her no. She wants me to tell you her brother is looking for a wife. He is a widower. She will introduce you."

Kiria clamped her teeth together to stop herself from laughing out loud. "Thank her for me. Tell her my husband died of AIDS and I am still in mourning. Tell her to use the condoms."

Mary Elizabeth coughed slightly before translating the refusal. The woman's bright yellow face assumed an expression of horrified sympathy. She dug a few more condoms out of the box, then turned and walked through the crowd to break the bad news to her brother.

When all the condoms were distributed and the slum women had returned home to prepare the midday meal, Mary Elizabeth and Kiria folded up the banner and threaded their way through the narrow streets of the slum toward the main road, followed by a comet's tail of children.

"Thank you, Kiria. You made such a difference." Mary Elizabeth smiled down at her new friend. "Usually, I can only talk to a few women and give out a dozen condoms. You draw crowds."

"No problem. Happy to be the white freak." Kiria grinned back up at Mary Elizabeth. "You're pretty good yourself. For a woman who's never been married, you really know your way around a condom."

By now Mary Elizabeth was accustomed to Kiria's strange humor. She smiled but said nothing.

"Why aren't you married?" Kiria continued. "Everyone here thinks marriage is so important for a woman. How did you talk your family into letting you choose a career?"

"I did not choose a career. I would have liked to marry. I am very homely."

"Homely? Mary Elizabeth, you're one of the most beautiful women I've ever seen. You're tall and elegant and I know women who paid money for cheekbones that aren't as good as yours."

"Paid money?"

"Plastic surgery."

Mary Elizabeth nodded. "I understand. Here, we pay money

for fairness cream. I am too dark and too tall to be beautiful. But a beautiful woman can be homely too."

"Then it must mean something different. Where I come from, 'homely' means plain."

"Ah. In India a homely woman is one who likes to cook and keep a nice house."

"We would call that domestic. So if you wanted to get married, why didn't you?"

"After my mother died, my father needed me to care for him. But we were never rich. Even before my mother died, my dowry was too small to make a suitable match."

"Dowry? But you're a Christian."

"I am. I am Anglo Indian. That is why I am too dark."

"I thought that meant you speak English."

"Why don't you come home with me?" Mary Elizabeth suggested. "My father loves to tell the story of my great-grandfather and it is one of the things he can still do. Then you will understand Anglo Indian."

For just a moment, Kiria thought longingly of the air conditioner in her hotel room. But her curiosity about Mary Elizabeth's great-grandfather won out. "Okay. Can we pick up some of those egg puffs from the Ajantha Bakery on the way? I'm starving."

"MY GRANDFATHER'S family came to India from England in 1885," John Alexander Johnstone said in the flat, whispery voice of advanced Parkinson's disease. "In those days, India was run by the British. My grandfather's father was a major in the British Army and my grandfather was born here. He should have been sent back to England for schooling when he was seven, but he was an only child and his health was poor. His mother would not allow it. And so he grew up more Indian than British."

John Alexander stopped speaking. His eyes lost focus in the present; his shaking fingers pulled at the blanket on his lap. Sitting on the horsehair love seat opposite his wheelchair, Kiria wondered if the frail old man had forgotten he was telling a story. Almost a full minute passed before he resumed speaking.

"When he was nineteen, he fell in love with the daughter of a wealthy Madras merchant and she returned his love. They met in secret, knowing that if his parents discovered their love, he would be forbidden to see her. She became with child and could not hide this from her family. When she would not name the father, the merchant became angry with his daughter and threw her out of his house."

As John Alexander recited the story of his grandparents' courtship and elopement, Kiria heard the stilted cadence of a beloved fairy tale, told and retold until the words never changed. Somewhere under the archaic language, the true story of the English boy and the merchant's daughter might still remain, but if so, it was locked in John Alexander's failing mind. This narrative was like a Bollywood movie, full of true love and honor and highly unlikely events—a myth that hid darker realities.

On the other side of the room, Mary Elizabeth listened to the family story with closed eyes and a contented smile. Her heart had never been tested by love. She heard her father's words with the same delight as when she was a child, sitting beside him on the roof in the evening, hearing them for the first time. For just a while she stopped being a spinster social worker struggling to care for a dying father. She turned her thoughts away from worry over medical bills and fear of what would happen when her father died. The enchanted recitation of her great-grandparents' romance washed over her and she allowed herself, if not to hope, at least to dream.

Patting the Lion

DO YOU KNOW THE BIGGEST cause of failure? Fear. Fear of loss. Fear of success. Even fear of failure. The truth is, to succeed you have to take risks and make hard decisions. And that's pretty damn scary.

When people ask me about the secret of my success, this is what I tell them. I also tell them I owe it all to my mother. If they assume this means she was a loving and supportive parent, I don't confuse them with the details.

My mother was a bitter, disappointed woman. She knew what she wanted from life: a suburban house, a successful husband and a brood of adorable kids. She never gave up on her dream, but all she managed to achieve was a two-room walk-up on the wrong side of the tracks, a succession of waitressing jobs and an illegitimate child. I grew up thinking her unhappiness was my fault; if I hadn't been born, she would have had her perfect life. It wasn't until I had to face my own tough decisions as an adult that I realized I had nothing to do with her unhappiness. She was the victim of her own decisions, just as we all are. More than anything else, it was Mom's inability to take responsibility for her life that gave me the courage to make tough choices and live with them.

So the day after getting back from India, I did what I always do when I have a really big decision to make. I went to sit on my mother's grave. It really focuses my mind.

It's one thing to watch a couple of National Geographic specials on lions. It's another thing entirely to pat a filthy, flea-infested animal with rotten breath. When Santoshi rescued me, I patted the lion. There were so many things wrong in her life: poverty, slavery, starvation. She'd survived all that. She'd made herself a success of sorts, clawed her way up to the pinnacle of possibility in her world: a drudge job for pennies a day and a cement floor shared with fifty other women at night.

Santoshi's limits were set from the moment of her birth because she didn't have a penis. Like me, Santoshi had been raised to believe that the only decent life for a woman was as a wife and mother. But whereas my role models were the heroines of the women's liberation movement, hers were the spinsters and widows eking out existence on the fringes of a society that had no place for them. Under Indian law women have equal rights, but it's a bit like giving a sports car to a two-year-old. Their cultural legs are too short to reach the pedals, much as mine were when I got married.

(Oh yes, I was married. It's not something I put in my bio. Ted was a lawyer and incredibly handsome. My mother adored him; I think our wedding day was the happiest day of her life. It was certainly the worst night of mine. He was so remorseful afterward that I told the doctor in the emergency room I'd fallen down the stairs, but it just got worse and I left Ted a few months later.)

Every time I thought about Santoshi, I felt a spike of rage

drive into my chest. Despite her formidable intelligence—how many people do you know who could teach themselves to read?—she really saw herself as an inferior human being. She lived a life so far beneath her abilities that happiness wasn't even a dream, let alone something worth fighting for. I knew my anger was excessive, a projection of my own past. It didn't matter. It didn't let me off the hook. Santoshi's world was wrong and I wanted to fix it. Although not even my exemplary problem-solving skills could make a dent in a culture shared by over a billion people, I was fairly sure I could do something to improve her standard of living and even her sense of self-worth.

Improving Santoshi's housing conditions wasn't a problem. All she needed was a safe place to live with dignity and within her means. I could throw money at that one. Mary Elizabeth had told me about the hostels for unmarried professional women. They were too expensive for Santoshi and required references, something a shelter dweller could not provide, but it would be possible to subsidize a hostel for poorer women and, given the fifty-to-one exchange rate of rupees to dollars, not terribly expensive.

The real problem would be to give Santoshi a sense of her true value as a human being. Self-esteem can't be bought. It has to be mentored, modeled, mirrored. No one I met in the male-dominated culture of India, not even the estimable Mary Elizabeth, saw Santoshi as anything other than an embarrassing inconvenience. The only person I knew who had the means and, more important, the motivation to foster Santoshi's self-esteem was me.

This was out of the question. I had a company to run. NOVIO had never issued shares, so I didn't have stockholders or a board of directors to report to, but two hundred people depended on me to keep NOVIO profitable and their jobs secure. I couldn't just take off and go to India for the benefit of one cleaning lady.

I sat on Mom's headstone all afternoon, but no solution came to me. Then three weeks later, on the last leg of a promotional tour for NOVIO, I saw a man standing at the back of a conference room in Toronto. He was slightly taller than Ted and his shoulders were broader, but there was no mistaking the aristocratic nose, Marlboro Man jaw and limpid, window-to-the-soul eyes.

After seeing my son, the decision to go to India was a no-brainer.

The Bitch and the Doorknob

❁ ❁ ❁ ❁ ❁

EVA HANDED A PR FOLDER to the last interviewer, a freelance journalist hoping to sell an article on Kiria to *Canadian Women Magazine*. "I'll e-mail you the transcript of the interview later this afternoon," she said as she ushered the young woman into the foyer of the hotel suite and opened the door. "If you have any questions about NOVIO or Kiria, our e-mail address is on the cover sheet."

The journalist stopped in the doorway and hiked her laptop bag higher up on her shoulder. "Thanks again for writing up the interview."

"No problem. I have to do it anyway for our files."

"I just feel so stupid about forgetting my power cord."

"Nonsense," Eva replied, fighting an urge to physically shove the girl out into the hall. "Everyone forgets things." She moved the door a couple of inches. The journalist took the hint and left.

Eva crossed the sitting room of the suite and entered the bedroom where Kiria, already changed into jeans and a red polo shirt for the last event of the day, stood in front of the full-length mirror.

"That was a waste of time," Eva said, picking a tan suede jacket from the foot of the bed.

"Maybe. And maybe someday, she'll be writing for *Time.*" Kiria pulled at the pieces of her hair that had been flattened by pulling on the polo shirt. "Everyone starts somewhere."

The beads on the ends of the extensions attached to Eva's cornrows clicked as she shook her head. "Not that one. She didn't even have any questions prepared." She held up the jacket for Kiria to slip into. "Thank God we're going home tomorrow."

Kiria shrugged into the jacket and pivoted to face her friend. "You're not the only one. Five cities in seven days. I'm getting too old for this."

"You don't have to go down there. Piet's the big draw for this group." Eva adjusted the collar of the polo shirt over the suede lapels. "Stay in the room."

"It's only an hour. I'll survive." Kiria leaned toward the mirror. "God, I look like a zombie. You go down. I've got to fix this."

Eva checked her watch. "You've got fifteen minutes. See you downstairs."

She took the elevator down to the mezzanine level and crossed the hallway to the hotel ballroom. It was a larger space than NOVIO normally booked for a press conference, but already the seats were filled and a number of people were sitting on the floor or leaning against the back and side walls of the room. Bloggers, unlike business journalists, turned up in hordes, all wearing what Eva privately thought of as the geek uniform: jeans, high-end sneakers and sweatshirts with slogans like "Byte Me." It cost a lot to book a ballroom and feed a crowd of this size, but the money saved by using gamers as beta testers for new video games and the increased sales generated by blog reviews more than made up for the extra expense.

Despite twelve years as Kiria's personal assistant, Eva did not understand the lure of technology. To her, computers were tools, no different from microwave ovens and lawn mowers. Piet, on the other hand, swam in these waters like a shark. Earlier in the day, at the real press conference, he'd looked lost and uncomfortable in the suit and tie appropriate for a director of research and development. Now, with his jacket and tie abandoned and his sleeves rolled up, he looked relaxed and confident as he stood by the podium, surrounded by a group of admirers. Eva watched him draw shapes in the air with his hands as he talked, and wondered, for what felt like the thousandth time, why she couldn't have fallen in love with a poet, or an accountant, or even just a man who wasn't almost a decade younger.

She walked to the small desk behind the podium and began checking the wiring that ran from her laptop to the amps and the screen. Piet broke away from his fan club and came to stand beside her.

"I checked it already," he said.

"Why am I not surprised?" She sat down at the desk to increase the distance between them and opened her laptop. "Looks like quite a crowd. Do you think we've got enough demo copies?"

Piet pushed up his glasses and scanned the crowd. "I hope so. I'm always underestimating these guys."

They both looked up as the noise level in the room rose. Kiria stood in the entrance to the ballroom, short and sturdy and radiating confidence. She moved toward the podium like a politician, waving at familiar faces, smiling and nodding. It was an act, one that Eva had seen many times before, but never done with so little enthusiasm. Usually Kiria chatted with the crowd and ad-libbed her presentations. This trip, she was just going through the motions, sticking to the script. Eva looked over at Piet. He shrugged back at her. The word "India" hung unsaid between them.

Kiria arrived at the front of the room, picked up the collar mike from the podium and clipped it to the lapel of her jacket. Piet moved to stand behind her. Eva fired up the first PowerPoint and the opening graphics filled the screen on the wall behind them.

Kiria spread her arms and grinned out at the room. "Hello, Toronto!"

All the bugs had been worked out of the presentation in Seattle and Los Angeles. Now it was just a matter of following Kiria's timing. Eva concentrated on moving through the slides as Kiria introduced the audience to NOVIO's newest game, Sharp-End. Unlike the real press conferences, this event was more of a demonstration and an opportunity to hand out beta test sets to expert gamers. Kiria moved across the front of the room with crackling energy, augmenting her words with wide gestures and making eye contact with the crowd. The audience, their attention on the rapidly shifting slides and not an empathic group to start with, never noticed that her smile went no higher than her cheeks.

When they came to the preview of the new commercial, signaling the end of the presentation and the beginning of the question period, Eva started up the video, then poured Kiria a glass of water from the pitcher on the desk and carried it over to the podium. Piet stepped up to stand on Kiria's other side. The three of them watched the room, gauging reactions.

It took Eva a moment to connect the wetness on her leg with the water glass rolling across the carpet. She turned her head and saw Kiria, irises reduced to a thin crystal rim around dilated pupils, staring at the ballroom entrance. The object of Kiria's interest was easy to spot. The man would be noticeable even if he weren't the only person in the room wearing a three-piece suit. He was easily the handsomest man Eva had ever seen.

As she watched him turn and leave the ballroom, Eva leaned toward her boss and whispered, "Who is that?"

Kiria ignored the question. She tugged the microphone off her lapel, thrust it into Eva's hand and strode toward the doorway.

The video ended and Kiria still hadn't returned. Eva handed the microphone to Piet and together they completed the presentation. When the last of the bloggers had picked up a beta test package and left, Eva went looking for Kiria. She found her in the sitting room of the hotel suite. Two miniature bottles from the bar stood on the coffee table. Kiria sat with her legs curled up beneath her body at one end of the sofa, holding a tumbler of bourbon. She'd been crying, but her face was composed and the hand holding the glass remained rock steady as she raised it in greeting.

"Are you okay?" Eva asked.

"I am now."

"Who was that guy? Do you know him?"

Kiria responded with a mirthless hiccup of laughter. "I can honestly say I've never seen him before in my life." She tossed back the last of her drink and placed the tumbler on the coffee table. "I think he's my son."

"Now I need a drink." Eva made for the bar. "Want another one?"

"Better not."

Eva got herself a miniature of rum, a can of Coke and a glass. She crossed the room and sat down on the opposite end of the sofa from Kiria. "So why do you think he's your son?" she asked as she popped the top of the can.

"Because he looks exactly like his father and he was born here in Toronto."

Questions tumbled through Eva's mind, but she merely turned her body toward her friend to show she was ready to listen. Kiria would tell only as much as she wanted to and would clam up completely if asked a question she didn't want to answer.

Kiria began in a flat tone. "I told you about my husband." She slid her fingers into her hair just above her left ear and rubbed at the scar on her skull. "What I didn't tell you is that I got pregnant. I was scared he'd beat the baby out of me. I told my mother, but she thought I was exaggerating, so I ran away from Albany, where Ted and I were living at the time. I went to Canada because I thought it would be harder for him to find me in a foreign country. I put the baby up for adoption here in Toronto."

"I don't understand. Why didn't you keep your baby?" Eva couldn't prevent herself from asking.

A brief smile flickered across Kiria's face. "Sorry. Of course you don't understand. You're too young to remember what it was like before the women's movement." She stood up abruptly and began pacing back and forth across the room. "I wanted my baby more than I ever wanted anything in my life, but it was different back then. Without help, a poor, single woman had zero chance of raising a child properly. I didn't want my son to have the same life my mother gave me, and I was terrified that if my husband found out, he'd force me back into the marriage.

"I didn't know what to do. Then about a month before the baby arrived, I was sitting on a park bench and this woman sat down beside me. We got to talking and she told me how lucky I was to be having a child and how she and her husband were trying to adopt. She was such a warm, loving woman. I realized that if I could know my child would be raised by someone like her, it would be easier to give the baby up. So I told her I was living in a home for unwed mothers and thinking about putting the baby up for adoption. A couple of days later, she and her husband showed up at the home. They invited me to stay with them until the baby was born and offered to adopt it. They were such wonderful people. They had everything I couldn't give my child. I did the right thing. I know I did the right thing."

"And you think that man we saw today could be your son?"

"I can't prove it, no. But I feel it"—Kiria stopped pacing and pressed both hands to her stomach, a gesture similar to the way pregnant women cradled their unborn children—"here."

"So, what are you going to do now?"

Kiria moved around the coffee table and sat back down on the sofa. "Nothing."

"What if he is your son?"

"What if he is? You saw him. He looks successful. He's probably married and has kids and is perfectly happy. If he thinks about me at all, he probably hates me. And he doesn't need his life turned upside down by my guilt."

"Okay. Good for him. But what about you? What are you going to do?"

"Same thing I've always done. Work harder and try not to think about it."

The idea of Kiria working harder made Eva sit up straighter on the couch. "Maybe you should go to India. Help that woman you've been talking about since you got back."

"I have a company to run. I can't leave NOVIO for that long."

"Why not?"

"Because people depend on me. I work twelve-hour days."

Eva set her glass down on the coffee table. "Actually, I was going to talk to you about that when we got back." She reached out to take Kiria's hands in both of hers. "No one is better at lining up the duckies than you are, honey. But we're all lined up right now. There's nothing at NOVIO that needs you. You've been micromanaging. It's driving everyone crazy. You're my dear friend,

Kiria, and I say this with love: please, for NOVIO's sake, go to India."

Kiria jerked her hands free. "I am not micromanaging."

"Are you kidding? You've been sitting in on every department's status meetings. You spent two days in finance tracking down a twenty-dollar discrepancy in the maintenance budget. You . . ."

Kiria held up a hand. "All right, all right. I get it. But there's no one to leave in charge. Piet's the only one who knows enough."

"So turn it over to Piet."

"I can't do that. He has fewer social skills than a doorknob."

"Personally, I think that's one of his strong points."

"How do you figure that?"

Eva grinned. "No change in management style."

Kiria grinned back. It was the first genuine expression of pleasure Eva had seen on her boss's face for weeks.

"Bitch!"

"Doorknob."

Santoshi Gets a New Sari

SANTOSHI SAT IN A CORNER of the shelter and added up the deposits in her bankbook for the tenth time. She loved her bankbook, although it represented only a fraction of her total savings. Santoshi never planned how to spend her money. She loved money for its own sake, especially the coins. As a child, her entire life had revolved around the acquisition of coins. Having coins in her hand gave her a feeling of comfort and safety. What for others was a means to an end was for her an end in itself.

She could not keep so much money safely in the shelter. The bulk of it was sealed in old jars and buried in empty lots and under paving stones throughout the city. She knew exactly where each jar lay hidden and checked on them frequently. The system wasn't perfect. She lost a jar once when a storm interrupted current to the street it was buried on and the city workers dug up the paving stones to find the faulty wire. It still made her feel ill when she thought about it. Banks were safer, but Santoshi could not open a bank account or deposit money herself. She depended on the warden to deposit money for her. If she asked for help, it would cost far more than the loss of one jar.

She filled about a jar a year. The current jar, almost ready to be buried, was locked in her suitcase. The money came mostly from tips earned by running errands for patients at the hospital. She hid the tips in her sari blouse before going back to the shelter and transferred them to the jar while she was locked in the bathing room. Occasionally, a patient would leave behind some clothing or a book that could be sold. Once she had found a new sari, still in its Madhar Sha store bag, under her bus seat and been able to return it for a full refund. She could have saved more money, but Santoshi would not steal, cheat or lie. She didn't count hiding her tips as lying.

The doorbell rang as Santoshi got up to return her bankbook to Warden. Priya looked up from her soap opera. Seeing the social worker, she tossed the gate key to Santoshi, who went to let in Mary Elizabeth. Santoshi usually liked to see Mary Elizabeth. As much as she trusted anyone, Santoshi trusted her social worker. But after two and a half years at this home, it was time to move on. Today, or someday very soon, Mary Elizabeth would be telling Santoshi to pack her things. As something of an expert in shelters, Santoshi had little hope that the food in the next one would be as good as it was here.

"Good afternoon, madam," Santoshi said as she opened the gate. "Have you eaten?"

"Good afternoon, Santoshi," Mary Elizabeth replied. "Yes, I have. And you?"

"Yes, madam."

"Priya?" Mary Elizabeth called out to the warden as she entered the shelter. "May I use your office to talk with Santoshi?"

Without looking away from the television, Priya extended her arm backward and flapped her hand in consent. Santoshi and

Mary Elizabeth went into the warden's room. Mary Elizabeth closed the door. This was unusual. Santoshi interpreted anything unusual as a bad sign. Today must be the day. Mary Elizabeth sat in the warden's chair. She gestured for Santoshi to sit down. Distressed, Santoshi preferred to stand.

"Santoshi, do you remember the tourist you helped last month?" Mary Elizabeth began.

"Yes, madam."

"She will be coming back to Chennai next month. She will be staying here for a few months. She will be renting an apartment. She wants a maid to come and live with her."

"Yes, madam." Santoshi couldn't see what this had to do with her.

"She asked for you."

"No, madam!" The denial exploded out of Santoshi before she could stop it.

"Santoshi, you cannot stay here much longer. I have not found you another home yet. This is all I can find for you." Frustration tinted Mary Elizabeth's voice. In three months of searching, she had been unable to find a shelter with space for a new inmate. The system was stretched to its limits.

"Madam, I will lose my job! When she leaves, I will have no home! I don't want to live on the pavement!" Santoshi's speaking so forcefully to a superior was a sign of how upset she was.

"I will find you another job, Santoshi. I will find you another home."

When Mary Elizabeth said she would do something, she always did it. But the next job could be anything. Only at the hospital could Santoshi make such good tips.

"The pay is very good," Mary Elizabeth continued. "It is three thousand rupees a month."

Three times Santoshi's current wage! A generous employer

often gave old clothes and other unwanted things too. Certainly living with a white woman would be far more interesting than living in a shelter. Her curiosity engaged, Santoshi began to consider the possibility. "What are my duties, madam?"

"You would keep house and cook."

"Cook? I cannot cook white persons' food, madam."

"She knows that. She says she will teach you."

An unusual skill was a highly marketable commodity. If she could cook Western food, Santoshi's chances of getting a job when Kiria Madam left would be good. There were risks, though. Santoshi did not like risks. "What should I do, madam?"

"You should take the job. We do not have any other choice right now."

Santoshi took a deep breath. She was going to take a risk! She hadn't felt so excited since she'd found the sari under her bus seat. "Very good, madam," she said.

"There is one condition."

"Yes, madam?"

Mary Elizabeth held out a five-hundred-rupee bill. "Kiria Madam says that if you want to work for her, you cannot wear that sari."

Unsuitable Accommodations

❁ ❁ ❁ ❁ ❁

YOU'VE HEARD THE SAYING MONEY talks? Well, in India, it screams like the lead singer at a heavy metal concert.

Within three days of my return to Chennai, using only a cell phone and the classifieds in the *Deccan Chronicle* newspaper, I had a school of real estate sharks swarming around me. Although it's hard to interpret motivation in an alien culture, my guess is they saw a foreign (=rich), white (=high-status) female (=stupid). From my side they looked like a pathetic collection of con artists vying to insult my intelligence. Seriously, if I'd said I wanted to buy the Taj Mahal, every one of them would have told me how lucky I was that it just went on the market.

Most of them came across as bullies too. I don't think this was intentional, more like lack of familiarity with the polite forms of English and limited experience in dealing with women. Still, it put me off. In the end I picked the only two agents who managed not to give me a direct order during their interviews. One was an excruciatingly formal young man named Sushil. The other was a fast-talking, middle-aged man whose full name was eighteen letters long and beyond my ability to remember. I called him Venkat.

The laws of supply and demand in India are pretty much just those of demand. With the exception of manual labor and high-end accommodations, it's an economy of scarcity. This made finding a property difficult. It should have made finding an apartment easy. The three I saw looked just fine, but Santoshi proved much harder to please.

Normally, no one considers the taste of the hired help when selecting a home. On the other hand, the hired help doesn't usually balk at an elevator either. After Santoshi insisted on climbing six flights of stairs to see the first apartment, I limited my search to lower-level accommodations. I discarded the second apartment when I saw Santoshi standing in the modern stainless-steel kitchen looking like she'd just learned she had terminal cancer. Finally, after watching her circle the bathroom of the third apartment looking for a wall tap and a floor drain, I canceled the rest of the viewings. Santoshi's self-confidence would never blossom in an intimidating environment.

I called Mary Elizabeth and explained the problem. She suggested letting Santoshi look for an apartment. I replied that a lifetime spent in the Shelter Sheridan hardly qualified Santoshi as an expert at assessing accommodation. Mary Elizabeth pointed out that Santoshi had been a maid in Chennai for over a dozen years. She may not have lived in any herself, but Santoshi knew a good apartment when she saw one. Comforted but not entirely convinced, I made a list of my minimal requirements—indoor plumbing, electricity, that sort of thing—and had it translated into Tamil by a friendly desk clerk at the hotel. Armed with the list, I invited Mary Elizabeth and Santoshi out for lunch.

I could do this because Santoshi was now quite presentable.

She had replaced her old sari with a cream-bordered navy one, a matching navy blouse, red plastic sandals liberally garnished with white daisies and a shiny, white plastic handbag. She had also taken to outlining her large eyes with kohl and wearing her hair in a tight braid that swung down her back, unfortunately accenting her stick-out ears. Other than the missing teeth, not really noticeable unless she laughed, which she rarely did, she looked like a respectable, middle-aged pixie.

I made the mistake of picking a traditional vegetarian restaurant and learned that cutlery is not a universal concept. While I struggled to restrict the inevitable mess of eating with my hand to the portion of my arm below the elbow, Mary Elizabeth explained to Santoshi that I wanted her to find us an apartment. At first Santoshi was upset with the responsibility. She could not possibly make such a choice for a white person. I said I wasn't happy with the fancy, expensive apartments the agents had shown me. She nodded. Her thoughts exactly. I said I needed a nice, homey place like a middle-class person would live in. She nodded again. I could almost see the little wheels turning in her head. It took some additional encouragement, but eventually Santoshi agreed to give it a try.

I gave her a thousand rupees in expense money and my list of the basics. She made a big performance of putting the money into a hot pink plastic wallet before holding the list out at arm's length and reading through it carefully. I made a mental note to take her to get reading glasses. After lunch, Mary Elizabeth and I stood on the steps of the restaurant and watched Santoshi walk out to the street, head high, plastic purse swinging jauntily from her arm. On at least one count, this apartment hunt would be a success.

I answered a knock on my hotel room door the next morning and found Santoshi standing in the hallway. She handed me a list with three addresses and phone numbers, and 968 rupees in change. I called the numbers and we went out to see them all that same day.

A tenement landlord in inner-city Detroit would have had trouble renting out those apartments. Basic didn't even begin to describe them. But they all had electricity and indoor plumbing and were structurally sound. Anything else I could handle myself. They were also phenomenally cheap.

I tried to ask Santoshi how she'd found those three apartments so quickly, but we soon found ourselves playing charades across the language barrier, a dismal failure given our lack of common cultural gestures. I'm not good with frustration. Later that afternoon I went out and bought a book to teach myself Tamil, which turned out to be the best investment I made during my whole stay in India.

Really Unsuitable Accommodation

❁ ❁ ❁ ❁ ❁

GEETA CLIMBED THE OUTSIDE STAIRCASE of her house to the first floor. Her short leg, the legacy of a childhood bout with polio, made climbing the steep risers difficult. She climbed like a child, placing both feet on each step. At the top she looked around and realized it had been years since she'd last tackled the staircase. The terrace was littered with old coconuts and decomposing leaves. She considered calling her daughter-in-law to tidy it up but quickly discarded the idea. Fortunately, the sweeper was still working in the courtyard. She leaned over the balustrade of the terrace and called down. "Jaya, come up here."

Jaya, decades younger than her employer, arrived a minute later.

"Clean this up," Geeta ordered, gesturing at the debris.

Jaya looked around, considering how much she could get for the extra work. "This is a large job, madam. I do not want to be late for my job at Mrs. Premila's. Mrs. Premila does not like me to be late." She left it there, waiting for Geeta to say the first number.

Geeta sidestepped. "This will not take very long. You will not be late."

"I'm very sorry, madam, but Mrs. Premila pays well. I do not want to anger her." Jaya's none-too-subtle reference to their last discussion on wages lobbed the ball back into her employer's court.

If she had the time, Geeta would have continued stalling or dismissed Jaya and done the job herself. But the white woman would be arriving in a couple of hours and Geeta did not want the mess outside the apartment door to put off such a prestigious prospective tenant. "Naturally, as this is extra work for you, there will be extra pay."

"How much, madam?"

"Five rupees."

"This is much work. I will be at least an hour late. Twenty rupees is fair."

"Twenty rupees! For a few minutes' work?"

Although the price had effectively been set at thirteen rupees when Jaya named her figure, the two women haggled for a few minutes longer, neither wanting to be perceived as a soft negotiator. Then, leaving Jaya to her task, Geeta unlocked the apartment door and went in to see what kind of a mess her useless daughter-in-law had made of cleaning the inside.

Geeta and her husband had aimed high when they went bride hunting for their only son. They needed a rich match to recover at least some of the cost of dowering five daughters. Blinded by the glitter of the girl's dowry, they managed to overlook the fact that the pampered youngest daughter of a wealthy man would be a poor fit for a less affluent family. Their daughter-in-law was an accomplished bharatanatyam dancer, could play two musical instruments and spoke five languages fluently. She held a bachelor's degree in computer science and was one year short of her MBA. But she did not know one end of a broom from the other. Geeta's dream of a submissive helpful girl who would alleviate the burden of caring for a family became a nightmare of poorly washed laundry, badly cooked food and, predictably, badly cleaned apartments.

As Geeta bent to pick up the broom left lying on the floor, a spike of pain shot through her back. With the practice of decades she pushed the pain aside and began sweeping.

Because her husband's sister's son had worked in America, Geeta knew that Americans were punctual. She positioned herself near the front door five minutes before the prospective tenant was due to arrive. As expected, the white woman arrived exactly on time.

"Good afternoon." Geeta opened the door and greeted the white woman in stiff, heavily accented English. "Please come in."

"Good afternoon. Thank you." The woman removed her sandals and entered. "My name is Kiria, and this"—she gestured to a small woman standing hesitantly in the doorway—"is my housekeeper, Santoshi."

Both Geeta and Santoshi were embarrassed by this casual introduction of a hostess to a servant. Santoshi tried to recover the social faux pas of her mistress by ducking her head. Geeta shrugged it off, focused on how much extra rent she could charge a tenant with a housekeeper.

"My name is Geeta. Please be seated."

Geeta led the way into the hall. The room was sparsely furnished with an ornately carved wooden bench and a small round table between two carved wooden chairs. A glass-enclosed cabinet against the far wall contained an eclectic assortment of photographs, china figurines and dusty stuffed toys. Kiria sat on one end of the bench. Santoshi entered the room and remained standing by the door.

"Would you like coffee?" Geeta asked.

"No, thank you. No coffee."

"Perhaps tea?"

"Yes, I like Indian tea. Thank you."

"Laxmi!" Geeta's voice hardened as she switched to Tamil. "Bring tea for our visitor. Bring tea for me."

The older women made stilted small talk while Santoshi stood silently by the door. Geeta politely inquired what Kiria had eaten for breakfast. Kiria commented on the weather. Geeta asked what country Kiria was from. Kiria then made the mistake of inquiring about Geeta's family. Geeta was halfway through describing the glorious wedding of her third daughter when the tea arrived. It was served in china cups carried in on a tray by a slender young woman with a pretty face.

"Auntie," she said, holding out a cup to Kiria.

"Thank you." Kiria sniffed the contents of the cup. "Is this spiced tea?"

A worried expression creased Laxmi's forehead. "Did you want spiced tea? I'm so sorry. I'll make some." She reached to take back the cup.

"No, this is fine. I was just wondering. Your English is excellent. You have no accent. Where did you learn?"

"From my tutor, Auntie." Laxmi handed the other cup to Geeta, who offered no thanks. "Excuse me, I have to turn off the rice cooker." Laxmi walked gracefully from the room.

Kiria turned to Geeta in surprise. "Your maid had a tutor?"

"Laxmi is my daughter-in-law," Geeta replied stiffly. She was beginning to wonder if the status of having a white tenant would be worth the aggravation.

"Oh, really?" Kiria groped for words to repair her mistake. "She's very pretty." The room filled with silence as the two women sipped their tea. Finally, Kiria said, "Perhaps we could look at the apartment?"

Geeta had no intention of climbing those stairs twice in one day. "I will have Laxmi take you up. Laxmi!"

Laxmi led the way up the outside staircase to the apartment. She removed the padlock from the door and stepped back to let Kiria and Santoshi enter first. The apartment had a front hall, a sitting room, two bedrooms, a room Kiria assumed to be a kitchen due to the presence of a sink, and a simple bathroom containing a Western-style toilet, a small sink and a wall tap. While Santoshi scurried from room to room trying every light switch and tap, Kiria stood on the terrace with Laxmi in the shade of a magnificently blooming bougainvillea tree.

"So, how long have you been married?" Kiria asked.

"Six months, Auntie."

"My name is Kiria. Why do you keep calling me Auntie?"

The corner of Laxmi's mouth quirked upward, creating a dimple. "It is how we politely address older people. We call them Uncle or Auntie. My in-laws would think me very disrespectful if I called you Kiria." She had a sparkle to her voice that matched the dimple.

Kiria, curiosity engaged by the interaction between Laxmi and her mother-in-law, decided to try for more information. "Tell me if I'm out of line here, but you just don't seem to fit with this house and this family."

"You marry a man, you marry his family," Laxmi replied philosophically. "My husband suits me very well. I can adapt to his parents."

Santoshi joined them on the terrace.

"So, Santoshi, house okay?" Kiria asked.

Santoshi nodded solemnly, trying not to show her approval of the apartment in front of the owner's daughter.

Kiria took one last look around the terrace and sighed. She didn't think much of the apartment herself, but that wasn't the point. "Okay, let's go talk rent," she said, and led the way back down the stairs.

Lovers' Quarrel

❁❁❁❁❁

THEODORE MEGLER CAME OUT OF the bedroom on Saturday morning to find his husband seated at the kitchen table, a half-eaten croissant lying ignored on the plate beside the laptop. Rik's long hair was still confined in its work ponytail. He'd unbuttoned the neck of his tunic. Light stubble shadowed his jaw, accenting high cheekbones.

Theo walked over behind the chair and placed both hands on Rik's shoulders. "Just get in? How was your shift?"

"Not great." Rik tipped his face up for Theo's kiss.

"Busy?"

"We had almost a hundred people through the ER last night. It's like everyone goes crazy around Christmas."

"Well, you're off for a couple of days now." Theo squinted at the laptop screen. "What're you doing there?"

"Winding down. It's a game. Chronography."

Without his contacts Theo had to lean down to make out the bright graphics. "Kids' game?"

"Not really. More of a thought experiment. You get to go back in time and change things to fix stuff in the future. I'm trying to prevent the Mars/Venus Water Wars." Rik clicked up a statistics display. "See this? I tried assassinating the president of the Earth Federation. All that did was start the war sooner. Now I'm thinking Sugarman is going to have to defect so that the Martians invent the FTL drive first." Rik clicked on the reload button and the game returned to the main menu.

Theo froze. The words "Copyright 2004 NOVIO" jumped out at him from the bottom right-hand corner of the screen.

"Now you're buying her games?" He shoved Rik's shoulders lightly.

"It's a good game," Rik defended himself. "And she's my biological mother-in-law. I'm interested in her. I Googled her. That got me to the company Web site and I found this. I didn't buy it. It's free."

"Whatever. I don't want to talk about it." Theo went over to the counter and poured himself a mug of coffee. "Thanks for making coffee."

"You're not fooling me. Ever since you saw her, you've been dying to know about her."

"Know what? What's to know? Some hard-ass bitch abandoned her kid for her job. That's all there is."

"You can't know that."

"I saw it, Rik. You didn't. You didn't see her, working the room, manipulating them, telling them about her wonderful company and her fantastic new game."

"So she's some hotshot businesswoman now. She wasn't then."

Theo sat down across from Rik. He put his elbows on the table and propped his forehead on his palms. "I should never have let you talk me into asking Mom about her."

Rik reached over to place his palm on Theo's forearm. "We

asked your mom because you feel abandoned by your birth mother, and the kids we adopt are going to feel the same way. If you can't deal with it yourself, we can't help them deal with it."

"She said it wouldn't do me any good. She was right. I feel worse now than I did before."

"That's not what she meant and you know it. She didn't think you'd be able to find Kiria. Your mom's old. She has no idea about the Internet or video games. She'd never have told you Kiria's name if she knew you could just Google it."

"But I did, and I've seen her and it was a mistake."

"If she was as hard as you think she is, she'd have had an abortion. Kiria Langdon is the only person who knows why she put you up for adoption. You have to ask her."

"I can't do that to Mom. I can't betray her like that."

Rik rose and walked over to wrap his arms around Theo's shoulders. "Your mom loves you. She wants you to be happy. She won't feel betrayed."

Theo sighed and leaned his head back against his husband's chest. "I can't. I'm just not ready. I need time."

"Then getting you ready is what we do next." Rik squeezed Theo's shoulders. "But not right now. I need to sleep and maybe you should finish up your dad's stuff first."

After breakfast, Theo sat on the floor of the den with the last of the boxes. Sorting through these papers was his final task as executor of his father's estate. Theo had loved his dad, but their relationship as adults had been rocky. Arthur Megler had never completely overcome his homophobia when he learned his son was gay. In a way, being made executor of the estate was a vote of confidence, a posthumous apology from the old man for the difficulties between them. Theo pulled the lid off the box and picked up the first folder.

In the bedroom, Rik was just dozing off when Theo's shout jolted him back to full consciousness.

"Rik! Rik! Come see this."

Rik rolled off the bed, hitched his Care Bear pajama bottoms up on his hips and went to the den.

"See what?"

"Look. Look at this." Theo, seated tailor fashion on the floor, surrounded by folders, held up a piece of paper in a shaking hand.

It looked like a page torn from a ruled notebook. Rik took it and began reading the heavily slanted handwriting.

Dear Mr. and Mrs. Megler,

I am returning the money you gave me to travel to the States. I know you said I didn't have to pay you back, but it bothers me, makes me feel like I sold my baby. A money order is enclosed.

I promised I'd never come back, and I won't. But it's harder than I expected. I think about the baby all the time. I'm afraid if you send me a letter or a picture it will be too hard, so I'm not putting a return address on this letter. I'm in Oregon. I have two jobs, cleaning houses during the day and offices at night. With no degree and no references, it's the best I can get right now. But I've enrolled in the business program at the university here. My classes start in the fall.

I can't imagine what would have happened to my baby if you hadn't sat beside me that day in the park, Alicia. I know that you are the best parents possible and you are giving my baby all the love I wish I could.

Thank you both, for everything. I will always be grateful.

Kiria

Rik handed the letter back to Theo. "Well," he said as he wiped the tears from his cheeks with the palms of his hands, "whatever the reason, I don't think it was because she didn't want you."

Clandestine Romance

❁ ❁ ❁ ❁ ❁

"THREE HUNDRED RUPEES! NO! VERY small trip. One hundred rupees." Kiria did her best to look like she knew what she was talking about. After her first week in Chennai, she had developed a system for bargaining with auto drivers: divide by three and move up in increments of ten. She'd tried dividing by two, but the number of times her first offer was accepted convinced her she was starting too high. Dividing by four caused the drivers to pull away instantly. Three seemed to be the magic number. It wasn't working today, though. This driver, like the five before him, just drove away.

Kiria continued walking along the street scanning traffic for an empty auto and a driver more willing to bargain. She was hot and tired and thirsty. Her ankles were swollen. Across the street she saw the now familiar logo of the one decent coffee shop chain in Chennai. Kiria decided to postpone her search for transportation in favor of an iced tea and half an hour of air-conditioning.

Rajkumar glanced up when the bell over the coffee shop

doorway chimed. He saw a gray-haired white woman standing with her eyes closed under the air conditioner mounted over the door. She looked hot. Sweat trickled down her temples and the armpits of her green churidar were soaked.

Mary Elizabeth turned around to see what had taken Raj's attention. "Oh no!" she exclaimed, and quickly turned back to face him.

"You know her?" he asked.

"It's Kiria. The woman I told you about? The one who wants to build a women's hostel."

"Is that so? She is not what I expected. She looks soft."

"Do not be fooled. She has been in Chennai only two weeks. Already she has found an apartment and has two real estate agents looking for property."

Raj's curiosity was piqued by the idea of such a forceful woman. Most of the women he knew at least pretended to be submissive. He rose. "We must invite her to join us."

Mary Elizabeth laid a hand on his wrist. "Raj, she does not know about us," she whispered.

"Then we will not tell her," he whispered back, patted her hand and walked over to where Kiria was standing.

"Excuse me. My name is Raj. Mary Elizabeth and I"—he gestured behind him—"are having coffee. Would you like to join us?"

Kiria looked past the short, portly man and saw Mary Elizabeth sitting at a table in the corner. Kiria smiled broadly. "I'd be delighted." At the table, she leaned down and gave Mary Elizabeth a loose hug. "So this is social work on a Tuesday afternoon. We never did this when I came with you."

A waiter brought over an extra chair and took Kiria's order for iced tea. Mary Elizabeth performed introductions without making eye contact, then asked Kiria what she was doing in Anna Nagar.

"Furniture shopping for the apartment. I went to Mylapore, but it's so expensive there. It's not like I'm going to be here for long. The money is better spent on the hostel."

"And did you find furniture?" Mary Elizabeth asked.

"Oh yes. Geeta, the landlady, told me about this department store. Rathna? They had everything. And getting it all there saved time. I only had to go shopping once."

"You furnished your house in one day?" Raj looked surprised.

"One morning, actually. But I still have to find an air conditioner. So, what's all this?" Kiria gestured at the folders spread out across the tabletop.

"Do you remember Meeta, the little girl you accidentally hit at the shelter the day we met?" Mary Elizabeth touched a folder. "Her mother is Gowrie. This is Gowrie's court case and Mr. Rajkumar is her legal adviser. We were discussing what to do next."

Kiria, having noted Mary Elizabeth's embarrassment during the introductions, did not think that was all they had been discussing. "Can Gowrie afford a lawyer?" she asked.

"At the moment she cannot," Raj replied. "If we are successful, though, she will be a wealthy woman."

"What is her case about?"

"We are trying to protect Meeta's inheritance," Raj explained. "When Gowrie was married, her family made a gift of land to her husband."

Kiria looked confused. "A dowry? I thought that was illegal."

"Since 1961. This was a gift." Raj's deep voice gently stressed the last word. "When her husband died last year, his family did not want to keep Gowrie. They returned her to her family. Her brothers refused to take her back unless the land was returned to them. Gowrie says her older brother is a gambler and has lost a great deal of his family's money. Gowrie does not want him to lose her daughter's inheritance as well."

"So he can't get at it because . . . ?"

"Gowrie has the deeds showing the land was owned by her husband."

"Then she inherited it, right? I don't see the problem. It's hers."

"But she cannot collect the income from the land. Her brothers have rented it out for rice growing and they are collecting the money. What they really want is to sell the land. They locked Gowrie in a shed to make her give them the deeds. They threatened to harm Meeta. She escaped and came to Chennai to hide from them, to protect her daughter."

"Why doesn't she go to the police?"

Raj marveled at the innocence of the foreigner. What kind of a world did she come from where police could be trusted to uphold the law? "That would not be wise. She would have to go back to her town to file the complaint. She would have to give the police the deeds. Her family is powerful there. Perhaps"—Raj hesitated for emphasis and delicately stressed the next two verbs—"some police official could be encouraged to lose the deeds."

"What about her husband's family?"

Mary Elizabeth took up the story. "Gowrie and her husband were a love match. His family is very, very traditional. They never wanted Gowrie. They only agreed to the marriage because he was a youngest son and the gift was large enough that she would not cost them money."

"But Meeta is their grandchild," Kiria protested.

"Their grand*daughter*," Mary Elizabeth corrected.

Kiria shook her head and took a sip of tea. "Poor Gowrie. Will the case take long?"

"If she produces the deeds, it's a strong case. Perhaps a year or two. She does not trust me enough to show me the deeds yet." Prompted by curiosity, Raj decided it was Kiria's turn to answer some questions. "So, Mary Elizabeth tells me you want to build a women's hostel?"

"Yes." Kiria turned to face Mary Elizabeth. "Actually, I was going to call you tonight. One of the agents has a property for me to see. I was hoping you could come along with me, tell me what you think."

"I know nothing about property," Mary Elizabeth protested.

"But you know a lot about the women who would use the hostel, where they work, what they need. You could tell me if the location is good. I have a viewing appointment on Saturday afternoon. You wouldn't have to take time off work." Kiria smiled hopefully.

Although she did not have any expectations for the success of Kiria's project, Mary Elizabeth felt flattered to be asked for her opinion and curious about what kind of place the agent had found. "I will be happy to come. I will ask Selvi to stay with my father."

"And I know quite a bit about property. Perhaps you would like me to join you?" Raj offered.

Kiria suspected Raj's offer was not entirely motivated by a desire to see the poor women of Chennai well housed, but she responded as though it was. "Would you? Thank you. I need all the opinions I can get."

"Where are you staying?" Raj asked, pulling a small notebook out of his briefcase. "I'll come pick you up."

"By then I'll be in Periyar Nagar. New number fifteen, old number thirty-seven, Circular Temple Road," Kiria said, giving him the address in both the new house-numbering system and the old one that most houses still displayed.

Raj wrote down the address. "I'll pick up Mary Elizabeth on the way. What time?"

"I don't know. I don't know where the property is either. I'll call the agent. What's your phone number? I'll call you when I know."

Raj reached into the breast pocket of his immaculate pale blue shirt and pulled out a business card, which he handed to Kiria. "My cell number is the best way to reach me."

Kiria took one of her own cards out of her purse, wrote her Indian cell number on the back and handed it to Raj.

"I should get back to the hotel." She pulled up the legs of her pants to expose hugely puffed ankles. "I'd better handle these before they get any worse. See you both on Saturday."

Raj and Mary Elizabeth said good-bye and watched Kiria leave. As the door closed, Mary Elizabeth turned a resigned face to Raj. "She knows."

"Yes, my love, I think she does. A very interesting woman. Tiring, though. I'm exhausted just talking to her."

Mary Elizabeth giggled.

Outside the door of the coffee shop Kiria successfully negotiated a fare back to the hotel with the first auto driver she flagged down. Sitting on the bench in the back of the auto as it pulled away from the curb, she looked back.

"A lawyer in love," she muttered. "Not bad. Not bad at all."

A Blind Man Sees Things Differently

❁ ❁ ❁ ❁ ❁

ON SANTOSHI'S LAST DAY AT the Radhakrishna Short Stay Home for Women and Children, Warden announced that there would be a special lunch in celebration of Santoshi's new job. No one actually believed this was Priya's real intention, because she assigned Santoshi to prepare the meal.

Although she had never been formally taught, Santoshi was undoubtedly the best cook at the shelter. After years of offering willing hands to the cooks in the houses where she worked, she had acquired a repertoire of recipes and techniques that were the envy of her fellow inmates, and it was generally agreed that Priya's sudden generosity was prompted more by a desire for one last dish of Santoshi's Chettinad chicken than any intention to celebrate. Still, the women welcomed any excuse for celebration in the bland, gray life of the shelter, especially one that came with meat in the middle of the week.

Santoshi herself did not mind cooking on her last day. There were many helping hands, and she preferred to be busy. The soothing work of chopping and stirring helped to calm her nerves, stretched tight over her fear of leaving the shelter for an unimaginable new life. She rose early and worked steadily through the morning, assigning tasks and chatting with those who came to help as the morning progressed.

Just before eleven, Gowrie entered the backyard where Santoshi was tending the pots of rice, sambar and rasam simmering over small fires. Gowrie carried her daughter, Meeta, on one hip and a large parcel, wrapped in newspaper, on her head.

"I could only get six chickens." Gowrie set Meeta and the parcel on the ground. "But two of the chickens are large. I got all the organs and I made the butcher chop the birds into small pieces."

Santoshi opened the parcel and studied the mound of chicken pieces. There was enough for a full serving for Priya, and everyone else would get either one large piece or two small pieces. "We should make beans as well," she decided. "Can you help me pick them over?"

"Let me do that." Banu came out the back door. "The doctor says I must use my hands as much as possible to make them strong again." She raised her arms and flexed her newly mobile fingers proudly. Banu's spirits had risen since the operation on her hands, just as Mary Elizabeth had promised. Now that she could feed herself and dress herself, Banu no longer wanted to die.

Santoshi nodded her thanks and returned her attention to the chicken. Banu went to the storeroom. Gowrie sat on the stone doorstep and held Meeta on her lap, away from the open fires. Meeta, exhausted from the long walk to the butcher and the excitement of watching the chickens being killed, leaned back against her mother's breast and fell asleep.

"Do your hands still hurt?" Gowrie asked Banu when she returned from the storeroom with a small sack of beans and a large pan.

"No, not like the burns. They just ache at night. It is hard to sleep."

"Perhaps you should not do so much with them," Gowrie suggested.

Banu pulled a handful of beans from the sack. "It is a joy to be useful again. It is good pain."

Gowrie placed her daughter gently on the ground and went over to help Santoshi pick stray feathers off the chicken pieces. "Warden will miss you, Santoshi. We all will. Are you excited about tomorrow?"

"Yes. But I am afraid too. I left my job. I am losing my place here."

Gowrie found this hard to believe. She envied Santoshi. "I wish some rich white woman would pay me so much to do so little."

"You are brave," Santoshi said. "You are young and pretty and someday you may find another husband. For me, this is only a short time between the shelters."

"I am not brave. But I would do anything to leave the shelters." Gowrie looked over at the sleeping child. "This is no place to raise my daughter. But why come back to the shelters? You said the white woman wants to build a place where women can live independently."

Santoshi rose and rinsed her hands in a pan of water. "There will be no hostel. She will give up. She will go home to her soft life." She lifted the lid of the rice pot. "And even if she does not, what woman would want to live there? Unprotected."

"I would." Gowrie rose as well and resumed her seat on the doorstep. "I will. When the hostel is ready, I will be the first woman to apply for a room. I would rather live alone and unprotected than rot within these walls."

"Better to return to your family." Santoshi picked up a ladle to stir the rice. "If it would not bring shame on my family, I would return to them."

"No." Gowrie shook her head. "I cannot go back now. My only hope is the hostel, and my job at the sari shop."

"And your court case," Santoshi reminded her.

"Yes, of course." After months of practice, the lie came easily to Gowrie. "But the lawyer says that could take years. I am not living here for years."

Banu stopped laboriously sorting through the beans and squatted back on her haunches. "I am sick of listening to you two whine about your good fortune." Her damaged mouth pulled down into an angry scowl. "How sad for you. Let me help you. I will take your strength, Santoshi, and your rich white woman and you can have my place here." She looked over at Meeta, sleeping by her mother's feet. "And I will take Meeta, Gowrie. And you can be the woman who will never have children because she is too ugly for a man to even look at." Banu's voice broke. Tears flowed a twisted course down her scarred cheeks.

Gowrie stared down at her dusty feet in their worn sandals. "I am sorry, Banu," she whispered.

Santoshi finished stirring the rice and replaced the lid on the pot. "What about a blind man?" she asked calmly.

Gowrie choked. Despite herself, Banu felt the corners of her scowl tug upward. The two women looked at each other and burst out laughing. What made Santoshi's remark even funnier was that everyone knew she had no sense of humor.

Death of a Butterfly

KIRIA SAT ON THE BALUSTRADE of the terrace outside her new apartment waiting for the furniture delivery van. Across the street, a woman in a ragged sari picked through a heap of garbage. Two small girls sat in the shade of the bougainvillea tree, the oldest holding an infant. Kiria hadn't noticed the garbage while looking at the apartment, and felt far from pleased to be discovering it now that she'd paid the deposit.

Santoshi came out of the apartment door and handed Kiria her ringing cell phone.

"Hello?"

"Hi, Kiria. It's Eva. Happy New Year."

"Eva! Happy New Year. How are you? How was the hangover?"

"It was awesome. I still have the headache. How are you?"

"Sweating and bathing in deet."

"No sympathy. Moving to India was your bright idea."

"I seem to recall being strongly encouraged."

"Okay, a tiny bit of sympathy. Listen, we have a kind of good-news, bad-news situation here. You know that chandelier you hate in reception?"

"The Kinky Butterflies. What about it?"

"You're never going to see it again."

"That must be the good news. Why?"

"That's the bad news. Remember Jim, the new guy in sales?"

" 'Call me Jimbo.' Yeah."

"He went over his limit at the office party on Monday night and had a Tarzan moment with the chandelier. Pulled it out of the ceiling."

"Oh my God! Is he okay?"

"Oh yeah, he's fine. Five stitches in his hand. He broke the fish tank."

"Anyone else hurt?"

"Well, Red and Ginger weren't too pleased."

"Oh dear. I'm sorry. You liked them."

"I still do. They're fine. I threw them in the toilet."

"Let's hope no one flushes."

"I didn't leave them there! They're on my kitchen counter in my grandmother's crystal punch bowl. Thought I'd get them out of the office until the repairs were done."

"So? All's well that ends well."

"It's not over yet. I had a contractor in to look at the ceiling today. He doesn't think there's any structural damage, but the estimate to replaster and paint is five thousand."

"That's peanuts."

"Not for Jimbo. He just bought that Porsche."

"Back up. Why is Jim paying for it?"

"Piet thinks he should. I tried to tell him you wouldn't like it, but he went all righteous on me."

"Righteous?"

"Yeah. Like people have to learn to take responsibility for their actions. Weird, eh? I don't think he likes Jim. Anyway, I told Piet to call you so you can straighten him out."

"Me? That's your job."

"I can't."

"Why not? You never had any problems setting me straight."

"Ummm . . . I might have encouraged Jim."

"To swing from light fixtures?"

"Well, I didn't think he'd do that. It's just that Piet was being such a stick and the party was dying and Jim was funny and . . ."

"Maybe you should pay for it. Just kidding. I'll talk to him. I wanted to find out how the integration tests are going anyway."

"Thanks. So there's one more thing. A lawyer called today asking for you. I told him Piet was filling in for you, but he said he could only talk to you. I told him I had to check with you before giving out your number."

"Did he say what it's about?"

"He said it was personal and you'd know what it was about."

"Did he give you his name?"

"Megler. Theodore Megler."

"Oh dear."

"Do you know him?"

"No, but remember that guy in Toronto? The couple who adopted my son were named Megler."

"Oh my God! You think he's your son?"

"Could be."

"How can you sound so matter-of-fact? This is exciting!"

"Depends on why he wants to talk to me. Think about it. He knows who I am, he's thirty-seven years old and this is the first time he's tried to contact me. There aren't a lot of warm, fuzzy explanations for this."

"I see your point. Oh! Maybe he's sick and it's something genetic!"

"Oh, well, that makes me feel so much better. Just give him my number and personal e-mail and let's get some facts to work with."

"You're right. I'll do it before I go to bed. You going to be okay?"

"I'll be fine."

"Well, call me if you need to talk."

"I always do. Meanwhile, it must be close to midnight there. Tell Piet to call me tomorrow morning."

"Okay. Take care of yourself. Bye."

"Bye, Eva."

Kiria and Santoshi spent the day setting up house. By early evening, Santoshi was in the kitchen rolling out chapatis while Kiria sat in a lawn chair on the terrace hanging up from her third call to the Nexus store. She put the cell phone down on her new patio table, pursed her lips and said a nasty word. There would be no air conditioner delivered tonight. The best she'd been able to achieve was a promise to have the van out first thing in the morning. She was thinking of checking into a hotel when the phone rang. She stared at it through two rings, then took a deep breath and picked it up.

"Hello?"

Piet's voice came down the line. "Hi, Kiria. It's Piet."

"Piet! It's you!"

"Of course it's me. Eva said you wanted to talk to me."

"I do. How's the testing going?"

"So far so good. There's a few problems, but nothing serious. We're running the last scripts today. Franklin's going to compile the results over the weekend. I'll tell him to e-mail them to you."

"Fantastic. So how's everything else going?"

"Not bad, except for Eva."

"What about Eva?"

"We're not working well together."

"She's being rude?"

"Nothing like that. I don't think she likes me."

"Oh, I'm pretty sure it's not that. Can you give me an example?"

"Well, you know the new guy in sales? Jim? He got drunk at the office party last week. He hit on Eva and she encouraged him, and then he started showing off for her and he pulled the chandelier out of the ceiling in reception. I mean, he was really drunk. So, anyway, we got an estimate for repairs and I told her to send it to Jim, and she refused!"

"Hmmm."

"What, 'hmmm'? 'Hmmm' as in it's okay to refuse an instruction?"

"No, 'hmmm' as in we paid for the alcohol. Have you talked to anyone in legal about this?"

"No. Should I?"

"Can't hurt. But it's your decision. You know, if Eva disagrees, she probably has a good reason. Looking at things from all sides is a big part of running a company. Listen to her advice. You don't have to take it."

"She just said you wouldn't like it."

"Well, personally, I'd think twice about punishing someone for getting drunk on liquor I provided. Listen, whatever you decide, as long as it's fair, I'm good with it. Have you had any other problems with Eva?"

"I just get the feeling she's avoiding me."

"Are you using your deodorant?"

"Very funny."

"Seriously, give it a few weeks. You're a new boss. She's just being careful until she knows how you work. Oh yeah, one more thing. Can you put the reception desk out by the elevators until the repairs are completed?"

"Eva did it yesterday and put some plants around it to make it look like it's supposed to be there."

"Does it?"

"How the hell should I know? I'm a geek."

"You and me both. Happy New Year, Piet."

"Happy New Year, Kiria."

Kiria hung up, swatted a mosquito on her neck and went in to apply more insect repellent.

Matchmaking

HAVE YOU EVER TAKEN ONE of those *Cosmo* quizzes? You know the ones. How Adventurous Is Your Sex Life? What Kind of an Animal Are You in Bed? With the exception of my friend Ally, who claims to have scored Tigress since puberty, the rest of my female friends admit that their libido scores have swung wildly over the years. Every woman has a different biological clock, but as the ovum countdown approaches zero, most of us have one last hormonal frenzy somewhere around our midforties. The lucky ones get through it by eating half a ton of chocolate and watching reruns of *Dirty Dancing* or *Pride and Prejudice* (BBC version). Those of us who are less lucky end up with dyed hair, a closet full of plunging necklines and, if we're single, at least a couple of humiliatingly short romances.

In the Victorian moral climate of India, cleavage was not an option for Mary Elizabeth, and if she dyed her mass of black hair, I couldn't tell. But the minute I saw her with Raj, I knew she was deep into romance territory. Nothing else could explain a forty-eight-year-old woman making cow eyes at a man who was three inches shorter, at least ten years older and—not to mince words here—chubby.

What he lacked in physical sex appeal, Mary Elizabeth's heartthrob made up for in presence. Raj was a lawyer. He dressed well, listened well and had a compassionate, generous nature. He came from a background of wealth and education, which gave him a broad worldview and an easy charm. All that and he adored Mary Elizabeth too. I couldn't believe my luck.

No one just waltzes into a foreign country and sets up shop. There are laws, customs. Anyone who doesn't know them won't get far. I expected to be hiring advisers, especially lawyers. With Raj I hit the jackpot. His enthusiasm for the hostel project had more to do with increased access to Mary Elizabeth than with any burning desire to help poor women. I was okay with that; better than okay, actually. A man in love will move a mountain with a teaspoon.

I don't care for romance personally, not having had much luck with it myself. Most romances are doomed if for no other reason than human beings cannot sustain that level of deception for any appreciable length of time. But theirs was more doomed than most. Mary Elizabeth was an Anglo Indian Roman Catholic. As a Brahman, Raj stood at the top of the heap in the Hindu caste system. Both were tediously conservative about their social standing. They hid each other from their families and never even considered dating, let alone marriage. Before I came along, their only contact had been a weekly coffee shop conference over Gowrie's court case. At this level, their romance would have smoldered along until the case ended, then died for lack of opportunity. Working on the hostel brought them together daily, if not in person, then by phone, and if not by phone, then in an endless series of instructions to me. "Ask Raj if he thinks . . ." "Tell Mary Elizabeth to meet us. . . ." Any excuse to mention the other's name.

Raj became my fixer, my go-to guy, the alpha male who pulled the strings I couldn't even reach. He enticed Mary Elizabeth into the project. Her motivations weren't any higher than his, mind you. At times I didn't know if I was building a hostel or running a dating service.

Raj proved his worth on our very first outing. Not knowing Chennai, I hadn't been able to give the real estate agents much in the way of direction other than I didn't want anything within half a mile of a river. The first property Venkat found backed onto a river, a slimy, stinky, oozing, sewage-clogged travesty of a river. The building itself, a dilapidated three-story apartment block in the Egmore district, featured a row of seedy shops on the street side and forty feet of weedy land at the back. Even if it hadn't been on the river, I wouldn't have considered it. It was fully occupied. I nearly fired Venkat on the spot.

Fortunately, Raj took charge and proved the old adage about getting more flies with honey. Which is a very odd expression when you think about it. Who exactly wants these flies? Entomologists? Any entomologist worth his salt should know that you get the most flies with shit.

Venkat, clearly expecting to run a snow job on a clueless foreign woman, found himself pitching to a very well-informed man. Raj went over the building with a magnifying glass. He was polite, even friendly, but poor Venkat was left in no doubt as to the depths of Raj's disappointment that such an unsuitable property should even have been presented to him. At the end of the viewing Raj stood looking out over the river. He said nothing, just shook his head slightly. River frontage was not a feature of any subsequent property Venkat showed us.

Boiling the Midnight Oil

SANTOSHI WOKE IN THE MIDDLE of the night gasping for breath. She lay back on the mattress, forced herself to breathe slowly and waited for her heart to stop hammering at her ribs. It was the same dream. Falling alone in the darkness.

She had feared many things when taking the new job, but nightmares had never crossed her mind. After a week of them, she was exhausted and afraid of sleeping. What if they never stopped? She sat up and hung her legs over the side of the bed, knuckling her eyes like a child. There was a faint line of light under her bedroom door. Perhaps Madam had left a light on.

Santoshi slid off the bed and opened her door. The light came from the front hall. Her bare feet made no sound as she crossed the living room. When she got to the hall door, she saw Kiria sitting at the table under the fan, drawing something from a book.

"Madam?" she said softly.

Kiria startled. "Oh my God!" Air currents from the fan whipped the paper off the desk.

"Sorry, madam," Santoshi apologized, picking up the paper. It was covered with wobbly drawings of what looked like it might be the Tamil letter "dhii."

"It's okay, Santoshi. No sleep?"

"No, madam."

"Too hot?" Kiria made a fanning motion in front of her face.

"No, madam." Santoshi felt chilled when the temperature fell below ninety degrees. Tonight the temperature was a comfortable ninety-five degrees and the humidity a pleasant eighty percent.

"Is something wrong?"

"Bad . . ." Santoshi did not know how to say "dream" in English. "Fall sleep, madam."

"Bad fall sleep, bad fall sleep," Kiria repeated. She mimed sleeping, then waking up afraid. "Bad dream?"

Santoshi nodded. "Yes, madam. Bad dream. You bad dream?"

"No. Too hot." Kiria suppressed a jolt of annoyance. The air conditioner had finally been delivered, but the installers were proving harder to motivate. Well, since Santoshi was up, perhaps she could make a cup of tea. Kiria wanted one but was afraid of the gas ring that took the place of a stove in their kitchen. "Santoshi, want tea?"

"Yes, madam."

Santoshi returned with the pot of Earl Grey and two cups on a tray. Kiria smiled. At first, Santoshi had been shocked at the idea of drinking tea together. Now her passion for Earl Grey was insatiable. Kiria poured. Santoshi added five spoons of sugar to her cup and sat with it on the floor.

"Book, madam?"

"Tamil book," Kiria said, handing the book down.

Santoshi opened the book and gasped. It had English words and Tamil words side by side! She traced the English letters with her fingers, wishing she knew their sounds. "Madam teach Tamil," she said.

Kiria had no idea what this meant, but it gave her an idea. "Book teach Tamil." She pretended to pluck a Tamil word from the book and push it into the top of her head. "Santoshi teach Tamil." She made the same gesture, this time pretending the word came from Santoshi's mouth.

Santoshi wobbled her head from side to side. Kiria had originally thought this gesture meant no. She now interpreted it as "I'm listening" or "Okay."

Kiria picked up the paper and pointed to her drawing. "Good?"

"No, madam. Bad, madam." Santoshi stood, picked up the pen and drew a letter. "Dhii."

Kiria thought her letters looked like Santoshi's, but she took the pen, traced over Santoshi's letter and tried drawing it on her own.

"No, madam." Santoshi pointed to Kiria's letter. "Dhi." Then she pointed to her own letter. "Dhii."

Kiria tried again. To her they looked and sounded the same. Obviously the little loopy thing at the end was important.

"I teach English," Santoshi said.

Kiria finally got it. She drew two stick people. She pointed to the one with short, scribbled hair. "Kiria." She pointed to the other with the long braid. "Santoshi." She drew an arrow from Santoshi to Kiria. "Santoshi teach Tamil. Kiria learn Tamil." She drew an arrow in the opposite direction. "Kiria teach English. Santoshi learn English." She emphasized the verb in each sentence.

Santoshi traced the last arrow with her finger. "Santoshi learn English," she repeated softly. "Thank you, Kiria Madam."

Dawn found the two women sitting at the table practicing each other's alphabets.

Santoshi's nightmare worried Kiria. After breakfast, she called Mary Elizabeth and put her on the phone with Santoshi to find out what the dream was about.

"She says she has the same dream every night," Mary Elizabeth reported when Santoshi returned the phone to Kiria. "She dreams she is falling alone in the dark. She says it started the day you moved in. She is sorry if it bothers you. She will try to be quiet."

"She has them every night?"

"That is what she told me."

"Does she know why she's getting them?"

"I do not think so. She says she feels frightened and lonely when they happen."

Kiria sighed. "Okay. Thanks for talking to her."

An hour later Kiria dialed Mary Elizabeth again.

"It's the bed!" Kiria almost shouted.

"The bed?" Mary Elizabeth did not understand. "Why?"

"She's used to sleeping on the floor, right? The bed is too soft. Not enough pressure."

"Maybe." Mary Elizabeth did not sound convinced.

"Well, it's worth a try. Would you explain it to her? Ask her if she wants to try sleeping on the floor tonight."

Kiria handed the phone to Santoshi. After a few minutes of conversation Santoshi handed the phone back to Kiria.

"She says she will try it," Mary Elizabeth said. "You should try leaving your bedroom door open too."

"My bedroom door?"

"She has always slept with many other people. Never alone."

"It makes sense, but I'm not sure I can do that. I'll think about it."

During the afternoon Kiria insisted on rearranging the living room furniture. That night when Santoshi went to bed, Kiria was still up watching the television, which now stood close to the door of Santoshi's room. Santoshi lay down on the floor. She fell asleep in minutes and slept dreamlessly through the night.

Kiria sat under the fan in the living room with her feet in a bucket of water. She flipped through channels, hoping to find one showing an air conditioner installer dangling upside down over a vat of boiling oil.

The Right Choice

❁❁❁❁❁

KIRIA WAS JUST EASING HER swollen feet into a bucket of cool water when the call came. She picked her cell phone up from the coffee table and very nearly dropped it into the bucket when she saw the Toronto area code in the caller ID display. Closing her eyes, she muttered, "You can do this," then flipped open the phone.

"Hello?"

"Hello. Is this Kiria Langdon?"

"It is."

"My name is Theodore Megler. Do you know who I am?"

"I think so. Was that you I saw at the conference in Toronto, at the back of the room?"

"You knew it was me?"

"You look exactly like your father—I mean your biological father. I followed you out, you know. I watched you wait by the elevators."

"I didn't see you."

"I hid behind that big plant. I didn't want you to see me. I just wanted to look at you."

"That's funny. That's why I went there. I saw on the NOVIO Web site that you were going to be in town promoting SharpEnd, and I wanted to see you."

"And then you left. So why are you calling now?"

"I found your letter."

"What letter?"

"The one you sent from Oregon, returning the money. I've known I was adopted since I was ten. Up till I saw that letter, I always thought you didn't want me. But now I don't think that's true. I want to know why you put me up for adoption. I asked my mom, but she said you never talked about it."

"I couldn't. I was too afraid. It's not a good story."

"I don't care how bad it is. I just want to know. What were you afraid of?"

"I was afraid your biological father would find us."

"Us?"

"You were always a person to me, even before you were born. The truth is, I married a very violent man, and when I found out I was pregnant, I was afraid he'd . . . Well, I almost lost you. We were living in Albany, New York, at the time. I ran away across the border to Toronto. But I got sick. I couldn't work and I ended up living in a home for unwed mothers run by nuns. The nuns tried to make me put you up for adoption. But back then all adoptions were closed and I didn't want to give you away. Then I met Arthur and Alicia. I realized they could give you more than I could, everything I couldn't. So I agreed to an adoption with them. It was best for you."

"Mom said you stayed with them before I was born."

"For two months. That's how I knew I could trust them with you."

"But you didn't want to see them after I was born."

"Is that what they thought? No. I would have loved to see them again. It was you I couldn't risk seeing. When you were born, the first sound you made was this croaky little cry. I knew that if I saw you, I wouldn't go through with it. So I closed my eyes and told the delivery nurse to take you out of the room and tell Alicia and Arthur I didn't want to see them again."

"You just walked away."

"You've obviously never given birth. More like hobbled away. But yes, that's basically what I did. Alicia wanted to be your only mother. Everyone told me she was right: the nuns, the social workers, the lawyer who wrote up the papers. So I promised to stay away. Actually, does Alicia know you're contacting me? Is she okay with this?"

"Why would you care?"

"Of course I care. She's your mother, much more than I am."

"I intend to tell her. She's got a lot to deal with right now. My dad died three months ago. I found your letter while I was going through the last of his papers."

"I'm sorry. Arthur was a good man. I remember how in love your parents were. It must be very hard for Alicia. I'm glad you called, but your relationship with Alicia is more important than talking to me. When you can tell her and if she's not upset by it, and if you're willing, I'd like to talk with you again. In case it doesn't work out that way, can I just ask you one thing?"

"I hope I can answer."

"Were they good parents? Did I make the right choice?"

"They were great parents."

"Then I'm happy. Good-bye, Theodore."

"Good-bye . . . Kiria."

Kiria waited for the click from the other end of the line before closing the cell phone. "Well, that was different," she muttered, and put her feet into the bucket.

Cranky

❁ ❁ ❁ ❁ ❁

HAVE YOU EVER BEEN ON a diet? Okay, stupid question. Who hasn't? You know how there's always one thing you can't have that somehow becomes the most delicious food in the whole world? With me it was doughnuts. I could go for months without even thinking about doughnuts. But as soon as I went on a diet, I yearned for them, even dreamed about them. Eventually, I'd break down and eat one and be surprised, every time, by how much better they tasted in my imagination.

In many ways, the first time I talked with my son was exactly like breaking a diet. I knew it was coming; Eva had told me. I prepared myself for anger, accusations, even avarice, since I didn't know why he'd waited so long to contact me. I was ready to feel guilt, remorse, overwhelming love. But none of that happened. He asked me why I put him up for adoption. I told him. We hung up. It felt just like a doughnut—a big, fat, slightly awkward doughnut. I was shocked by my response, or rather my lack of one. I had stronger feelings about the air-conditioning installer.

Twenty-four hours after moving into the new apartment, I had cable, broadband, drinking water, cooking gas and screen windows, because none of these providers got paid until the job was completed. However, I foolishly paid for the installation of the air conditioner at the time of purchase, resulting in a sixteen-day delay between delivery of the unit and the arrival of the installer. I tried everything to get him to come out sooner: enticement, threats, bullying; I think I even cried. Nothing worked. He evaded capture with abject apologies and incomprehensible excuses. "So sorry, madam, but today Pongal Festival. Must help my mother wash cow."

During this period I averaged two hours' sleep a night. If Santoshi hadn't picked an apartment with great cross-ventilation, I probably wouldn't have gotten that much. The extra six hours of consciousness I spent with my feet in a bucket of water, learning the Tamil alphabet. Aside from giving my Tamil skills a leg up, sleep deprivation resulted in unpredictable mood swings. My days fragmented into a thousand shards of conflicting emotions coated with a thick layer of crankiness. This ultimately saved me a great deal of money.

Sushil and Venkat showed us nine properties altogether. Five of them were occupied; I had no intentions of evicting anyone. One was a collapsing ruin, not even worth an attempt at restoration. Two were miles outside the city, an impossible commute for working women. One had real possibility. It was a sprawling old barracks that had housed British railway personnel before independence and, until recently, had been used by the railway company to store old machinery. Everyone liked it. Tropical climates are not kind to buildings, but Raj felt it could be made habitable for a reasonable amount. Mary Elizabeth and Santoshi liked the location. It had a fair amount of land that I thought could be turned into a safe playground for children. Consensus had been reached. Negotiations began.

The railway company assigned an anal-retentive little *t* crosser with a side order of obsessive-compulsive as our primary contact. Well, perhaps that's a bit harsh. But he was really very, very annoying. He stalled. He dithered. He checked everything with his superiors. He went out of station, which is Indiaspeak for out of town, without telling us. And when he finally showed up at the second rescheduling of the third meeting, it became apparent he wanted an outrageous amount for a bribe.

Now, I'm not opposed to graft, per se. As long as it doesn't cross legal boundaries, it's reasonable compensation for additional services rendered. A whole profession has developed around political graft; in America we call them lobbyists. But the demands of the briber must be proportionate to the benefits for the bribee. This guy wanted a Range Rover just to pass me up to the next level.

If I'd had air-conditioning, I probably would have gone as far as a new bicycle or a secondhand motor scooter. But sleep deprivation impaired my judgment and I really disliked the little shit. I tried to get him down to roller skates. Negotiations exploded in a spectacular display of name-calling and fizzled out entirely after my halfhearted apology via voice mail got no response.

It was about this time that Santoshi started disappearing during the day. Taking care of me was hardly full-time employment, and next to my landlady, Santoshi was about the most money-obsessed person I had ever met. She could squeeze a rupee to powder and clutched every paisa with an iron grip. When she asked me if she could leave my lunch in the fridge and go out for the day, I assumed she'd found a second job. This was good news for two reasons.

Santoshi had seemed a little shell-shocked when we first moved in together, sitting in her room when her work was completed, as though, after years of being told what to do, she couldn't imagine doing anything without instruction. Finding a second job was a huge step toward independence for her, not to mention it got her out of my hair.

After I'd lived alone for so many years, sharing my home with another person, however self-effacing, got on my nerves. I'm not a hermit, not even a recluse. But I like my solitude. After a couple of weeks with Santoshi I needed space, time to scratch my mental butt, talk to myself and make voodoo dolls of air-conditioning installers.

How to Do Laundry

AS SANTOSHI FINISHED PEGGING OUT the morning's laundry on the line strung across the terrace, she heard the creaking of the hand pump in the yard below. She walked to the back of the area and stood looking down at Laxmi trying to pump water for her own laundry.

Laxmi held the pump handle in both hands, battling it like an enemy. Instead of finding the rhythm of the water flow and allowing the handle to rise on its own, she pushed both down and up. The water erupted from the spout in jerky spurts, some of it falling outside the water jar.

Santoshi had watched this performance every second day since moving in and could not understand it. Why was Laxmi using the pump at all? Why wasn't she getting her laundry water out of the tap from the roof tank? Santoshi found her own arm muscles contracting in sympathy. Suddenly she could stand it no longer. She trotted down the stairs and around to the back of the house.

"Miss? Miss? Let me help you."

Laxmi stopped pumping and straightened up, placing her left hand on the small of her back to ease the strain. She looked through the kitchen window to make sure neither of her in-laws was there to see her, then smiled sadly at the little maid. "I would like that. But I cannot pay you."

"No reason to pay, miss. I will show you how to make the water flow. Please step back."

Laxmi stepped down from the pump platform. Santoshi stepped up. "You should hold the handle in one hand and rest the other," she instructed. "You should only push down. Feel the pump return to the water. Watch." Santoshi gave the handle a few downward pushes. The water began to flow in a steady stream. "You try." Santoshi stepped off the platform.

Laxmi took her place. Grasping the handle at the end, she pushed down hard, then relaxed her arm while the handle rose back up. As it neared the top, she actually did think she could feel the piston contacting the water below. She found the rhythm after a few pushes. The water flowed steadily. "This is much easier!" Laxmi exclaimed.

Santoshi pointed to the tap in the pipe coming from the roof tank. "You should fix this, miss."

"It's not broken." Laxmi continued to pump.

"Then why are you pumping by hand?"

Laxmi glanced at the kitchen window again. "Electricity costs money," she said in a low voice.

"But you are rich!" The exclamation burst out before Santoshi could stop it.

"I was rich. Now I am a married woman." Laxmi's head jerked toward the house. "I do as I am told."

Never having been married herself, Santoshi had often felt envious of the pretty young woman with her handsome husband

and her lovely clothes and the status of a family. The idea that this girl was being forced to pump water softened the edges of envy with pity.

Laxmi wasn't sure why she was saying these things to a servant. Perhaps it was gratitude. In two minutes Santoshi had done more to make Laxmi's life easier than Geeta had in six months of angry tutelage. Perhaps it was just that this was a real conversation and not a harshly uttered command.

"Do you like working for the white woman?" Laxmi asked to prolong the conversation.

"Kiria Madam is very good. But . . ." Santoshi paused, searching for a way to explain her loneliness without saying anything bad about her mistress. "There is too much time. Not enough work," she finished lamely.

"Not enough work?" Laxmi sounded incredulous. Her life was nothing but work.

"One person to care for does not make much work. And Western food is very easy to cook," Santoshi explained.

"You cook Western food? I love Western food. What do you cook?"

"Sandwiches. Kiria Madam likes sandwiches. And soup. And pizza. I do not cook pizza. It is delivered. And salads. She likes salads."

"Pizza! I adore pizza." Laxmi closed her eyes and remembered meeting with her classmates at Pizza Hut. "Do you like it?"

"There is much bread. We are not sick. I prefer rice."

Because she had been raised in more affluent circumstances, Laxmi did not share Santoshi's old-fashioned belief that leavened bread should be eaten only by sick people. She liked leavened bread and missed having morning toast. But it cost forty rupees a loaf and Geeta would never buy it. Laxmi worked the pump handle and thought about how lucky Santoshi was to be able to use the water from the roof tank and eat food like pizza.

The first water jar was filled. Santoshi moved it aside and placed the second jar under the pump spout. Then, because she too was enjoying her first real conversation since moving in, she said, "I will pump the next jar."

The women exchanged places. Santoshi began to pump and Laxmi poured some water into a bucket and started to add soap powder.

"Less soap, miss," Santoshi advised. "You will need too much water to rinse."

"How else does it get clean?"

"With soaking. Leave those to soak. I will show you when we finish pumping. Why do you wear this sari, miss?"

"This?" Laxmi forgot about looking for her in-laws and sat on the pump platform. "Because I don't want to get my good clothes dirty."

"But this is a good sari."

"It was once." Laxmi fingered the gold-embroidered pink fabric. Her voice was sad. "My father bought me this for Deepavali, two years ago."

"Where is your family?"

"In Bangalore."

"Do you see them, miss?"

"My parents are ill. They cannot travel. I want to call them but . . ."

"We do not need a maid!" Geeta's shout came harshly through the kitchen window.

Laxmi leapt up from the pump platform. Santoshi stopped pumping.

Geeta came limping out of the kitchen doorway. "We will not pay you."

Santoshi ducked her head.

"We were just talking," Laxmi protested.

"You were talking. She was working." Geeta turned to Santoshi. "What are you doing here?"

Santoshi's first instinct was to run, but she fought it down. "This is my water, madam," she said. She stepped down from the platform, picked up the half-full water jar and balanced it on her hip. "I will bring back the jar shortly, madam." She forced herself to walk away slowly.

"Why did she pump water?" Geeta asked after Santoshi had disappeared around the corner of the house.

"She didn't say." Putting an empty jar under the spout, Laxmi stepped back up on the platform and began to pump.

Back on the roof terrace, Santoshi found Kiria sitting by the balustrade, talking on the phone as usual.

"Eva? Eva? Calm down. He's just . . ." Kiria rolled her eyes upward. "No, I don't think he meant you're fat. Hang on a second, I've got to talk to Santoshi. Just hang on." She pulled the phone away from her ear. "Good morning, Santoshi. What's the water for?"

By now Santoshi was able to understand most of Kiria's simple sentences by means of ignoring all the filler words. She said the first thing that came into her mind. "Hair wash, Kiria Madam. Breakfast, Kiria Madam? Dhosa?" she asked hopefully.

"Toast, please. And coffee. Thank you, Santoshi." Kiria pressed the phone back to her ear. "Look, Eva, we'd both like to enroll Piet in Tact 101, but I'm certain that in this case the 'substantial' remark was about your organizational skills, not your backside. . . ."

Santoshi carried the water jar into the bathroom, then went into the kitchen, feeling slightly nauseated. Bread again. She put a pot of water on the gas ring to boil, placed two pieces of bread in the strange toasting machine and wondered how it could be that she felt sorry for Laxmi, a woman who had everything Santoshi would never have.

Service to family was a woman's duty. Laxmi should be proud to wash clothes for her husband and his parents, to cook for them, to serve them. Perhaps it was that Laxmi had no homely skills. Perhaps her mother had not thought them important for a girl who would marry into a wealthy family. But Laxmi had not married well and now she must pump water because her mother-in-law was bad tempered. It seemed harsh that Laxmi must be punished for her parents' mistake.

Santoshi poured the bitter black coffee that Kiria Madam liked so much into a mug. Her small nose wrinkled as she spread the disgusting peanut butter on Kiria Madam's toast. Picking up the tray, she decided to skip breakfast this morning.

Later, after Geeta had left to do the marketing and Kiria Madam had gone to take her bath, Santoshi took the water jar back downstairs and finished the laundry lesson.

Family Dynamics

❁❁❁❁❁

WANT TO PUT YOUR BRAIN in a blender? Try working out family dynamics in an alien culture.

As I watched the comings and goings of the family living in the main house below the apartment, I soon found myself addicted to the real-life soap opera taking place daily under my nose. To understand my enthrallment, you're going to need a short introduction to the cast of characters and a précis of the plot.

- Venu: titular head of the household. Early seventies, usually home, rarely awake. If napping were an Olympic sport, this guy would have taken the gold back to India. I know this because his room was directly below my terrace and he could have snored for India as well.
- Geeta: Venu's wife. Midsixties, usually home. Partially crippled by polio as a child, actual head of household,

although she always pretended to defer to her husband and attributed all decisions to him.

- Mani: Venu and Geeta's only son. Late twenties, home some evenings, charming and easy on the eyes. Very, very easy on the eyes.

- Laxmi: Mani's wife. Early twenties, always home, pretty and lively.

They were the stars of the show. The supporting cast included:

- Venu and Geeta's five married daughters and their husbands, children and in-laws. I met them all at one time or another but never did get their names straight.

- Prakesh, a young man who came over every day for lunch. (Prakesh had been raised in America until he was eighteen and was one of the few people I met in India that I could have a normal conversation with. Because his standards of hygiene were American, he had given up looking for a maid who could satisfy them and consequently did all of his own household chores. This uncharacteristic obsession with housework by a man was the primary cause of his reputation as an eccentric in the neighborhood.)

- A clutch of nosy neighbor ladies who stood on the street chatting with Geeta from time to time.

- Santoshi, who had formed a clandestine friendship with Laxmi.

Like all good soap opera plots, this one revolved around a love triangle. Geeta and Laxmi were engaged in a battle to the death for Mani's affections. Mani loved Mani, but he was so charismatic that neither woman noticed. Or perhaps they did but didn't care. Venu's narcolepsy may have had something to do with avoiding his female relatives, but he was very old, so perhaps he was just tired. When he did stick his nose out of the bedroom, it was generally to order Laxmi to make him tea.

Geeta's weapons of choice were maternal privilege, cruelty and backbiting. She slathered her son in affection like mayonnaise on potato salad. She treated Laxmi like an unpaid servant, ordering her around and inventing ways to make her life harder. Geeta complained constantly—to her husband, to Mani, to the neighbors, to her daughters and even, when I let her, to me—about Laxmi's laziness and incompetence. To be fair, Geeta was a very hard worker herself.

Laxmi fought back with passive aggression and sex. She did exactly what she was told to do, never more, never less and never well. This last one could be attributed to her privileged upbringing. When her husband was around, she became a caricature of a Tamil movie siren. Again in fairness, I have otherwise perfectly normal friends who turn into goo at the merest whiff of testosterone.

Mani accepted the adoration of both women as his due, flattered them when it didn't inconvenience him and was not above being conspicuously affectionate toward one when he wanted something from the other. In his defense, he was the baby of the family, born after his parents had given up hope of having a son. Venu and Geeta spoiled their precious scion rotten. He grew up convinced that he was the center of the universe.

Add to this hackneyed plot the married sisters and nosy neighbors in Geeta's camp, eccentric lunch guy and Santoshi as

Laxmi's only defenders, and I had a daily dose of drama that kept me spellbound.

In illustration, let me just recount my all-time favorite episode: "The Laundry Lesson."

Instead of teaching her daughter-in-law how to do chores properly, or even just doing them herself, Geeta preferred to let Laxmi struggle and then redo the work. The laundry was rich territory because Laxmi was pathetic at it. On wash days, Geeta inspected the laundry hanging on the line in her backyard closely, pulled off the items that didn't meet her standards (unless they were Laxmi's garments) and rewashed them.

I watched from the back of the terrace one morning as Santoshi gave Laxmi a laundry lesson. Geeta came out for inspection and found nothing to rewash. She rechecked the line, literally turning garments inside out in her search for dirt. Then, and I'm not making this up, she pulled a shirt off the line and dropped it on the ground. She called Laxmi out, pointed to the shirt and berated her.

Laxmi just stood there and took it with her head up and her arms hanging relaxed at her sides. When Geeta finally ran down, Laxmi picked up the soiled shirt, pegged it on the line and walked back into the house. My Tamil wasn't yet up to getting the gist of Geeta's complaint, but it had to be something along the lines of bad pegging.

Now, here's where the little gray cells hit the whirling blades. Why?

Why did Geeta pick a wife for her son that she disliked? Or, if she had originally liked Laxmi, why did she change her mind?

Why did clever, well-educated Laxmi choose such a weak defense strategy? Why did she put up with it at all?

Why did Mani encourage the rivalry between his mother and his wife?

Why did the sisters and the neighbors seem to approve of Geeta's cruelty?

Why did the eccentric Prakesh side with Laxmi?

Why did Santoshi and Laxmi hide their friendship? For that matter, why were they friends at all?

Mulling over these questions and watching the domestic drama unfold below my terrace kept me pleasantly occupied in the doldrum days between moving in and finally finding the location for the hostel. Then I had something much more perplexing to ponder, because it was Santoshi who found the property for the hostel. Where Venkat had failed miserably and Sushil had lost his commission to my temper, Santoshi had triumphed, finding not only the perfect property but the perfect vendor.

First the apartments, then the hostel. How did she do it?

Santoshi Saves the Day

LAXMI ANSWERED A KNOCK AT the front door late one afternoon to find Kiria standing on the doorstep.

"Oh good, it's you," Kiria began with her typical bluntness. "I'm sorry to bother you. I need a favor. Have you got a few minutes?"

Laxmi opened the door wider, gesturing Kiria into the hall. "Of course. Come in. Have you eaten?"

"Yes, thank you." Kiria had not eaten, but it was faster to lie and avoid the inevitable twenty-minute discussion required to politely reject the mandatory offer of food. She stepped into the hall but remained standing by the door. "Santoshi came home just now and she's very agitated. She's teaching me Tamil and I'm teaching her English, but I can't make out what she's so upset about. I tried calling my friend to translate for us and she's not answering. Would you mind coming upstairs for a few minutes and translating?"

"I'll be happy to." Laxmi would be more than happy to.

Anything that postponed sweating over the stove was a blessing. "Just give me a minute to tell my mother-in-law where I'm going."

Laxmi found Geeta in the back bedroom, making entries in the family account book. The old woman's withered leg was propped up on the bed. Sweat trickled through the wrinkles on her neck. She had not turned on the fan. "You use too much cooking gas," Geeta said without looking up. "Use less."

Laxmi felt a spike of annoyance. By birth and education, she was trained to think of money in terms of ability to buy comfort. She despised her in-laws for their brutal frugality but was careful never to let this show. Dropping her shoulders to calm herself as her yoga guru had taught her, she replied meekly, "Yes, Mother." She remained standing in the doorway until Geeta looked up.

"What?"

"Our tenant has asked me to translate something for her."

"What?"

"I don't know."

"Have you chopped the onions?"

"Not yet."

Geeta knew perfectly well that Laxmi was showing defiance. Permission cannot be granted where none is asked. However, after this morning's work on the family budget, Geeta had no intention of offending the tenant. "Go!" she said, trying to make it sound like an order. She waited until Laxmi was almost out of hearing range before muttering, "Idiot."

It was Laxmi's first time inside the upstairs apartment since it had been furnished. She expected it to be cold because of the air conditioner, but it was only a few degrees cooler than outside. The hall contained a square wooden table and four chairs. A laptop stood open on the table, headphones plugged into the side. Kiria led her through to the living room, which was furnished with an upholstered sofa, a glass coffee table and a wide-screen television on a stand against the far wall. The furniture was awkwardly positioned, the cable for the television looping across the floor from where it entered the room to where the television stood. The walls were undecorated and the built-in cement shelves, neatly lined with newspaper, were almost empty. To Laxmi it looked cluttered and somehow bleak at the same time.

"Have a seat." Kiria gestured at the sofa. "Would you like some tea? We have Earl Grey or regular milk tea."

"What's Earl Grey?"

"It's black tea flavored with bergamot, a kind of mint. Santoshi likes it."

"I think I'd like to try that. Are you comfortable here?"

"Getting there. Santoshi takes good care of me and it's much better now that the air conditioner has been installed."

"I expected it to be set lower."

"It's a compromise. Santoshi gets sick if it's too cold."

Santoshi came out of her bedroom as her name was spoken. At the sight of Laxmi, she burst into a flood of intense Tamil. Her hands, normally folded at her waist, flapped at her sides. Her head bobbed up and down. She looked like a bird about to take off.

After a few sentences Laxmi's eyebrows drew together in confusion. She held up her hand to Santoshi and turned to Kiria. "Are you looking for a mental institution?"

It was Kiria's turn to contract her eyebrows. "A what?"

"She says she has found a mental institution for you."

Kiria's expression changed from confused to excited. She turned to Santoshi. "For sale?"

"Yes, Kiria Madam." Santoshi, who rarely smiled, was beaming.

"Ask her if it's occupied," Kiria said to Laxmi, then suddenly changed her mind. "No, wait. You'll translate better if you understand. Santoshi, make tea, please? Earl Grey."

"Yes, Kiria Madam." Santoshi went into the kitchen.

Kiria sat on the sofa beside Laxmi. "I came to Chennai to build a hostel for poor working women. A place where a woman like Santoshi can live safely."

"You mean a shelter?"

"No. A hostel. One that doesn't ask for big deposits and references. One that charges rent poor women can afford."

"But there are shelters. They are free."

"Yes, but women shouldn't be locked up just because they are poor. And many women who don't want to be locked up live on the streets. This is about safety with dignity."

Laxmi could hear the passion in Kiria's voice but didn't understand it. In her world safety came from one's family, and dignity came from obedience to one's family. The idea of women living independently chilled her. What kind of a life would that be for a woman? She tried to explain this to Kiria. "India is a culture of family. Indian women do not live independently."

"They do," Kiria insisted. "I've seen them. In the shelters. On the pavements. Women whose husbands have left them. Women whose families have rejected them. I've met them."

"They are ragpickers, prostitutes," Laxmi discounted.

"Exactly," Kiria said triumphantly.

Laxmi suddenly found herself teetering on the edge of a cultural gap at least as wide as the oceans separating their two countries. She felt physically dizzy.

"So," Kiria continued, "the plan is to create a hostel, with bunk rooms for single women and private rooms for women with children. I want it to have a communal canteen and a day care center. Close to schools and some land to make a safe playground for the children and—" She stopped abruptly, then finished up. "Well, you get the picture."

Laxmi didn't understand, but she did indeed get the picture. "And Santoshi has found this asylum for sale and it might be what you're looking for?"

"If it's big enough and if it isn't occupied. I'm certainly not going to evict mental patients."

"That would be difficult," Laxmi agreed.

Santoshi came back into the living room, carrying the tea tray. She set it down on the table. Surprised to see three cups on the tray, Laxmi stared at Santoshi, who ducked her head.

"If I don't drink, she will be upset, miss," Santoshi explained in Tamil.

"Do you know what she's doing?" Laxmi asked.

Santoshi nodded. "Yes, miss."

"This idea is outrageous. To make a hostel for prostitutes."

"Not prostitutes, miss," Santoshi protested. "Decent women."

Kiria picked up the teapot and began to pour. Santoshi sat on the floor on the opposite side of the coffee table.

Laxmi noted the corners of Kiria's mouth twitch downward when Santoshi sat. "Is something wrong?" she asked.

"I don't understand why she insists on sitting on the floor when there's an empty chair just over there," Kiria replied with annoyance as she handed a cup to Laxmi.

"She does it to show you respect," Laxmi explained as she accepted her tea. "Have you asked her to sit on a chair?"

"I didn't realize I had to." Kiria stood up and walked to the dining table. Picking up one of the chairs there, she carried it back to the coffee table and placed it beside Santoshi. "Would you please sit in the chair, Santoshi?" she asked, gesturing to make her request clear.

Santoshi seemed confused by the request, but she picked up

her tea and added her customary five teaspoons of sugar before perching hesitantly on the edge of the chair. Kiria returned to sit on the sofa and drank her tea without adding sugar. Laxmi decided to compromise and used two teaspoons of sugar. She sniffed the perfumed steam rising from her cup, then sipped cautiously. Strange, but not unpleasant.

"Please ask Santoshi about the place she found. Ask her why she thinks it's good," Kiria requested.

After a few minutes of talking, Laxmi interrupted Santoshi. "This is too much. I must take notes."

Santoshi got up and went to the living room shelf. She came back with a pen and notepad. Handing them to Laxmi, she reseated herself on the floor and continued talking.

Despite her opinion of the project, Laxmi found herself drawn into the logistics of creating a hostel community. This was much more interesting than gouging the rotten spots out of cheap onions. Kiria sipped her tea and watched the two women from opposing ends of the social spectrum gradually forget to hide their friendship as the discussion became animated. After twenty minutes of increasingly intense conversation, Laxmi finally ran out of questions. She leaned back and reviewed the notes she'd taken. Santoshi picked up the tea tray and headed for the kitchen. Kiria could almost hear the thump of the social barrier between the two women slamming back into place.

"I think you will find this very promising," Laxmi said, and began her report.

The Loony Bin

❁❁❁❁❁

"IS THIS IT?" KIRIA PEERED out the tinted window as the Mercedes turned off the street and stopped in front of an ornate iron gate set into a lavender concrete wall topped with gold lotus-bud finials.

"This is it. The Ravichandran Mental Health Centre." Raj powered down the driver's window as a sturdy watchman in a pale blue and navy uniform approached the car. The two men spoke for a few seconds; then the watchman swung the gates wide. Raj drove into the grounds and parked the car in front of a small building just inside the gate, shaded by a magnificent Flame of the Forest tree. Mary Elizabeth and Santoshi climbed out from the back of the car. Raj and Kiria got out of the front.

"Someone really likes lavender." Kiria looked around as she adjusted her dupatta. "This place looks like Barbie's Palace."

In her mind's eye she stripped away the ornate decoration and bright paint. She saw a U-shaped two-story concrete building. A deep balcony ran the full length of the second story, supported by almost Ionic columns and overhung by an extended roof. The building was set well back on the property behind a large courtyard with a wide shallow fountain at its center. Formal gardens bordered the courtyard and the fifteen-foot lavender wall enclosed the entire property.

"It looks expensive," Mary Elizabeth said, shaking the front folds of her sari into alignment.

"Raj! How nice to see you! How are you?" A tall white woman came out of the small building. She wore her gray hair pulled severely back in an elegant chignon. Her pale blue silk sari rustled softly as she crossed to shake Raj's hand.

"I'm happy to see you too, Sally. I was very sorry to hear about Ravi. How have you been?" Raj took her offered hand between both of his.

"I'm getting along. I miss him so much sometimes. I didn't expect you. You should have called. I'm afraid I haven't much time right now. I'm waiting for someone."

"That would be me, Mrs. Ravichandran." Kiria stepped forward and offered her hand. "Kiria Langdon. I called earlier."

"Ms. Langdon. Pleased to meet you."

The two women shook hands.

"Call me Kiria. This is Mary Elizabeth Johnstone and this is Santoshi and it seems you already know Raj. They have been helping me assess property."

"Welcome, welcome. Call me Sally." Sally smiled at Mary Elizabeth and Santoshi, then turned back to Raj. "And here I thought you'd come to see me. Well, you hardly need to see the place at all. You know it as well as I do."

"Yes, Raj, that's interesting. How do you know the Ravichandran Mental Health Centre? And why didn't you tell me about it being for sale?" Kiria smiled to soften the accusation.

"Because I didn't know it was. When did you decide to sell, Sally?"

"Oh, I can't run this place. I decided months ago, but it took a while to find places for the patients. In three weeks' time everyone except Old Viji will be relocated. I don't know what I'm going to do with her, but something will come up. So, shall we take a look around?"

As Mary Elizabeth, Raj and Santoshi began walking toward the main building, Kiria placed a hand on Sally's arm and held her back. "You haven't put this place on the market yet?" she asked.

"No. I was quite surprised when you called. How did you find out?"

"Santoshi told me." Kiria looked perplexed. "What I can't figure out is how my housekeeper knows all this stuff. I say look for an apartment; she finds three in one afternoon. I say I want a hostel; she finds one that isn't even on the market yet."

"Ah, that explains it."

"Not to me."

"Well, I gave most of the staff notice last week. Told them I was going to sell the Centre. I imagine Cook told the ironing man. She's had her eye on him since his wife died."

"The ironing man?"

"You haven't been in India very long, have you? The street grapevine here, my dear, rivals CNN. It's usually maintained by the ironers, you know, those people who iron clothes on street corners. My guess is that your Santoshi has been making the rounds."

"So that's where she was. I thought she had a second job. Damn."

"Damn what?"

"I just realized that if I buy this place, Santoshi probably deserves some kind of commission, since she found it. If I pay her what the real estate agent would have charged me, she won't need to work for me anymore. Well, show me around. Maybe I'll hate the place."

"My dear, you cannot possibly hate this place as much as I do." Sally tucked her hand into Kiria's elbow and they began to stroll toward the main building. "Let's catch up with the others."

Kiria looked ahead to where Raj and Mary Elizabeth stood close together at the foot of the steps leading up to the door of the main building. "No hurry," she said. "How long have you lived in Chennai?"

"Almost forty years. I met Ravi when I was eighteen." Sally's eyes focused on a distant memory. "We fell in love at first sight." She sighed and returned to the present. "And after we got married, I moved here to Madras."

"Good move?"

"Oh yes. Nothing is perfect, but Ravi's family made it so easy for me. I converted to Hinduism, you know, just before my son was born. Do you have children?"

"I have a son."

"They're such a miracle, aren't they? When I sell this place, I'm going to San Francisco. My son and his wife and my grandchildren are there. Do you have grandchildren?"

"Not yet." Kiria decided to change the subject. "Why do you hate this place?"

Sally stopped walking and stared down at her visitor. "My dear"—she enunciated her reply with Shakespearean clarity—"it's a *lunatic asylum*."

TWO HOURS later, Kiria, Raj, Mary Elizabeth and Santoshi sat in the gatehouse drinking sweet spiced tea from small steel beakers. Sally had discreetly excused herself to return to the main building and discuss something with the head nurse.

"It's perfect," Kiria said. "Well, aside from the color. And I can't afford it."

"Color good, yes, Kiria Madam." Santoshi's new English skills fell short of colloquialism.

"I agree. It is a pretty color," Mary Elizabeth said.

"You don't know how much it costs," Raj pointed out.

"Location, Raj. Location, location. Look at the area." Kiria gestured toward the gate. "Look at the lot size. A smart developer could put four or five high-end condos in this place. And except for the broken sewer, it's in great shape. I can't afford it."

"The back wall and the balcony need repairs," Raj said. "The wiring is old."

"Oh yeah. That just makes it so much cheaper," Kiria said.

Although she still had a low opinion of Kiria's plan to build a hostel, Mary Elizabeth did not think a better place for one could be found. "It has water in almost every room," she pointed out. "It has two small buildings. It has a big kitchen. This room could be the office. There is a bus stop just outside the gate."

"Right. It's getting cheaper by the minute." Disappointment dropped Kiria's voice an octave. "I just hate it that we can't afford this place."

Raj drank the last of his tea. "My advice to you is remember Old Viji. I think you will find that Sally does not care so much for money. She can be very accommodating under the right circumstances."

AFTER DROPPING Kiria and Santoshi back in Periyar Nagar, Raj drove Mary Elizabeth home. Alone in the car, with the tinted windows hiding them from the eyes of the people on the streets, they held hands.

"It is a wonderful place," Mary Elizabeth said.

"Yes, my love, I think our search is over. What? What's wrong?"

A single tear slid down Mary Elizabeth's cheek. "I will miss this time. Now I will only see you over coffee again."

"Nonsense." Raj squeezed her hand and shook it gently. "Kiria cannot do this alone. She needs my help. And she needs *your* help."

"My help? What can I do?"

"Think about it. How will Kiria find tenants? How will she know who to accept? How will she collect rents or handle disputes? Look at her. She cannot live here. She has only been here six weeks and her face has aged a year."

"She is thinner, yes. And you think I can do this for her? Raj, I need to work. My father is so ill now. His medicine costs so much. Soon I will have to take a loan."

"You will not take a loan. This much I can do for you." His tone was final. "And you will be paid. Kiria is a businesswoman. She expects to hire an administrator. She will hire you."

Mary Elizabeth sat silently for a minute, considering the idea. "Perhaps. If she offers."

"She will."

Raj pulled the car up outside Mary Elizabeth's house and shut off the engine. He turned in his seat, cradled the side of her face in his hand and gently wiped the tear track from her cheek with his thumb. "We cannot let your father see this," he said.

Truth and Consequences

❁ ❁ ❁ ❁ ❁

"ARE THESE OKAY, HON?" RIK asked, tossing his head as he came into the den.

Theo looked up from the laptop screen and studied his husband's head critically. "They're really good. They look real."

"You don't think they're too short?" Rik pulled at one terry cloth ear.

"On you, yes. On an eight-year-old, they'll be perfect. She'll be the best-dressed bunny in the pageant, thanks to Uncle Rik. Are we driving over to your sister's tonight?"

"No, they're coming over here to pick up the costume. Probably stay for lunch." Rik walked across the room and bent over Theo's shoulder to look at the papers spread out on the desk. The bunny ears flopped down by his cheeks. "How's it going?"

Theo rubbed the bridge of his nose with his fingertips. "Not bad, actually. It's all circumstantial evidence and she did well on the stand. If I don't screw up on this closing, she's got a good chance."

"You never screw up." Rik massaged Theo's neck. "It's one of the reasons I married you."

"Oh, that feels good. What's the other one?"

The doorbell rang.

"That's my sister. I'll tell you later. Tonight." Rik finished the massage with a squeeze and a quick kiss on the top of Theo's head. "You finish up here. Come down when you're ready." He left the room, ears swinging wildly.

Theo leaned back in his chair and closed his eyes. Through the open door of the office he could clearly hear the visitor's high nasal voice floating up the stairs.

"Mr. Lachapelle?" Rik must have nodded because the voice continued. "I'm Mrs. Walden, from Children's Aid. I'm here to inspect your home." After a few moments of silence from Rik she continued, "You were informed there would be a surprise inspection, weren't you?"

A picture of Rik's face, bunny ears flapping, formed behind Theo's closed eyes. He leaned over and hit his forehead against the desktop twice before going downstairs.

"I BLEW it!" Rik slammed the dough he was kneading on the counter. A blizzard of flour puffed up around him. "I blew it! I blew it!"

"You didn't blow it." Theo pulled a bottle of Chardonnay from the fridge. "Making costumes for school plays is a good thing."

"Yeah, but wearing bunny ears around the house when you're gay isn't." Rik punched at the dough again.

"Don't go there, Rik." Theo reached out and grasped Rik's bicep, turning him around. "You pulled me out of the closet. Don't you go back into it now."

The muscles of Rik's arm flexed into steel as though he intended to pull away. Then, gradually, he relaxed and leaned against Theo's chest. Theo put his arms around his partner and waited.

"I've got flour all over your sweater," Rik whispered finally.

"Not my problem. It's your week to do laundry." Releasing the embrace, Theo turned to pull open a cupboard. He took out two glasses and picked up the wine bottle. "Leave the bread. Let's have a drink."

They carried their glasses into the living room and sat close together on the tan leather sofa. Rik stared into his wine and came to a decision. He'd pushed the adoption idea. It was up to him to take the next step. Placing his glass on the coffee table, he reached over and took Theo's free hand. "If this doesn't work out, maybe it's time to give up."

"No!" Theo protested.

"But you're only doing this for me."

"Not anymore. I want this now."

"Why? What's changed?"

"Remember I told you about Kiria asking me if she picked the right parents?"

"Yeah. You said it was the only time you could hear emotion in her voice."

"Well, the more I think about it, the more I'm grateful to her. My parents loved me. I always knew that. Even when Dad couldn't cope with me being gay, I still knew he loved me." Theo put his glass down beside Rik's and turned his body to make eye contact. "When we looked through the files to find Eddie and Jason, know what bothered me most? All those kids who won't get adopted. All those kids growing up with no one to love them."

Rik reached out and laid a palm against his husband's cheek. "I know. I felt the same."

RIK WAS almost asleep when the thought came to him. He sat up and shook Theo's shoulder.

"Theo, wake up."

Theo sighed. Time for another midnight brain wave. He raised himself on his elbows. "What?"

"If we adopt Jason and Eddie and someday they want to know about their birth mothers, I don't want them to think they have to go behind my back. I'd want to help them through it. Wouldn't you?"

"Of course."

"Then you have to tell your mom you talked to Kiria. You're not doing her any favors by hiding it."

Long after Rik's breathing had slowed into the steady rhythm of sleep, Theo lay awake, staring into the darkness.

Lady Sarah

❁ ❁ ❁ ❁ ❁

DO YOU BELIEVE IN GUARDIAN angels? I can't decide. If they do exist, most of them have to be pretty incompetent, right? And if they don't, then how do you explain people like Sally Ravichandran?

Shortly after touring the loony bin, I met Sally for high tea at the Madras Gymkhana Club, one of the better legacies of the British Raj in India. The club was conceived and built in the 1880s on an island in the mouth of the Kuvam River to provide a venue where senior British Army officers and Indian royalty could pursue the then-popular sport of pigsticking. The river, of course, can no longer be considered a desirable feature of the location. Fortunately, pigsticking has been replaced by golf as the club's sport of choice. Once I got the hang of breathing through my mouth, I spent a very pleasant afternoon there chatting with Sally.

If guardian angels can be equated to cars, then Sally had a gold-plated Rolls-Royce. Born just three years after Prince Charles, Lady Sarah, as she was known to her friends back in England, spent her sunny childhood years in preparation for the day when Charlie would drop by for tea and pop the question. She practiced good posture and studied the finer points of dinner seating under the tutelage of her loving mother, while her adoring father ensured that his darling daughter became an expert horsewoman and a crack shot. Even granting the eccentricity of the British peerage, I can't help but wonder why the duke felt familiarity with firearms would be critical to his daughter's success on the throne of England.

When she was eighteen, this Lana-Turner-on-a-good-day look-alike fell in love with Ravichandran, an Indian psychiatrist visiting at the London hospital where she volunteered, the occupation of all debutantes who are too upper-class to work. You'd think the duke and duchess would have raised some objection to this flagrant waste of education, right? On the contrary, her enlightened parents gave her their wholehearted blessing, a fabulous London wedding and a honeymoon in Hawaii.

So maybe when she moved to Madras with her new husband, she had difficulty adapting to the climate or the food or his family? Exactly the opposite. She luxuriated in the heat, became expert at cooking Indian cuisine and enchanted Ravichandran's wealthy and equally enlightened parents by giving birth, after less than four hours in labor, to a son.

Ah, but what about the husband? Did he turn out to be a philanderer? A gambler? A wife beater? Disappointing as this must be to you, Ravichandran was a kind and gentle man with no bad habits and a whole catalog of good ones, who loved his wife passionately from the day he met her until the day he died. Which, to forestall your next question, was peacefully in his sleep at the ripe old age of eighty-eight.

Enough questions. I asked them all. Trust me, Royce was one hell of a guardian angel: no major illnesses, no childhood traumas, no tragic events, not even a serious case of Delhi Belly after living in India for nearly forty years. Sally Ravichandran was the poster girl for good fortune. She'd never even flown coach.

Aside from her being a statistical freak, or maybe because of it, I'd have to say that Sally was just a tad shallow. She had the attention span of a butterfly, flitting from one interest to another, never completely engaged. But she did have that aristocratic noblesse oblige thing. So when her husband died and she found herself responsible for twenty-one mentally impaired scions of Chennai's wealthiest families, she really did try to keep the hospital up and running, with predictable results. By the time I met her, Sally just wanted out. And the only thing between her and the exit was Old Viji.

Back in days before genetic theory made its way to India, it was common for Hindus to marry their daughters to maternal uncles. This practice is fading out in modern times, though still far from extinct. Marriage to such a close relative is something of a gamble. It skews the genetic dice in favor of birth defects, and Old Viji was the unfortunate result of just such a bad roll.

Old Viji wasn't actually all that old. She'd come to the Centre as a ten-year-old in the early eighties when her increasing size and disability made home care impossible. Ravichandran had originally diagnosed her as severely autistic but began to suspect she had Rett syndrome when her body began to twist asymmetrically in response to a curving spine at the age of fourteen, a diagnosis later confirmed by DNA testing. She'd lived her entire life at the Centre, floppy limbed and drooling, head twisted to the side, eyes staring up and to the right. She could no longer walk and had never learned to talk, although she had a large repertoire of hoots, grunts and shrieks. She had never managed to catch on to potty training either.

Despite these handicaps there was something about Old Viji, some spark that made Ravichandran think there just might be a real person trapped inside that useless body. When her father died and payments for her maintenance stopped, he continued to care for Old Viji, waiving his fees and paying for her full-time caretaker out of his own pocket. Now that her husband was gone, Sally was footing the bill. She would have been delighted to pay some other reputable institution to care for Old Viji but could not find one willing to take on a new patient without a guardian's consent. Old Viji, an only child, had outlived her few traceable relatives.

Fortunately for me, Ravichandran and Raj's father were old school friends. At first I thought this was stretching coincidence a bit too far. But Sally told me that when she came to Madras, the Brahman community had been very tight-knit, living in the same areas, sending their children to the same schools, marrying their children within the community. It would have been almost impossible for the two families not to have known each other. Raj knew a great deal about Sally and he pointed out that Old Viji was my best bargaining chip.

I did a little research. At her age there was nothing that could be done to improve her condition. All she really needed was a place to live out the rest of her life. So I proposed a deal whereby Viji and her caretaker would become tenants of the hostel under the oversight of the administrator, while I set up a small trust fund to pick up the tab for the caretaker's monthly salary, which was less than I'd normally have spent on lattes in a week.

Sally could by no stretch of the imagination be characterized as an astute businesswoman. Focused on freedom from responsibility, she was so delighted with the plan that she practically tried to give the place away. But that would have been unethical, even for me. I couldn't pay her the full value of the property, but I did manage to talk her up to slightly over two-thirds of what Raj and I thought she could get for it if she put it on the market.

As soon as Sally's car pulled out the front gate of the club, I was on the phone to Raj, asking him whom I could get to draw up the offer.

Baby Steps

❂ ❂ ❂ ❂ ❂

From: meglertheodore@rogers.net
To: kiria@novio.com
Subject: Questions

Hello Kiria

You said on the phone that you'd like to talk to me again, so I hope that you'll be willing to answer some questions. I didn't realize how great the time difference is. It must have been after midnight your time when I called. It seems easier to e-mail.

First, you should know that Mom knows I contacted you. I thought she'd be upset. But when I told her what we talked about she said she's okay with this. She asked me to say hello to you and tell you she understands now why you never spoke about yourself.

I want to know something about my father and my grandparents. Do I have any other relatives?

You don't have to answer this last one if you don't want to. Do you ever wish you'd kept me?

Theo

From: kiria@novio.com
To: meglertheodore@rogers.net
Subject: Answers

Hi Theo

These are difficult questions. I'm glad you chose to e-mail, it gives me time to think about how to answer.

I am not the best person to tell you about your biological father or his family. His name was Edward Chaswell the Third. He was a lawyer in Albany, New York, in 1975 when we got divorced. I know nothing after that. If you want to look him up, you should know that I never told him about you.

Actually, I never told anyone. After you were born, I came back to the States and went to Oregon. I let everyone assume I'd gone there when I ran away from Albany. Ted would never have agreed to a divorce if he knew he had a child, and my mother would have been needlessly unhappy to know about a grandchild she could never see.

My mother was estranged from her family. She told me they were very religious and did not approve of her. I'm her only child and illegitimate so don't know who my father was. My mother never wanted to talk about him and I was never curious enough to push her. She came out to live with me when she started treatment for breast cancer and died fifteen years ago. I never remarried and have no other children.

The first few years after the adoption were very difficult, much harder than I expected, like a hole in my life that couldn't be filled. But I never regretted giving you to Arthur and Alicia. It's hard to explain this, but as much as it hurt me to do it, it was my responsibility to give you the best life possible and back then that wasn't going to be with me. Even if I could go back and do it over, the circumstances would be the same and I'd make the same decision. I'm not the kind of person who regrets what can't be changed. I'm sorry if you find this disturbing, but it took courage for you to contact me, and for that you deserve the truth.

Feel free to ask me anything else.

I also have questions. I never expected to know anything about you at all. Now that we've talked and e-mailed, I must admit to being curious. Perhaps it's some residual sense of maternal responsibility.

I would like to know if you are happy with your life. Do you have a relationship? Children? And I wonder why, since you've known you were adopted almost all your life, it was important for you to contact me now.

Please tell Alicia I'm grateful for her understanding and I think she and Arthur did a fine job.

Kiria

From: meglertheodore@rogers.net
To: kiria@novio.com
Subject: Answers and more questions—but easier ones

Hi Kiria,

Thank you for answering my questions honestly. It's been very helpful. When I answer yours, you'll understand why. I don't mind answering, by the way. I feel the same curiosity about you.

Nothing is perfect, but I am for the most part very happy with my life. Much of this is due to my husband, Rik. I'm sorry if this shocks you, but I stopped hiding who I am a long time ago. I'm a criminal lawyer in a small firm that specializes in Legal Aid cases, which makes me something like a public defender in the U.S. The people I defend are often basically good people who've had tough lives. I like to believe that my work helps them build better ones. I think I get this from Dad. He worked a lot at the free health clinics downtown.

The reason I contacted you was because Rik and I are trying to adopt children. I always thought you put me up for adoption because you didn't want me. I resented that and didn't want to pass my feelings on to our children. So I asked my mother about the circumstances of my adoption. She told me your name and what she remembered of you. I looked you up on the Internet, but I didn't try to contact you until I found your letter in Dad's papers. I was worried, not sure what to expect. But knowing turns out to be better than not knowing. So thank you again.

I have more questions for you, but I think you'll find these easier than the last ones. Rik and I love to travel. We've been all over Europe and last year we went to Thailand, which we loved. India's on our list, but we haven't made it there yet. Your assistant said you're there indefinitely. What's it like? Why are you there indefinitely?

Rik says hi and wants to know if there's a secret for getting to level eight in Chronography.

Theo

From: kiria@novio.com
To: meglertheodore@rogers.net
Subject: India

I had no idea there was a level seven in Chronography, let alone a level eight. I'll find out who's upgrading it and have them send you the link to the cheat pages. (Then find out why they aren't working on a profitable product. Employing engineers is like herding cats.)

I'm not shocked by your marriage. I'm pleased that we live in a time when it's possible. It amuses me that you're a lawyer, given that you come from a long line of them.

If you want to know what India is like, you've come to the right person. Honestly, I could write a book about this place. . . .

The Rebellion

SANTOSHI LIFTED THE LID OF the kitchen garbage pail, and compressed her lips tightly. Kiria Madam had taken out the garbage again. A quick check under the sink confirmed that the beer bottle, the tin can and the plastic bottle were no longer there. Three rupees gone. Waste!

There were many good things about living with Kiria Madam: water from taps, easy work for good pay, the joy of learning English and the beautiful new reading glasses that made it so easy to learn. But the waste! And the food! The bland, terrible food! Santoshi had never expected to miss shelter food.

She emptied the dustpan into the pail, snapped the lid shut and checked the wall clock. It was almost eleven, time to wash the vessels. She loaded them into the wash pan along with the soap bar and went out to the terrace to listen for the old man.

Kiria Madam was talking on her cell phone as usual. She smiled at Santoshi as she spoke. "No. She's never said anything about hating you. This is what's keeping you awake? . . . Well, I don't think she . . . but . . ." Kiria dropped her head and covered her eyes with her free hand. "Look, you can't just order people around. They have to feel you respect their opinions. . . . No, of course she doesn't know anything about the software. . . . It doesn't have to be about work. Tell her you like her earrings. Ask her to help you find some for your sister's birthday. . . . She always wears earrings. . . . It doesn't matter if your sister's birthday is in September. . . ."

Santoshi stood by the balustrade, waiting to be sure Venu was asleep. At the sound of his first snore she trotted down the stairs and around the house to the backyard, where she placed the wash pan under the wall tap.

"So many vessels?" Laxmi whispered through the kitchen window. "I saw the pizza delivered last night."

"They are mostly clean," Santoshi whispered back as she entered the kitchen. "What are you cooking today?"

Two days a week Geeta went out to visit one of her daughters. With Mani at work and the old man asleep, Laxmi's domestic education was coming on nicely under Santoshi's tutelage.

"Snake gourd." Laxmi held up a thin crooked squash. "And seerfish and beans."

"You know the fish and beans. Snake gourd is easy, like pumpkin." The two women moved into their now-familiar kitchen positions. Santoshi took charge of the cooking. "We need much garlic. You peel it. I will chop the ginger."

Laxmi picked up a head of garlic and began breaking off cloves. "Where is your mistress today?" The question was prompted by curiosity. Both Santoshi and Laxmi knew that Kiria approved of Santoshi's efforts to help Laxmi.

"She is on the terrace, talking on the phone again." Santoshi's clever fingers pared paper-thin slices of ginger from a gnarled root. "Did your husband like the chicken sixty-five?"

"Yes, he ate twice. Who does she talk to?"

"Mostly a woman who thinks her bottom is fat and a man who tests something and can't sleep. I think it is her job."

"What does she do?"

"I don't know. On her business card it says C-E-O."

"That means she runs a company. Do you know the name of the company?"

Santoshi put down her knife and pictured Kiria's card in her mind. Madam's name in black letters. Then "CEO." Then in big red letters, "N-O-V-I-O," she spelled the unfamiliar word out loud.

"NOVIO!" In her excitement, Laxmi forgot to keep her voice low.

"Shhhh," Santoshi hissed.

Both women listened. Reassured by the continued snoring from the front bedroom, they continued.

"Is it important?" Santoshi asked.

"It's a technology company. They develop computer games." NOVIO had been a case study in the relationship between private ownership and innovation in Laxmi's management-strategy course during her last year at university. Laxmi realized she had Kiria *Langdon* living upstairs. "She's famous."

"Why?"

"I can't explain it."

Santoshi found this not-very-polite way of telling her she wouldn't understand slightly annoying. She knew she could understand, just like she now understood many of the words in the English children's books when Madam told them to her. She decided to change the subject. "Have you bought the sari for your husband's father's brother's son's wedding yet?"

"No," Laxmi said shortly. She picked up the snake gourd and began violently hacking it into pieces.

"Not like that!" Santoshi hissed. "You are ruining it. Stop. What is wrong?"

Suddenly Laxmi dropped the knife and sank to her haunches on the kitchen floor. She tucked her head between her knees and covered it with her hands. "I can't do this anymore," she whispered. She flung back her head and shrieked at the ceiling. "I CAN'T DO THIS ANYMORE!"

The snoring from the front room stopped. The two women froze. Laxmi rose, ran into her bedroom and slammed the door. Santoshi stood alone in the kitchen for a moment, then scurried through the back door to pick up her unwashed vessels and run back upstairs.

MANI CAME home for lunch to find his father shouting at Laxmi through the bedroom door.

"Papa, Papa. What's wrong?" Mani hurried over to where his father stood.

Venu turned his anger on his son. "Your wife has gone crazy! Mr. Prakesh came and went without lunch. I have not eaten. She will not come out of the bedroom and cook." He turned back and slammed his palm against the door. "Come out, you lazy girl! Come out and cook my lunch!"

"Papa, calm yourself. Come." Mani took his father gently by the arm and led him to the dining table. "Please sit. Tell me what happened."

Venu sat and folded his arms across his chest. "I heard her shout. I came out of my room to see what was wrong. She has locked herself in her room and will not come out. Then Mr. Prakesh arrived and there was no food. We are shamed," he finished dramatically.

"How long has she been in there?"

"Over an hour."

"I will talk to her." Mani walked to the bedroom door and knocked gently. "Laxmi? Are you ill?"

"No, I'm not ill." Laxmi shot back the bolt and opened the bedroom door for her husband. "Unless you mean mentally." She crossed the room and sat on the bed.

She had changed from her sari into the blue jeans and orange T-shirt that had been her favorite outfit in university. Her unbraided hair was pulled into a high ponytail that swung down her back. Mani thought his wife looked Western and sexy.

"Why did you lock yourself in the bedroom?" Mani sat on the bed and put his arm around his wife's shoulders.

Laxmi leaned her head against her husband's chest. "I'm thinking."

"Thinking?"

"Yes, thinking. I used to be very good at it." She hesitated, unsure of how to explain to her husband exactly what she had been thinking, then began with, "Mani, I am not a good wife."

"You are a very good wife," Mani said, squeezing her shoulders. "My friends are all jealous."

"I mean I'm not a good housewife."

"Well, you are getting better. That chicken sixty-five was delicious. What are you making for lunch?"

"Nothing."

"But Father is hungry. I am hungry, Laxmi."

"Go to Ashok's and get biryani."

"Okay." Mani liked Ashok's biryani. It had lots of mutton. He stood up and walked to the door. Just before leaving the room, he thought of something. "Don't forget to change before Mother gets home."

Laxmi rose and slid the bolt back into the socket after he left. It had not escaped her notice that once his own problem was solved, her husband had no interest in hers.

Laxmi finally came out of her room in the late afternoon, wearing a sari, with her hair neatly braided again. She went into the kitchen and began preparing chapati dough for the evening meal.

Geeta, hearing the noise of the pans, came out of her bedroom and entered the kitchen. Her husband had told her of Laxmi's strange behavior that afternoon. Thinking the girl might be pregnant, Geeta kept her voice mild. No good came from upsetting a pregnant woman. "What happened today?"

"You mean, why did I lock myself in my room? I found out who our tenant is." Laxmi began to knead the dough. "She is Kiria Langdon. I learned about her in school."

"She is famous? An actress?" Geeta liked the idea of having a famous tenant.

"No, a businesswoman. One who has built a successful company with a reputation for producing innovative technology."

"I don't understand."

"Yes, but I do understand. That's the problem. Mother, I will never be a good housewife. You know this. But I can be good in business. I can make much money for this family with a job."

"A job? How much money could you make?" The thought of extra money snagged Geeta's attention away from her disappointment that there would not soon be a grandson.

"Enough to pay for five maids, all better at making chapatis than I am." Laxmi dropped the dough into a bowl and put a plate over it. "Perhaps enough to buy a car in two or three years."

Right up until Laxmi's last word, Geeta had been intrigued. At the word "years," she came to her senses. "No. You must have a child. Your husband needs a son."

"Then let me work until children come."

"Working is too stressful. And people would think your husband cannot support you."

Laxmi restrained herself from pointing out that nothing could be more stressful than living with Geeta. "Housework is stressful for me. An office job would be easy. Many women work now. Mani has many friends with wives who work."

Venu came into the kitchen, folding the bottom of his lungi high over his sagging little paunch. "Where is my tea?"

"I will make it now, husband." Geeta turned on the flame under the milk pan. "This foolish girl wants to get a job."

Venu looked at Laxmi where she knelt by the pantry shelf sorting tomatoes for the evening chutney. "What are you saying, girl?" he demanded harshly, still upset by the shame of not feeding Mr. Prakesh the lunch he had paid for.

Laxmi made an effort to respond mildly. "I want to work in an office, Father. I want—"

"Are you saying that my son cannot support his wife?" Venu's outraged shout surprised both women.

"No, Father. I am only saying that I am not—"

"You! You cannot even cook my lunch. You should be grateful that we do not send you back to your father. He cheated us. Sending us such a useless wife for our son. And barren. Eight months and no sign of a grandson."

Laxmi, who had spent the afternoon in the bedroom fueling her own anger, suddenly felt overwhelmed. She rose violently to her feet, sending the tomatoes she had gathered into the skirt of her sari rolling across the kitchen floor.

"I work like a bullock in this house!" she shouted back at Venu. "It is you who cheated my father. Telling him you had two maids and a cook."

"Why should we pay for maids when you are here?" Geeta could not resist joining in. "Do you think silk saris are cheap? Do you think that diamond in your nose came out of the garden?"

"What good are silk saris to me?" Laxmi rounded on her

mother-in-law. "I never leave the house. Can I wash the floor with a silk sari? And do not talk about diamonds. My father paid for this." She turned back to face Venu. "And it is your son who is never here to give you a grandson. It is your son—"

"Silence!" Venu roared. He raised his arm and took a step toward his daughter-in-law. His foot landed on a soft tomato. Arms flailing wildly, he fell heavily to the floor.

"Aiee!" shrieked Geeta. "You have killed him!" She fell to her knees beside her husband.

As suddenly as it had come, Laxmi's anger left her, replaced by fear. What had she done? She bent over her father-in-law and tried to help him sit up.

"Get away from me!" Venu swatted at her hands. "Get out of my sight."

Laxmi burst into tears and ran from the kitchen. A few seconds later her bedroom door slammed violently shut and the bolt snapped into place for the second time that day.

Cooped Up

❁ ❁ ❁ ❁ ❁

DID YOU KNOW THAT IN a crowded chicken coop the lowest-status hen can be identified by its back? I know this because I worked on a farm one summer as a teenager.

The dominance hierarchy in chickens is maintained by pecking. A lower-status bird, when pecked by a higher-status bird, immediately turns around and looks for an even lower-status bird to peck, resulting in one neurotic chicken scurrying around the coop with a bald, bloody back. As much as we would like to think otherwise, dominance in human social groups is maintained exactly the same way it is in chickens, by violence and displaced aggression. Of course, unlike chickens, human beings have imagination. We are not limited to physical violence. I suppose you could say we've improved somewhat on the poultry model. But the point is, we still do it.

Although she was smarter and better educated than anyone else in the downstairs household, Laxmi was the bloody-backed chicken of her family by virtue of being the daughter-in-law, the lowest rung on the traditional Indian extended-family ladder. The disparity between her abilities and those of her higher-status family members created a pressure cooker of unresolved emotions in Laxmi. So, unlike her family, I was far from surprised on the day she finally exploded.

Santoshi and I were sitting on the terrace one evening having our daily language lesson when the decibel levels from the kitchen downstairs rose beyond ignorable levels. My Tamil wasn't up to full comprehension of the exchange, but with Santoshi's help I managed to understand that Laxmi wanted to get a job. Given Laxmi's housekeeping skills, I thought this was an excellent idea. Apparently her in-laws did not share my opinion.

When Venu tried to assert his dominance with vocal violence, Laxmi, surprisingly, counterattacked with increased volume of her own. Geeta, predictably, backed up her husband by shouting at Laxmi too, at which point I was certain Laxmi would back down. Instead, she took them both on, forcing Venu to resort to physical violence.

There was a crash and a thud. Geeta shrieked something. Venu yelled. A door slammed. Laxmi's sobbing wafted up to the terrace from her bedroom window for an hour or so. Mani got home late in the evening and spent a while pounding on the bedroom door and shouting drunkenly at his wife.

The next morning, as I was taking out the garbage, Geeta came out to apologize to me for any inconvenience the previous evening's hysterics may have caused. Unaware that I knew enough Tamil to have a basic idea of what had happened and apparently forgetting that Santoshi spoke the language fluently, Geeta gave me a highly edited account of events in which Evil Laxmi goaded Poor Venu beyond the bounds of endurance while Saint Geeta tried to make peace between them. Her account of Laxmi's attempt to kill her father-in-law by throwing tomatoes on the floor, complete with a dramatic reenactment in the kitchen, had me chuckling for the rest of the day.

Laxmi remained locked in her room for five days. During that time I could scarcely tear myself away from the terrace as the comedy of the family trying to reestablish a pecking order in the absence of their normal scapechicken unfolded below.

Day one: Venu gives up his narcolepsy. Mani does not go to work. Three daughters show up in the morning. Long discussions, presumably reviling Laxmi, are paused when Prakesh shows up for lunch, then continue late into the night, punctuated by various family members pounding on the bedroom door and shouting at Laxmi from time to time.

Day two: Venu is still awake. Mani again remains home from work. One daughter shows up. Prakesh again interrupts a Laxmi-bashing session. Around the middle of the afternoon, Mani and Venu have an argument. Geeta takes Mani's side. The daughter seems to support Venu. By early evening, no one is bothering to pound on the bedroom door any longer.

Day three: Venu remains awake again. Mani goes to work. No daughter visits today. Venu starts a fight with Geeta in the morning. When Prakesh shows up for lunch, he does something that causes Geeta and Venu to resume pounding on the bedroom door as soon as he leaves. (My guess is that Prakesh asked if Laxmi was ill, and the family suddenly realized that she hadn't had anything to eat or drink for three days. Or so they thought. Santoshi was taking food and bottles of water down at night and passing them through the bedroom window. We even got extra pizza one night and sent it down with a can of pop.) Mani comes home from work and pounds on the door a while.

Day four: Venu is awake in the morning. Mani stays home from work. Geeta leaves the house, presumably to seek solace with one of her daughters. Mani and Venu take turns pounding on the bedroom door while they argue with each other. Venu is unable to sustain diurnal consciousness and retreats to his bedroom for a nap. Mani takes off on his motorcycle. Prakesh shows up for lunch but leaves when no one answers the door. Geeta comes home, yells at Laxmi through the bedroom door for a while, then wakes up Venu and starts a fight. Mani comes home, late and drunk. Geeta tries to start a fight with Mani, who gets back on his motorcycle and zooms off into the night.

Day five: Venu returns to full-time narcolepsy. Mani stays home from work, probably sleeping off a hangover. Aside from the resumption of Venu's snoring and Geeta's angry bashing of pots in the kitchen, the morning is fairly quiet. Prakesh comes for lunch as usual and is still there when the carpenter comes to take out the bedroom door. Prakesh becomes very agitated and races out of the house. The carpenter leaves without taking out the door. Mani and Geeta shout at each other sporadically for an hour or so until Prakesh returns with a police officer in tow, forcing Venu, as titular head of the household, to wake up. Laxmi releases herself from incarceration. The police and Prakesh leave. With Laxmi once again available, Geeta, Mani and Venu stop pecking at one another and gang up on Laxmi to reassert their dominance.

At which point I'd had enough. Or, to be more precise, I'd had enough of Santoshi crying in her bedroom while I tried to hold a videoconference with the development team to find out why beta revisions were now four weeks behind. Between the anvil chorus downstairs and Santoshi's heartbroken sobbing in the next room, I had no choice but to reschedule the call and handle the on-site situation.

Santoshi had been calm while Laxmi remained locked safely in the bedroom. I think she even enjoyed those clandestine little feeding forays. She always came back from them in a cheerful mood. But after a couple of hours listening to Geeta, Venu and Mani berate her friend, Santoshi broke down. Now, she was a tough and secretive woman, not the kind to cry easily and certainly not the kind to cry out loud, which meant that whatever was going on downstairs was relatively serious.

The fastest way to get your nose bloodied is to stick it into someone else's business, especially someone else's family business. But I felt I had to do something. I went downstairs to sort out the chickens.

Women's Liberation 101

❁ ❁ ❁ ❁ ❁

KIRIA STOOD IN THE DARKNESS outside her landlord's back door and studied the family group in the kitchen.

Geeta stood by the gas ring, frying some green vegetable. She talked loudly, punctuating her words by jabbing the metal spoon she held in Laxmi's direction. Venu sat in a chair at the end of the kitchen table, arms folded across his chest, an open beer bottle on the table beside him. From time to time he interrupted Geeta to shout at Laxmi himself. Mani stood silently in the interior doorway, one hand in his pocket, the other holding the neck of a beer bottle. In the corner Laxmi crouched on the floor, pushing a heavy stone roller over a flat granite slab covered in coconut paste. One side of her mouth was swollen and dried blood crusted her chin. She was crying silently, her tears falling into the lap of her sari.

Kiria could not understand all of what was being said, but tones of voice and facial expressions told her that Geeta and Venu were venting and clearly had a good deal more to get off their chests. Mani was trying to avoid being drawn into the argument and looking for a way to escape. In the corner, Laxmi seemed broken and defeated.

Kiria stepped into the light from the doorway. "Excuse me," she said loudly.

Geeta, Venu and Mani looked up, startled. Laxmi quickly pulled her hair down over the side of her face and bowed her head over the roller.

"I'm very sorry for your problems," Kiria began. "I've come to see if I can help."

"This is a family problem." Venu scowled at her. "This is not your concern. Please leave."

"Well, I'm glad we agree your family business is not my concern, Mr. Venu. However, you've been sharing it with me for the past five days and my home has become uninhabitable. That *is* my concern. It would be very inconvenient for me to move. You and your family have been very helpful to me. If there is anything I can do to help you in return, I really would like to do it."

"I am sorry we disturbed you. There is nothing you can do. Go away." Venu's reply lacked aggression, but was clearly meant to be dismissive.

Kiria ignored the order. "Are you sure? I don't know what the difficulty is, but I understand it has something to do with Laxmi getting a job, and if money is a problem, I would be happy to loan you some."

"See!" Geeta exclaimed in Tamil, shaking her spoon at Laxmi. "I told you people would think your husband cannot support you."

Laxmi's head drooped lower. Mani frowned and drank from the bottle he was holding.

"There is no money problem," Venu said sharply.

"I'm sorry," Kiria apologized. "I didn't mean to offend you.

And I certainly don't think that Mani is unable to support his wife."

"You know Tamil?" Venu asked in surprise.

"Not much, but I understood that. I see how careful Geeta is with the household expenses and you don't have a maid or a car like so many other families on the street. You rent out part of your house. Mani works so much overtime. It seemed like a logical conclusion."

Kiria carefully avoided looking at the beer bottles. She liked a beer herself from time to time and knew that Venu and his son were drinking more than Geeta had spent on her family's meals for the day.

Silence followed Kiria's explanation. Even the rhythmic grating of the stone roller stopped. No one knew how to respond to this catalog of observed poverty. From talking with Santoshi, Laxmi knew that Kiria was perfectly well aware Mani went out drinking with friends every night. Why was she lying? Venu and Geeta looked at each other. Was this how their family was perceived through a stranger's eyes? Mani, who had recently been warned by his supervisor about taking days off and leaving work early, stared down at the floor.

Noting this, Kiria decided to twist the screw one more time. "There is no need to be modest, Mani. I'm sure your parents are very proud that you work so hard," she said gently. When no one leapt in to correct her, Kiria decided she'd taken that one as far as it would go and changed direction.

"Well, whatever the reason, I will soon be hiring some employees myself and I'll be happy to consider you for a position, Laxmi." She looked at Laxmi and smiled, but the young woman kept her head down. "Well, as you wish."

Kiria started to leave, then turned back in the kitchen doorway to face the family. "Oh, yes, one more thing. After this week, it's hard to believe that Laxmi's injury is accidental. However, I was wrong about your financial situation and I'd like to be wrong about this. But if I'm not"—she paused and looked at each family member in turn—"and you want to talk to a family counselor, I have a friend who can recommend one." She turned away again and walked into the darkness.

After Kiria left, the family remained silent for a few minutes. Mani drank from his bottle. Geeta went back to stirring the vegetables. The grating of the stone roller resumed.

Finally Venu stood up. "I'm tired," he announced. "I'm going to bed." He walked past Mani to his bedroom.

Mani finished his beer. "I'm going out." He handed the empty bottle to his mother and followed his father out of the kitchen.

Geeta held the bottle and looked after her son. She thought about the price of beer. She thought about how much money Mani would spend with his friends that night. She thought about the electricity and water bills she would pay as soon as she received the rent from that nosy tenant. Suddenly, Geeta felt very old and tired. She turned off the gas flame and left the kitchen without saying a word.

In the corner, Laxmi stopped rolling coconut paste and wiped the tears from her face with the skirt of her sari. Normally, without instructions from Geeta, she would have left the kitchen as well. But tonight she felt pity for the tired old woman and knew Geeta would be upset at the waste of food tomorrow. Laxmi rose and began to put away the uneaten meal.

THE NEXT morning Kiria was in her kitchen making a peanut butter and jelly sandwich. She did not like the kitchen. She did not like the stone sink or the stained concrete work surface and walls. She especially did not like the gas ring and its feeble-looking connection to the propane cylinder resting on the floor.

But Santoshi was out marketing and it only took a minute to make a sandwich.

Kiria was cutting the sandwich into quarters when the doorbell rang. She opened the front door to find Laxmi standing on the terrace holding a reed broom.

"I'm sorry to bother you," Laxmi said. "I just came to thank you for the food. The pizza was nice."

"Don't thank me—it was Santoshi's idea. Come in." Kiria opened the door wide.

"I shouldn't. I should get back to sweeping."

"Okay, if you want. But I'd like to talk to you, and if we stand out here, you're more likely to be seen." Kiria nodded down toward the street.

Laxmi looked around almost furtively, then leaned the broom against the balustrade and stepped inside the apartment.

"Does it still hurt?" Kiria looked up at Laxmi's swollen face.

Laxmi touched her split lip lightly. "Yes, but not so much."

Kiria leaned in and examined the injury. "You should get that stitched. It's going to leave a scar. Come sit down. I want to tell you something."

She led the way into the living room. "Would you like something to drink? I have some juice boxes with straws."

"No, thank you." Laxmi sat on the edge of the sofa and looked up at Kiria with curiosity. "Why did you lie last night?"

"About Mani working so hard? Partly to get their attention away from you. Partly to get your attention. There are some things you have to know about your situation."

"What do you know about my situation? You aren't even married."

"Not now, but I was." Kiria sat down on the sofa and parted the hair above her left ear, revealing a jagged three-inch scar. "I know something about your situation."

Laxmi's eyes went round. "Your husband?"

"Yes. My husband." Dropping her hair, Kiria took Laxmi's hand. "Now, listen. People hit because they can. Anything you do is just an excuse, not a reason. Once it starts, it won't stop unless you do something."

"What can I do? I have no money."

"You have diamonds in your nose and gold around your neck. You have more money than half the women in Chennai."

Laxmi placed her free hand on her chest. "This is my tali," she said with force. "It's like a wedding ring."

"Actually, it's much more symbolic than that." Kiria could not resist sharing her opinion. "It's a noose. People put those on cows." Laxmi looked shocked. "Okay, forget I said that. What about the diamond stud?"

"It was a gift from my father. I can't sell it."

"Well, I'm not qualified to make suggestions for how you run your life, Laxmi, but if you don't do something, it's going to be a very painful one. What about your parents?"

"I can't go back to my father's house. He is ill. That's why I had to get married."

"I don't understand."

"My father was worried he would die before he found me a husband. He chose this family because he thought it would be a good place for me."

"He was wrong. Tell him."

"No. It is too shameful. I can't tell him. He would be too upset."

"You mean you haven't told him about how you are treated? He doesn't know?"

Laxmi shook her head. "He has a bad heart. He is too sick."

"And your mother?"

"She would not understand. She would send me back."

"To a man who beats you? Why would she do that?"

"Mani didn't hit me!" Laxmi leapt to her husband's defense. "Geeta hit me with the spoon."

Kiria tipped her head and the corners of her mouth twitched. "You know, I shouldn't be so surprised at that. And neither Mani nor Venu tried to stop her?"

"You don't understand. It only happened once. It's not a good reason to leave my husband."

Kiria sat back and sighed. "So no one in your family will help you?"

Laxmi shook her head.

"Do you want to stay in this family?" Kiria asked.

"I love my husband. He's handsome and kind."

"But he's never home."

"Why should he be? He enjoys being with his friends."

"And he doesn't stand up for you with Geeta."

"He is showing proper respect for his mother. He is a good son."

Kiria gave up. This conversation was just pushing string. Laxmi wasn't ready to deal with her situation yet. "I'll take that as a yes. But think carefully. Your life is difficult now. It may get worse or it may stay the way it is. But unless you do something, it can't get better. And think about this too. Locking yourself in your room is just running away from the problem. There is no perfect solution for any problem, but a solution you choose is better than one chosen for you by someone else.

"Okay, end of lecture. Are you sure you wouldn't like some juice?"

Laxmi rose and moved toward the front door. "No, I've been here too long already. Thank you again for the food."

"Like I said, thank Santoshi." Kiria followed Laxmi and opened the door to the terrace. "The jobs are real, by the way. I'll be hiring soon. If you decide to apply for one, bring me your résumé."

Laxmi nodded. She picked up her broom and began sweeping down the stairs.

Kiria closed the door and went back to the kitchen to find a heaving mass of ants where her PBJ had been. The first few times this happened, she had sprayed down the kitchen with insecticide, but she soon learned it was faster, not to mention less toxic, just to remove the food and let the ants go away on their own. She lifted the sandwich with a spatula and dumped it into the garbage. Then she used the spatula to lift the plate into the sink and ran water over the plate and the spatula and her arms until all the ants were washed away.

"I hate this," she muttered. She wasn't referring to the ants.

Sari-itis

HAVE YOU EVER WONDERED HOW a sari stays on? Think about it. It's basically five to nine yards of uncut fabric, with no seams or fastenings, that has to be retucked, repleated and rewrapped every time it's worn. You'd think it would unravel at the first step, wouldn't you? But it doesn't. It's a miracle of engineering.

When I first came to Chennai, I had no intention of ever wearing a sari. Oh sure, I liked looking at them—as art. I admired the bright colors and designs of the material, even thought they might make nice curtains to take home with me when I left India. But as clothing? Three yards of fabric clogging up my legs and another yard or so flapping around my butt, getting caught on furniture and door handles, seemed more like an armless strait-jacket than an actual garment.

Gradually, as I watched the women around me, I came to see that a sari is more than a nice piece of material. It is quintessential couture. Saris are available in such a broad range of colors and patterns that you can walk the streets of Chennai all day and never see two women in remotely similar outfits. But if you happened to find two women wearing identical saris and placed them side by side, you would still be looking at two completely different garments. The pleats and tucks of a well-wrapped sari can create curves, hide bulges, add height and improve posture. Every sari is handcrafted every morning to perfectly fit the body of the woman who wears it.

I found myself illogically drawn to the idea of wearing one myself but assumed that sari wrapping was a difficult skill to master, honed over years of practice. And even after all those years, an expert sari wrapper would probably need at least an hour and a full-length mirror to achieve the graceful, flowing results that filled the streets all around me. You know what they say about assumptions. The truth, as I discovered one day when Mary Elizabeth borrowed my bathroom to change in, is that a sari is remarkably simple to wrap. After some practice it takes about ten minutes to put one on.

This discovery changed my whole sartorial philosophy. Although my churidars were comfortable, I was far from delighted with walking around looking like an embroidered washing machine with leggings. I'd seen some remarkably chubby women looking pretty damn good in their saris. Although I couldn't hope to achieve the ravishing results produced by Mary Elizabeth and Sally, I decided to buy one for myself and see if this magical garment would transform me.

Indians do not shop alone, at least not for saris. Shopping for a new sari requires the opinion of at least three female friends or relatives. For a really important sari, say, something like the mother of the bride, the entire extended family must advise the prospective buyer. As my only friend in India, Mary Elizabeth agreed to accompany me on my quest. There are many places to buy a sari in Chennai, from box stores with saris hanging over the counters to marble palaces devoted to the adornment of the female form. Of these, Madhar Sha and Chennai Silks are reputed to have the best selection. We went to Madhar Sha.

As we sat in the back of an auto, zipping through oncoming traffic at a brisk ten miles per hour, I told Mary Elizabeth about the arrangement I'd reached with Sally and that I wanted to reward Santoshi but couldn't figure out how to do it.

Santoshi never spent money if she could avoid it. She would walk for miles to avoid paying a six-rupee bus fare. She would starve to death standing in front of a bakery rather than spend eight rupees on an egg puff. As far as I could tell, aside from buying a couple of blessings from the priest at the local temple, Santoshi hadn't spent any of her salary at all. She thanked me for it, with a disturbing little gesture that involved touching my feet, then locked it in her suitcase. I tried to convince her to put it in the bank, but she was afraid of banks and wanted me to do her banking for her. That was never going to happen. I'd come to India to encourage Santoshi's independence, not to help her avoid it.

Other than making her suitcase too heavy to carry, a commission paid in cash was worse than useless to Santoshi because it would make her too rich to qualify as a resident of the hostel. Anyone who can't sleep alone or shell out bus fare is unlikely to embrace the idea of setting up her own apartment, and anyone who can afford her own apartment doesn't have much chance of getting back into the shelters. I wanted to reward Santoshi fairly for the work she did to find the property, not destroy her life.

Mary Elizabeth was too polite to express her surprise at the idea of paying the maid so much money for so little effort. She agreed with me that Santoshi would have no use for the cash and said she'd think about it as we pulled up in front of our destination.

Madhar Sha is a temple devoted to the worship of the sari. Huge columned rooms are lined with polished wooden counters. Behind the counters stand the salesmen. Behind the salesmen floor-to-ceiling wooden shelves hold thousands and thousands and more thousands of saris, all neatly folded and stacked so that the customer cannot see them.

To see a sari, the customer must peer at the slim sliver of color that is on display and then engage in an extended session of arm waving and verbal instructions to point out its location to a salesman. The shelves are organized by price, resulting in a large number of bored-looking salesmen leaning on the counters in the silk sections and a heaving, shouting mass of women clustered ten deep around the few harried salesmen at the nylon and polyester counters. It says volumes about the mentality of commerce in India that this system does not result in instant bankruptcy. Madhar Sha opened its doors in 1937 and remains at the pinnacle of sari retailers to this day.

We elbowed our way through children and grandmothers and great-aunts and second cousins twice removed until we squeezed in among the buyers and their support groups at one of the five-deep cotton counters. While Mary Elizabeth attempted to catch the attention of a salesman, I fingered through the mounds of saris waiting to be folded back onto the shelves. This counter contained plaid saris in squint-inducing color combinations predominated by crime-scene-tape yellow and life-jacket orange.

I had no intention of buying a plaid sari, but before I could tell Mary Elizabeth we should try another counter, my pale complexion attracted the attention of one of the salesmen. This rapid acquisition of assistance did not endear me to the other women at the counter, some of whom had probably been trying to flag him down since the previous week. I was stuck with shopping for something or getting lynched by an angry mob for impersonating a customer.

I told him I wanted dark and plain. He pulled an orange, purple and green tartan off the shelf behind him. Thinking that he'd misunderstood, I repeated my request for dark and plain. He pointed out that in the absence of sequins and mirrors and gold embroidery, it *was* plain, madam. In an attempt to cut short what was rapidly becoming a plaid nightmare, I scanned the counter looking for anything even close to attractive.

My eye fell on a speck of red. My heartbeat sped up. My pupils dilated. My hands shook as I reached out and gently pulled it from under the pile. I had contracted that dread disease, Sari-itis.

Sari-itis afflicts approximately one in ten Indian women. It is incurable. The disfiguring effects on its sufferers can only be controlled by placing limits on their credit cards. You see the victims on the streets of Chennai every day, pathetic women who have succumbed to the lure of the fabric and bought a sari whose pattern highlights all their figure flaws and even creates some they don't have. A short, fat woman will buy a silver sequined sari that makes passersby break into spontaneous disco dancing. A tall thin woman in red and white vertical stripes becomes an undulating optical illusion, causing cross-eyed drivers to swerve into one another as they attempt to avoid her.

I'd been infected by huge gold windowpane checks on a bright, cherry red background. Deep inside my little voice screamed, *"You idiot! It'll make you look like Mrs. Santa Claus!"* But, despite the fact that this was the first unambiguous warning my little voice had ever managed, I ignored it.

"I'll take this one," I told the salesman.

Mary Elizabeth, instantly and correctly interpreting my actions, tried valiantly to pull me to the cash desk, but I fought her and managed to snag a violently violet sari covered in orange and gold embroidery before we got there.

I wore my lovely red and gold sari only once. I was unable to control the compulsion to hum "Jingle Bells" the whole time. Thanks to Sally, I finally did manage to join the sari brigade. She had no use for her extensive sari collection when she left to become a full-time granny in San Francisco, and gave me twenty or so that she thought would suit me before she donated the rest to charity. Over the next few months, as I wore my secondhand saris, I gained an entirely undeserved reputation for excellent taste, which I maintained by never again setting foot inside Madhar Sha.

And, as always, Mary Elizabeth came through for me. In the auto on the way home she suggested that instead of paying Santoshi a commission, I offer her rent-free accommodation in the hostel for life.

Santoshi was grateful. At least I think she was. She touched my feet.

You Just Can't Give Good Help These Days

❁ ❁ ❁ ❁ ❁

STILL BASKING IN HIS LUNCHTIME euphoria, Prakesh stepped through the front gate of Venu's house and started walking back home to continue working. A voice called out from behind him.

"Prakesh! Prakesh! Have you got a second?"

Unlike most of the people in the neighborhood, Prakesh did not think the white woman living above Venu's house was an oddity. He had been raised in America. He found her direct manners and logical conversation far more normal than the roundabout ways of his other neighbors. After five years in India, Prakesh had given up trying to become a real Indian and accepted that he would be forever suspended between two cultures: the one that he loved and the one he was forced to inhabit.

Before Kiria's arrival in the neighborhood, the high point of Prakesh's day had been the home-cooked lunch he bought from old Geeta. It wasn't that the food was good. In fact, until quite recently, the food had frequently been barely edible. But he would have cheerfully eaten an old sandal if it was served by the divine

Laxmi. Now, with the added possibility of a conversation with Venu's tenant, lunch hours had taken on a golden glow.

He smiled broadly at Kiria as she approached. "Hi, Kiria. What's up?"

"Two things. First, I wanted to ask you how it's going with them after you brought in the police last week." Kiria tipped her head in the direction of Venu's house.

Prakesh rolled his eyes upward. "What a nightmare! Geeta had told me a couple of days before that Laxmi was sick. When the carpenter showed up to take out the door, I realized I hadn't seen Laxmi for almost a week. Geeta wouldn't pay what the carpenter asked for to take out the door. Venu was asleep. Mani just ignored the whole thing and kept eating his lunch. I thought Laxmi could be dying in there, so I went and got the police. Then Laxmi came out and she was fine and I felt like an idiot."

"And you're still having lunch there? Aren't they mad at you?"

"Well, I thought they'd be, so I came over the next day to get my money back because I'd just paid them for the week. But Laxmi invited me in and said she was sorry for the misunderstanding. Venu is upset, but when I apologized, he said it wasn't my fault that Geeta and Laxmi are always fighting. Mani is still pretending nothing happened."

"And Geeta?"

"Well, she's probably mad at me. But since Venu forgave me, she can't say anything. And I haven't actually seen her. Maybe she's avoiding me."

"Well, I'm sure she'll get over it in time. Listen, have you got a few minutes to help me with something?"

"What?"

"I'm trying to explain something to Nirmila, but my Tamil's not up to it."

"Who's Nirmila?"

"She's over there." Kiria pointed to the garbage heap across the street where a thin woman in a ragged sari was poking through the refuse.

"The ragpicker?" Prakesh could not keep revulsion out of his voice.

"You don't have to hug her. You just have to talk to her. You can stand upwind. You can take a bath when you get home." She smiled to show she was teasing.

"Well, I guess it won't kill me." Prakesh managed a strained smile in response. "What do you want me to say?"

Kiria explained as they crossed the street. "You know I'm building a hostel for poor women? So, I've been watching Nirmila from the terrace for the past few weeks and I think she's just the kind of person I'm trying to help. I've been bringing her my recyclables and trying to talk to her, but I can't understand what she's telling me. As near as I can make out, she's a widow and a pavement dweller, but that's as far as I can get."

Nirmila stopped poking through the garbage as the old white woman and the young man approached. She straightened up and gestured to her three girls to remain sitting in the shade of the bougainvillea tree. Very little in Nirmila's life had given her reason to trust people. She appreciated the bottles and cans and newspapers brought by the white woman, but no one talked to ragpickers. Few people even looked at them. The white woman's odd behavior worried Nirmila. What did she want? Why did she keep asking questions?

"Nirmila, this Mr. Prakesh. He from me to speak," Kiria said in crude Tamil. She turned to Prakesh. "Tell her I would like to ask her some questions to see if I can help her."

"This woman says she wants to help you. She wants to ask you questions," Prakesh translated, standing as far away as he could from the filthy ragpicker.

"Why? Why does she want to help me? What does she want?" Distrust sharpened Nirmila's thin face.

"Oh, that's a long story," Kiria said after Prakesh translated the questions. She thought for a minute, then reached into her purse, pulled out her wallet and extracted a five-hundred-rupee note. "Tell her I will pay her five hundred rupees to talk to me. She doesn't have to answer any question she doesn't want to."

Like most people who have never been poor, Prakesh felt a confusing blend of pity and revulsion when he put an individual face on real poverty for the first time, but as the three-sided conversation progressed, he gradually forgot his discomfort. He became interested in Nirmila's story, even began to admire her. If his own mother had shown half as much spirit when his father died, he'd still be living in America.

For her part Nirmila began, for the first time in many months, to feel hope again. When her husband died, she could have given her children to an orphanage or become a prostitute to support them. But Nirmila had a skill. She was the daughter of a ragpicker and the wife of a ragpicker. She knew garbage. Two days after the death of her husband she had placed her six-month-old daughter on her hip and, with the two older girls trailing behind, pushed her husband's cart along the familiar route through Periyar Nagar. But hampered by three children, she had been unable to find as much as her husband. And as a woman, she had been unable to obtain good prices for what she did find.

She could feed her girls only twice a day now. Her milk was drying up and the four-year-old was constantly ill. Just this morning Nirmila had come very close to renting the baby out to the beggar woman who slept beside the family on the pavements. If what these people said was true, her daughters might have a chance, not only to survive, but perhaps to go to school. And even if it was not true, her children would eat vegetables and meat for a month.

After twenty minutes of talking, Kiria and Prakesh left Nirmila to finish picking through the garbage heap.

"Thank you for your help, Prakesh. What did you think?" Kiria asked as they walked back toward the house.

"Well, it was interesting. Do you do this kind of thing all the time?"

"God no! That's one of the ten most depressing conversations I ever had in my life. I kind of admire her, though. I hope she comes back for an application."

"Me too."

It never occurred to either of them that Nirmila could not read or write.

"Let's talk about something less depressing. What are you translating now?" Kiria asked, referring to his job of translating English training manuals into Tamil for schools and colleges in Chennai.

"A paper on codependency from an American psychology journal."

"Codependency? That's like trying to translate water for a fish. I'm surprised there's even any words for the concepts in Tamil."

"Actually, there's a lot of words." Prakesh spread out his arms, palms up, in a gesture of helplessness. "But they mostly have positive connotations."

Bribery

❁ ❁ ❁ ❁ ❁

HAVE YOU EVER READ A Regency romance? I was addicted to those novels in my twenties. I checked them out from the library by the dozen, escaping my own problems in a world where the heroine's biggest dilemma was how to find her true love amid the devilish rakes and smooth-talking fortune hunters of a London Season. I never actually expected to find myself in this situation.

In the Indian system of graft, the party with the money is exactly like a Regency debutante at a ball. As the conversion of the Ravichandran Mental Health Centre into the New Beginnings Women's Hostel got under way, my dance card filled with dozens of suitors: suppliers, contractors, inspectors, all trying to convince me to grease their sweaty palms. They waltzed me around the bribery ballroom delicately whispering double entendres. I didn't know any of the steps and frequently didn't understand the first meaning, let alone the second one. But unlike a naive debutante, I had considerable experience with negotiating.

I won more than I lost, except with the inspectors who simply refused to show up and inspect without a "gift." On the plus side, they would approve just about anything for the right amount. The inspector from the electricity board managed to give himself a nasty shock while poking about in a junction box with a metal pen. He still passed the wiring, after a modest increase of a few thousand rupees in his remuneration. I hired an independent inspector for a second opinion to ensure my tenants wouldn't fry when they flipped a switch.

The commonest bribery tactic was The Stall. Some mysterious glitch would develop in finding materials or skilled labor that could be resolved only by the infusion of large amounts of cash. So during construction I made a habit of turning up at the work site every day to ensure that any crisis that developed was genuine and to check up on Old Viji.

I'd expected Old Viji to be upset by the construction activity. Instead, she seemed to enjoy it. She sat in her wheelchair outside her ground-floor room, hooting and flapping at the workers. When her caretaker tried to take her back in, Old Viji howled in protest and I wondered if she would appreciate more stimulation. There were a few televisions among the furnishings Sally left behind. I had one installed in Old Viji's room, and much to the delight of her caretaker, whose nightly struggles to get the disabled woman settled into bed could be heard halfway across Chennai, Old Viji became a Japanese-anime addict. She would sit quietly—well, as quietly as possible for a woman with a full-body twitch—through anything as long as the anime channel was on.

I myself soon became fascinated by the medieval quality of the construction process. There were no cranes or backhoes or forklifts. There were barely any power tools. Hard hats? Safety boots? Sissy stuff. Workers scrambled around the site in bare feet. Everything was done by hand with ancient tools and a rope-and-pulley mentality. Men dug out the old sewers using flat, short-handled, backward-facing shovels. Women in gaudy saris carried away the dirt in baskets on their heads. A few men seemed to be employed for the purpose of squatting around the site smoking and drinking tea. They turned out to be the supervisors.

Much to the amusement of the coolie women, I tried carrying a loaded basket on my head, just to see what it was like. It weighed about forty pounds and fell off my head after five steps. I limped for weeks, but X-rays showed my toe was not broken.

When the time came to fix the walls, the women carried baskets of sand, gravel and cement to a geriatric, miniature cement mixer, then carried baskets of the finished concrete to the men who clambered around on wobbly bamboo scaffolding. The women could produce more concrete in thirty minutes than the scaffolding crews could use in the same amount of time. While they waited to mix the next batch, they squatted around the cement mixer chatting. My Tamil was improving daily and some of the women had a basic English vocabulary, so I used my white-freak status to muscle in on the conversation.

It was a whole new world for me. Like all women they talked about men and children and food. Unlike the other women I'd met in India, they also talked fairly freely about drinking and sex. But by far the lion's share of gab time was devoted to marriage and dowry. All of them were either saving to dower a female relative, paying off a dowry loan or anticipating fat dowries for their unwed male relations. They had an endless interest in the price of iron bed frames, motor scooters and tin wardrobes, where to buy gold and silk cheaply and, most important, how to find the boy/girl and how much should be spent on the "gifts" to the boy's family. The mothers of daughters, naturally, held significantly different opinions on these last two topics from the mothers of sons.

Many Western people are horrified by the thought of arranged marriages. I'm not one of them. In my experience, love, or, more often, lust, is just about the worst possible criterion for selecting a life mate. People in love have impaired judgment. They should not be allowed to operate heavy machinery or make important decisions. Yes, true love is enduring. It is also rare. Everyone else is just temporarily insane. Great honeymoon sex is the only benefit of marrying for love, and who waits until they're married these days?

Dowry, on the other hand, is demeaning and occasionally dangerous. It's demeaning for the man, who is sold to the highest bidder, and for the woman, whose value is essentially a negative amount. Families frequently go into debt to finance a marriage. Dowry gets dangerous when someone decides to sell a kidney to raise the money or when the groom's family decides to capitalize on his resale value. In 1986 this was so common that the Indian Parliament added Dowry Death to the list of domestic violence crimes. Anyone who strays far enough off the tourist trail in India will soon run across its survivors.

I wasn't shocked. Let's face it. India is practically synonymous with poverty. People who are much better off will do far worse for considerably less. But I was confused by how a system that put its breeding population at such an extreme disadvantage could survive for millennia. Surely billions of revered mothers and beloved daughters over thousands of generations would have found a way to even their odds? The answer, when it came, was obvious.

I was squatting with the women around the cement mixer one day when the topic of inflation came up. Apparently the price of husbands had recently risen and some of the women were worried that by the time they saved enough, their daughters would be too old to marry. In an attempt to get a handle on the inflation rate, I asked an older woman how much dowry her father had paid. She spat out a glob of saliva, red from the betel nut many of them chewed, and said that her father had received about ten thousand rupees.

Misunderstandings were quite common between us given the remedial state of my Tamil. I assumed she'd said that her father *gave* ten thousand rupees or perhaps that her *husband's* father had received ten thousand rupees. But then a small bragging war started among the older women, and as each of them boasted about how much she had been worth, I realized that buying husbands was a fairly recent phenomenon. I asked each woman when she was married and discovered that as recently as thirty years ago at least some men paid for wives.

None of them could explain to me how this change in the flow of dowry came about. I suspect it had something to do with the great migration into the cities taking place at the same time. Women in the country had value as field labor. In the cities, where well-paid work was available only for men, women became an economic burden and the flow of dowry gradually reversed.

To me, a card-carrying member of the women's liberation movement, it seemed obvious that the way back to balanced gender values was for women to earn decent wages. I tried to talk with them about the benefits of spending money on educating their daughters instead of bankrupting themselves to pay this repulsive reverse ransom. But no one was willing to take the risk. They were terrified that without a dowry their daughters would never marry.

Although I thought they seriously underestimated the power of the sex drive, not to mention the fact that it's better to be an old spinster than a dead wife, I came to accept dowry in the same way I accepted sweat and ants and power cuts and corruption and a thousand and one other things about India that I didn't like and had no control over. I even helped a couple of the women out, when injuries, which were common on the work site due to the lack of safety equipment, prevented them from earning.

Okay. I fed the system. Sue me.

Lessons of Love

SANTOSHI CARRIED THE TEA TRAY out to the terrace where Kiria sat enjoying the ocean breeze blowing away the heat of the day, replacing it with the scents of night jasmine, incense and frying spices that filled the streets of Periyar Nagar after sunset.

Over the past months, Santoshi had come to look forward to the nightly ritual of tea and language lessons on the terrace. She loved English. Having mastered the alphabet in three lessons, she was now soaring through the crisp sounds of the consonants and the wild confusion of small words that filled the picture books Kiria Madam had bought for her at the Higginbotham's store. Tonight she would be reading from a new book, learning exciting new words.

For her part, Kiria did not enjoy the lessons as much. She found the elaborate Tamil grammar confusing and doubted she would ever speak it fluently. But she did value the insights gained from being able to understand some of what was said around her.

She had no expectations of ever being able to read Tamil, having learned 210 letters of the alphabet so far with no end in sight.

While Kiria poured the tea, Santoshi took out her reading glasses and hooked the arms carefully over her ears. She reached out and lightly touched the brightly colored cover of the book that lay on the table between them. "This new book, Kiria Madam?"

"Yes, it is. Are you ready to read?"

"Sugar first, Kiria Madam." Santoshi added five spoons of sugar to her cup and stirred carefully; she was not used to china cups yet and still feared breaking them. When her tea was sufficiently stirred, she took a sip, carefully wiped her hands on the skirt of her sari and picked up the book.

"*The Oogly Doooskling*," she began. "Kiria Madam, what 'Doooskling'?"

Suppressing the urge to add an article and a verb to the question, Kiria contented herself with correcting pronunciation. "Ugly Duckling. A duckling is a baby duck."

"What 'duck,' Kiria Madam?"

Kiria folded her fists into her armpits and flapped her elbows. "Quack, quack, quack," she said, hoping Indian ducks made the same sounds as American ducks.

Santoshi nodded and turned the page. " 'Once upon a time' . . . Kiria Madam, what 'upon'?"

Kiria sipped her tea while she thought. " 'Once upon a time' means long ago."

The reading progressed slowly with many explanations and corrections to pronunciation. Kiria sincerely regretted her choice of book. When her phone rang, she grabbed it with relief.

"Hello?"

"Hi, Kiria. It's Eva."

"Oh, not again. Just sleep with him and get it over with."

"Sleep with who?"

"Piet."

"Kiria! Anyway, I'm not calling about Piet. Shelly Korrel at CNN is planning a new series on self-made women. She wants to tape an interview with you in New York. I thought you might be interested. It's free publicity, and SharpEnd will be releasing soon. She said to tell you Mazatlán. What does that mean?"

"It means I shouldn't drink tequila."

"She's blackmailing you?"

"No, more like calling in a favor. Actually, I wouldn't mind a steak and a real shower right now. Okay. Find out when they're taping and book a round-trip and four days at the Plaza on my personal account. You know, I wasn't kidding about Piet. You like him. I can tell from ten thousand miles away."

"But he's so young!"

"Only eight years. Would you feel this way if he were eight years older?"

"That's different."

"Yeah. Younger men have more enthusiasm. Look, Piet may be the love of your life. Or not, in which case you'll just have great sex. There's no downside here."

"He hasn't asked me out."

"He likes you. Stop treating him like he's got bubonic plague and I'll bet he asks."

"You think so?"

"Pretty sure. Look, I'm in the middle of something here. Call me when you've made the bookings. And if you can't go out with him, at least cut him some slack. Before we get further behind in beta testing than we already are."

"I can try. Talk to you later."

"Bye, Eva."

Kiria pinched the bridge of her nose as she put down the phone.

"Head pain, Kiria Madam?" Santoshi asked.

"No. Heart pain."

Santoshi's face crumpled into a expression of such profound concern that Kiria laughed out loud. "Not real heart pain, Santoshi. In-love heart pain."

Santoshi had thought Kiria Madam too old for that. "You in love, Kiria Madam?"

"Not me. My friend. Are you in love, Santoshi?"

Santoshi looked down at the book in her hands. Kiria was about to apologize for asking a personal question when Santoshi looked up, smiling triumphantly.

"Once upon a time, Kiria Madam."

Banana Steps

From: kiria@novio.com
To: meglertheodore@rogers.net
Subject: Thanks for the pictures

I especially like the one of you and Rik on your wedding day. I see what you mean about the morning suits, particularly the top hats. You may be wrong about never wearing them again, though. They'll come in quite handy if you're ever invited to the Royal Enclosure at Ascot.

I'm on the banana diet once more, although this time the dysentery isn't as bad. Perhaps I'm developing immunity to whatever is causing it. Which remains a complete mystery because I haven't eaten out in weeks.

Remember I wrote you about the domestic drama downstairs? Well, it seems that Venu (by whom I mean Geeta, of course) has finally agreed to Laxmi getting a job. Laxmi brought up her résumé last night and she's surprisingly well qualified, so the problem of finding an office manager for the hostel may be solved. Now all I need is a reliable plumber.

Mary Elizabeth took me sari shopping last week. It turns out I have terrible taste in saris. I'm sending Rik the two I bought. Perhaps they'll come in handy for making Halloween costumes for his nieces, or café curtains, or something equally gaudy.

When you see Alicia, tell her the maple syrup arrived safely and thank her very much. When I can risk real food again, I'm going to teach Santoshi how to make pancakes.

Hi to Rik

Kiria

PS—I wasn't going to ask, but find I want to know. How did it go in Albany?

From: meglertheodore@rogers.net
To: kiria@novio.com
Subject: get well soon

Hi Kiria

Sorry to hear you're ill again. I hope you find whatever is causing it; meanwhile, good thing you like bananas. Rik says Hi back and stay hydrated. This is the one downside of being married to a nurse. They're very bossy. (***I'm bossy? Ask him about the SUV! —R***)

Albany was a bust. Rik and I took your advice and went to the library to check out the newspaper coverage of your divorce before trying to contact my father. His second divorce was even more spectacular. I've defended people like him. Nowadays he'd more likely be charged with assault, not divorced on the grounds of cruelty. If it was just me, I might have contacted him. People change, as you said. But I've got Rik and someday hope to have kids to think about. He's not a person I want in their lives.

Mom is taking an Alaskan cruise with her bridge buddies. This is the first time since Dad died that she's been excited about anything and I take it as a good sign.

Did I tell you our new neighbors are from Sri Lanka? We told them you were in Chennai and they invited us over for a traditional Tamil meal the other night. Do you have rasam soup in Chennai? That stuff is deadly. I was up all night. . . .

Hiring and Firing

KIRIA LOOKED AT HER WATCH and decided she had time to handle one more thing before Mary Elizabeth and Laxmi arrived. She sat in the shade of the Flame of the Forest tree and scrolled through the contacts in her cell phone until she found the plumbing contractor.

"Hello?"

"Mr. Karani? This is Kiria Langdon."

"Mrs. Langdon. How are you?"

"I'm good." Kiria got right down to business. "The plumber still hasn't come in to work. If he doesn't finish the toilets by the end of the week, the tiling will be delayed."

"He has a fever."

"Again?" Kiria didn't bother to hide her disbelief. "Well, is there anyone else you can send?"

"As I told you before, Mrs. Langdon, subcontracting to another plumber will increase the costs." Mr. Karani did not bother to hide his triumph.

"Then I'll have to find another plumber myself."

"We have a contract, Mrs. Langdon."

"Yes, of course. I'll have my lawyer send the dissolution papers to your office today."

"Remember, there is a cancellation penalty in our contract."

Although she had intended to keep the conversation pleasant, Kiria had learned long ago never to ignore a threat, even one as mild as this. She decided to show some claws. "There is also a timely-completion clause in the contract and unlike you, Mr. Karani, I intend to honor *all* of the provisions in our agreement, not just the ones I like. If you don't agree to the dissolution, that is your choice. When construction is completed, we'll know the full cost of this delay, and I'm sure our lawyers can work out who owes what."

Kiria shut the phone with a snap. "Take that, you coprolite!"

"What is a coprolite?" Mary Elizabeth sat down beside Kiria on the bench.

"Fossilized excrement."

Mary Elizabeth continued to look at Kiria blankly.

"Old shit," Kiria explained in cruder terms. "You're early."

"My father's appointment at the hospital did not take as long as expected."

"How is he?"

Mary Elizabeth sighed. "Not very good. They say it is just a matter of waiting now. I have decided it is time to hire a real nurse. Now that Father is not cooperative, he is too difficult for Selvi."

"Can you afford a nurse? Do you need help?"

"No, I can manage. But thank you. I appreciate that you offered. It is more than my family has done." Mary Elizabeth's well-to-do cousins had become mysteriously unavailable since illness had taken her father's mind as well as his body.

"We choose our friends, but we're stuck with our relatives. If you do need help, you just have to ask."

"Thank you. I wish I could spend more time with him. He is awake so little these days."

Kiria smiled. "Now, that is something I may be able to help you with. But let's wait until Laxmi gets here."

"Laxmi is coming?"

"Yes. She applied for the office manager job."

"Her family allows this?"

"Apparently."

"Why?"

"I don't know. Geeta just seems to have given up. It's been very quiet downstairs for the past few weeks."

An auto pulled up outside the hostel gates. Laxmi, wearing blue jeans and a white shirt, climbed out. Mary Elizabeth looked at Laxmi's clothes in shock. This was not proper attire for a job interview. Kiria, on the other hand, whose employees in Vancouver rarely wore anything as fashionable as the shirt, thought Laxmi looked quite nice.

Laxmi paid the driver and walked over to join the women sitting on the fountain. "Am I late?"

"Actually I think you're early." Kiria rose. "Let's go into the office. I'm starting to broil out here."

"You'll love it here next month," Laxmi said as the three women walked over to the small building by the gate. "It'll be summer then."

"I can hardly wait." Kiria flipped the switch to start the ceiling fan as she passed through the door.

The office was filled with discarded items from the main building waiting to be picked up by the medical-salvage company. Although most of the Centre's furnishings had been reusable, the specialized beds and equipment were too valuable not to be sold off. Kiria hiked herself up onto a bed beneath the fan. Mary Elizabeth sat on a wooden bench by the window. Laxmi decided to sit on a bed.

"Unless I can't find a decent plumber," Kiria began, "construction on the hostel should be finished in three or four weeks. It's pretty obvious I can't run this place. Aside from my pathetic Tamil, I have to go to New York soon."

"Your Tamil is good for a person who has only been here a few months," Mary Elizabeth assured her friend.

Laxmi thought Kiria spoke with a very low-class accent. She chose to comment on Kiria's departure instead. "You are leaving India?"

"Just for a few days, I hope. With luck I'll be back by the end of the month. Just in time for summer. Anyway, I need an office manager and an administrator and I need them soon. I think you would make a good administrator, Mary Elizabeth. And I looked at your résumé, Laxmi, and I'm willing to give you a six-month trial as office manager because I think you have some skills Mary Elizabeth needs but doesn't have."

"I do?" Laxmi looked surprised.

"You can use a computer, for one. You can set up documentation systems. Much as I admire the handcrafted quality of your files, Mary Elizabeth, I don't think it's a good use of my salary dollars to have employees wading through mountains of handwritten notes."

"Oh, Kiria, I'm sorry. I can't. My father is too ill." True disappointment showed on Mary Elizabeth's face.

"Don't say no yet. The job doesn't require you to be in the office all the time. Especially during the setup phase. It's all stuff like designing the application form and deciding on tenant qualifications and creating the hostel rules. You could work in the office a couple of mornings a week and work from home the rest of the time. I'm hiring you for your knowledge of the tenants, not for your ability to run an office. That's Laxmi's job."

"What else would I do?" Laxmi asked.

"Staffing and payroll, budgeting, bookkeeping, banking, repairs and maintenance and anything else that comes up."

"Repairs and maintenance!" Laxmi exclaimed. "I'm not a plumber."

"No, but you you'd be hiring them," Kiria told her.

Laxmi looked doubtful. "It's a very large job."

"Well, it will keep you out of the house." Kiria grinned at Laxmi, who touched the small scar on her upper lip and smiled back. "I don't expect you to do it alone. You'd be responsible for staffing. Hire help."

"And the pay?" Laxmi knew from her studies that the employees of NOVIO were extremely well rewarded by profit-sharing bonuses. She also knew large profits were not likely in this situation.

"Ah, now, there we come to the interesting part." Kiria slid off the bed and started pacing around the furniture. "Normally, I pay the middle of the scale and divide fifty percent of the net profit among all employees. But unless there's a miracle, I don't see how this hostel is going to break even, let alone make a profit. On the other hand staff turnover costs more than low wages save. So we need a plan to minimize operational costs that includes paying decent wages and a titanium budget."

"What is a titanium?" Mary Elizabeth asked.

"A very strong kind of metal. I mean we need a budget that has no soft spots. One that takes everything into account. So for starters I'm going to offer each of you a consulting contract for a three-month period. That way I can control the costs. The three of us will put together the plan and the budget. When I know how much loss to expect, I'll come up with a way to generate the shortfall and pay decent bonuses."

Kiria stopped pacing and looked at the two women. Mary Elizabeth seemed totally confused. Laxmi, who understood perfectly due to her business courses in university, felt a rising excitement. "Like a second business?" she asked.

"Yes. Something like putting in a row of stores against the street wall. Or a day care center. Or expanding the canteen to lunch catering. I'm open to suggestions."

"This will work!" Mary Elizabeth exclaimed suddenly. "I thought the hostel would fail, but this will work!"

"Why would it fail?" Kiria asked.

"Because you will not find many good tenants for it. People will take advantage, not pay rent or try to cheat. But now it doesn't matter, because you will not need the rent."

Kiria's eyebrows rose in surprise and she sat down on the bench beside Mary Elizabeth, overcome by a momentary sensation of vertigo. She wasn't surprised people would cheat or not pay rent. She was surprised she hadn't made a plan to handle it.

"Well, I don't know why you're so excited about me being cheated, but that's not going to happen. How do social workers deal with this? When people apply for assistance or a place in a shelter?"

"We visit their homes. We interview them."

"Does it work?"

"It works sometimes. Sometimes they still cheat."

Kiria put it aside for the time being. "Let me think about this. So, will you take the job?"

Mary Elizabeth thought about working from home and the large fee. Quitting her job was a risk, but she would have more time with her father. "Yes," she said.

With nothing to lose, Laxmi had no hesitation. "I will too."

"Good." Kiria stood up. "We'll start tomorrow at ten a.m. We'll work till one, then . . ." A movement outside the window caught her eye. "Oh no, you don't. Vijay! Vijay!" she shouted, hurrying out of the office to accost a thin young man in paint-stained shorts scurrying toward the gate. At the sound of Kiria's voice, he stopped abruptly. His shoulders sagged as he turned around.

"Vijay, why are there only three painters here today?" Kiria demanded.

A New Point of View

❁ ❁ ❁ ❁ ❁

THE DAY AFTER HER EMPLOYER left for America, Santoshi sat on the floor of her bedroom, counting the coins in her jar and wondering how she would fill the time until Kiria Madam returned. In the shelters, Santoshi had spent her free time talking with the other inmates or sleeping. But with Laxmi away all day there was no one to talk to and sleeping alone in the apartment was difficult.

The coins were not helping. They no longer felt comforting in her hand. Since coming to work for Kiria Madam, Santoshi's world had expanded. These useless coins could not fill the hole left after the excitement of looking for the hostel and the joy of English lessons. One day soon, Santoshi thought sadly, Kiria Madam would leave India forever and it would be time to move into the little room at the hostel and go back to a life of scrubbing pots and sweeping floors.

With a shock, she realized that she would be very unhappy back in that small life and she finally understood why Laxmi had shouted out in the kitchen on the day she locked herself in her room. A person could not be happy when mind and spirit were squeezed into too small a space. The idea of happiness as something that could be found by expanding one's world had never crossed Santoshi's mind. It was unsettling, strangely exciting. She rose and dumped the coins from the skirt of her sari back into the suitcase. As she shoved the suitcase back under the bed, the strangest thought of all occurred to her. Were the coins really useless?

Two hours later Santoshi stood outside the hostel gates, studying the foundations of the box stores that were being constructed against the outside wall. It looked like the store farthest from the gate would be larger than the others. The rent would be higher, but the longer shelves would hold more goods. The owner of that store would have more to sell.

"Santoshi! What are you doing here?"

Startled by Laxmi's voice, Santoshi told the truth. "I am thinking of my life in the hostel after Kiria Madam leaves."

"I suppose it will be very much like your life before she came. Except there will be no kitchen duty." Laxmi held up a tea tin and a small roll of butter biscuits. "I just got some tea for myself and Mary Elizabeth. Would you like some?"

"Yes, miss." Santoshi accepted the invitation with relief. For a while at least, she would not be alone.

Entering the office, they found Mary Elizabeth sifting through a pile of papers. "This is impossible!" she exclaimed without looking up. "How can Kiria expect me to interview all these people? This will take months."

"Why bother?" Laxmi set the tea tin down on the desk. "I found Santoshi outside. She is having tea with us."

"Santoshi!" Mary Elizabeth dropped the papers and smiled. "How are you?"

"I am good, madam." Santoshi sat on the bench beneath the office window.

"Yes, but you look tired." Laxmi took three metal beakers from a desk drawer and filled them from the tea tin. "Did you sleep? I didn't hear the television last night."

"I did not turn it on, miss. It is difficult to turn off the television when I am asleep." Santoshi accepted the tea and biscuit Laxmi handed to her. "Who are you interviewing, madam?"

"Applicants for the hostel." Mary Elizabeth sipped her tea. "Almost two hundred and fifty women have applied. Kiria wants to be sure that the women who are given a place qualify by the rules."

Laxmi sat beside Santoshi on the bench. "Waste of time. You said it yourself; they will lie. Kiria is a very smart woman in many ways, but she doesn't know what these people are like. You probably don't know them as well as you think either. I'll bet Santoshi could tell you some things about your clients in the shelters."

"I'm sure she could," Mary Elizabeth said. "I must at least talk to them all."

"Are there many rules, madam?" Santoshi asked, concerned that she might not qualify.

"Only three. They must not be beggars or prostitutes. They must be working and have a very small income. They must have no man to support them."

"And they must want to pay rent." Laxmi added her own rule.

Santoshi thought the three rules sounded simple. Most of the working women she'd met in the shelters would qualify. Even that ragpicker Kiria Madam was giving the bottles to . . .

Suddenly, Santoshi sat up straight and placed her tea beaker on the bench. "Let me help you, madam," she offered. "Kiria Madam still pays me, but I am doing nothing. I do not like to be alone all day. Laxmi is right. I can talk to these women in ways you cannot."

"You will do the interviews?" Mary Elizabeth was dubious.

"No, madam. I will wear my old sari and talk to the women and their neighbors. I will tell you if they are lying. Then you only have to interview the ones who are not."

Mary Elizabeth considered this. "Well, it would save me a great deal of time."

"Problem solved," Laxmi said, and bit into her biscuit.

Santoshi spent the rest of the day in the office studying the applications. She went home with Laxmi that night. The next morning she put on her old green sari and began the first day of what would be a most interesting three weeks.

"YES, I know her. She is not here now. She is working." The old beggar woman squatting by the temple gate looked warily up at Santoshi. "Why are you looking for her?"

"I have heard that she has found a place in a poor woman's hostel, Auntie." Santoshi had recently become very good at lying by telling the truth.

"A hostel!" The beggar hawked and spat phlegm into the road. "She is deceived. There is no such thing. The government wants to move us off the streets."

Two plump women approached the temple gate. The old beggar held out her hand reflexively. Passing through the gate, the nearest woman dropped a small coin into the cupped palm in an obviously familiar routine.

"It is a shelter," the old woman continued, tucking the coin beneath her.

"Perhaps, Auntie. But I would like to ask her about it. Do you know where she works?"

"You will be locked up with the rest of the fools," the beggar grumbled, but she gave Santoshi directions.

"Thank you, Auntie." Santoshi dropped a two-rupee coin

into the beggar's hand and walked away. She had taken only a few steps when she heard the old woman calling out after her.

"Why do you think the locks are on the outside?"

Although she had spent her childhood on the streets, Santoshi had never actually lived on the streets. For all of her life she had thought of the locked shelter gates in the same way she thought of the locked door of the room where her old master, Rahul, had taken his children at night, as protection for those hidden safely inside. Now, as she walked along the narrow alley between the woven palm-leaf walls of huts that offered the families within nothing more than protection from the elements, she thought of all the locked doors she had slept behind in her life and realized that the beggar woman was right. The locks were all on the outside.

At this hour of the evening, the normal hutment smells of sour sweat and old urine were temporarily overlaid by the homey scent of frying ginger and garlic with an occasional perfumed waft of incense. Chatting men sat in small groups drinking tea and coffee. Women laughed with one another across cooking fires. Children ran shouting between the huts or squatted intently in the road, playing games with pebbles. The noise of televisions came from almost every dwelling, powered by the frayed wires that looped between them. At first Santoshi had been fooled by the televisions into thinking these people were well-off. She knew now that the televisions were given out free by the government and were a valuable source of information for the many illiterate residents of the hutment who could not read newspapers.

Santoshi came to the road at the end of the alley and looked left as the beggar woman had instructed. A shabby hut leaned against an old tree trunk, its moldy palm-leaf walls disintegrating, just as the woman had described it. A man smoking a beedi squatted at the side of the hut. The acrid scent of the drug drifted toward the alley. Santoshi could clearly hear the rhythmic grunting of another man inside the hut.

Turning right, Santoshi walked until she came to an abandoned auto at the side of the road. She squatted behind it and pulled a small notebook out of the waist of her sari. She wrote the word "prostitute" beside the woman's name, tucked the notebook back in her sari and decided she had done enough for today.

When she got home, Santoshi shot the inside bolt of the front door and stood staring at it for several minutes before going into the kitchen to make dhosas for her supper.

Santoshi Saves the Day—Again

❁ ❁ ❁ ❁ ❁

DON'T YOU JUST HATE IT when people mess with the plan? It happens in every project. You turn your back, even for a second, someone gets a bright idea and the next thing you know, you're running damage control.

Just after construction on the hostel was completed, I had to go to New York for a few days. When I returned to Chennai, I learned Santoshi had somehow talked Mary Elizabeth and Laxmi into giving her the position of official hostel spy.

I had no idea why Santoshi decided espionage would be a good career move, but as with everything else she set her mind to, she turned out to be quite good at it. She spent her mornings in the office studying applications and writing up her findings. In the afternoons and evenings she resurrected that disgusting gray-green sari and wandered around Chennai chatting up the applicants and their neighbors.

With the real maid out snooping all the day, I had to become the maid. I learned three things from my first and only attempt to do laundry in a bucket:

1. It is possible to rinse one's clothing entirely in the sweat generated by scrubbing it.

2. Indian dirt is more tenacious than Indian fabric dye. My churidars and saris came out looking like Jackson Pollock's summer collection.

3. The ratio of excruciating back-pain days to bending-over-a-bucket hours is 2:1.

I bought a washing machine. And a vacuum cleaner. And opened an account at the local restaurant to avoid having to use that hideous gas ring. Despite the new modern conveniences, our standards of hygiene dipped slightly, primarily because next to "hot" the word "dusty" is probably the most frequently applied adjective in descriptions of India. The Indian tourism board would really like "incredible" to be the cliché of choice, but they have a long, hot, dusty road ahead of them. There comes a point where the discomfort of fighting dirt by far exceeds the discomfort of living in it.

Now we're just going to pause here and do a short recap of my efforts to improve Santoshi's life to date:

1. Over half of my savings account was now invested in a hostel that was guaranteed to run at a loss for years to come, if it ever got off the ground at all.

2. I had lost about thirty pounds in two bouts of dysentery. Oh, did I forget to tell you about those? Until I

caught her at it, Santoshi had been rinsing our salad vegetables in tap water. To be fair, she was entirely unaffected by it.

3. And now *I* was the maid.

About this time a normal person would have begun to wonder just how far she was willing to go before admitting defeat. For most of my life I have sincerely wished that I were just such a normal person. But I'm not. By now I was so engaged in the process, so in love with my fantastic idea, that the thought of giving up never crossed my mind. I was like the *Titanic*, steaming along with so much forward momentum it would take an iceberg to stop me. Unfortunately there are very few icebergs in the Indian Ocean.

Okay, back to the Saga of Santoshi the Spy.

Santoshi's summarized report, translated by Laxmi, disqualified about ninety percent of the applicants. I should not have been so surprised. Many of the people I dealt with in Chennai were like children, constantly pushing to see what they could get away with. Salespeople lied blatantly about the quality of an item and outrageously inflated prices. Total strangers asked me to take them back to the States with me. One enterprising young shoe salesman even expected me to find him a wife when he got there and specified her attributes: young, blond and beautiful, with big "boozzums." Some people just asked me to give them things outright, mostly my watch. And you'd never believe how many people mistook a gray-haired old lady for a drug-addicted sex tourist.

Coming from the bottom of the economic pyramid, our applicants showed remarkable ingenuity in testing the boundaries. There were prostitutes, whom we'd ruled out on the grounds that we didn't want them bringing clients home. There were beggars, who, as far as I was concerned, probably already had benefited enough from charity. Some applicants were not employed at all, making rent collection highly unlikely. A few were well enough off by Indian standards and just didn't want to pay market prices for their accommodation. Many of those who did qualify were actually fronting for people who didn't. Finally, despite the fact that the application clearly stated a woman must have no supporting male relative, a surprising number of the applicants were living harmoniously with husbands or boyfriends.

So there I was, with over forty vacancies and less than twenty possible tenants, including Gowrie and Banu, the two safe bets recommended by Mary Elizabeth. Where were all those women I'd met in the slums and in the shelters and on the pavements, whining about their hardship? Was Laxmi right? Were they all prostitutes and . . . hang on, why had Nirmila been disqualified?

Laxmi had translated only a summary of the applications; the applications themselves were in Tamil. I hadn't really mastered Tamil writing, and reading Santoshi's cramped little squiggles was far beyond my ability. Gathering up the applications, qualified and disqualified, I headed over to Prakesh's house and gave him a job. A week later he e-mailed his translations back to me. Nirmila's application wasn't there. Not in the qualified pile and not in the disqualified pile.

I watched for Nirmila from the terrace the next morning. When she appeared, I rang Laxmi's doorbell and took her with me to translate because I wanted to understand exactly why Nirmila hadn't applied.

When asked, Nirmila looked at me like I'd slapped her. Spittle flew from her lips as she shouted out her rage at me. Amid the accusations and hurt feelings, the gist of it was that she had paid someone to fill out the application for her and taken a day off work to submit it at the office. Having no address, she'd been told to come back to the office in two weeks to find out if her application had been accepted. When she did, she was told that all the units were taken. She spent considerable time dwelling on how she and her children had gone hungry to pay the man who filled out the form and the two days of lost income caused by the long walk to the office.

No matter how forcefully I asked, she would not tell me who had told her the units were all rented. But she didn't have to. There were only four people in the office, and two of them were standing right in front of her. I reimbursed Nirmila for her lost income and called a staff meeting.

Santoshi Loses the Day

❁❁❁❁❁

MARY ELIZABETH CHECKED HER WATCH. In an hour, Raj would be waiting for her at the coffee shop. Where was Kiria? It was very unusual for her to be so late. Mary Elizabeth shifted in her seat on the wooden bench beneath the office window. "Do you know what this is about?"

Santoshi looked up from the application form she was filling in for her room. "No, madam."

Now that her spying days were over, Santoshi had returned to her tightly braided hair and severely pleated navy sari. Mary Elizabeth could barely recognize the drudge who had gone to work for Kiria. In her place sat a woman who, with her reading glasses perched at the tip of her tiny nose, could be mistaken for a schoolteacher or an accountant. It wasn't just the crisp sari and the glasses. Santoshi's posture was erect, her voice firm. Although she hadn't lost her habit of suffixing every second statement with the word "madam," she made eye contact when she said it.

"Did you like being a spy, Santoshi?" Mary Elizabeth asked.

Santoshi gave the question serious consideration. "I enjoyed the thinking, madam. But it made me sad."

"Why? What made you sad?"

"The streets, madam. All my life I have been afraid of the streets. Now I know they are not as bad as I imagined. I stayed in the shelters because I was afraid of the streets. But I watched those people. Even though they have a hard life, it may be better than hiding in a shelter the way I did." Santoshi suddenly looked worried. "But I did not mean that I do not appreciate what you did for me, madam. You were very good to me."

"I did not know you were so unhappy in the shelters."

"I did not myself, madam."

"So, what will you do now? The hostel does not need a full-time spy."

"No, madam, but it does need other things."

"A cleaner? A cook?"

"If there is nothing else, but there is no future in that." Santoshi put down her pen and folded her hands on the desk in front of her. "I have been thinking, madam. I will never marry. I will never have sons to care for me when I am old."

"You are still young," Mary Elizabeth protested, partly because she herself still cherished the dream of marriage, even though her time for having children had almost passed. "There are many men, widowers, who would consider marrying you."

"But would I consider marrying them? I am small and I have no teeth. No man will want me. They will only want my dowry, my work. I have seen that kind of marriage. I have lived with women who had those marriages. Look at Gowrie. She was a rich woman. She lost everything." Santoshi picked up the rental form. "I would lose everything I have gained with Kiria Madam. I would lose my room."

"Gowrie's husband died, Santoshi. He did not take her money. How will you live alone?"

"Gowrie is alone," Santoshi said softly, then continued in a firm voice, "I will not dream. I will care for myself. Kiria Madam has told me this, and I believe her. I will open a provisions store, madam."

"A provisions store!" Mary Elizabeth could hardly believe she'd heard correctly. "Where?"

"Here. There is no provisions store on this street."

"We will have a canteen."

"Women need soap, madam. We need matches and ant chalk and many other things. And sometimes children like candy."

Mary Elizabeth sat back, silenced by the brilliance of the idea. She had always known Santoshi was clever, but this? Mary Elizabeth noted the reference to Kiria and wondered if Santoshi's newfound confidence would survive the loss of its mentor. Or the realities of commerce.

"Santoshi, it takes a great deal of money to open a provisions store. Where will you find this money?"

"I have it, madam."

"You need more than what you have saved in the bank."

"I have more, madam."

"Sorry we're so late." Kiria strode into the office, followed by Laxmi. "There was an accident at the Chintamani lights."

Kiria picked up one of the six plastic lawn chairs that made up the bulk of the office seating arrangements. She placed it directly under the fan in the center of the room and sat down. Laxmi, knowing what was coming, greeted Santoshi and Mary Elizabeth and sat down at the far end of the window bench.

"It's almost lunchtime, so I'll get right to business," Kiria said. "I have learned that there is at least one hostel application missing. Does anyone know what happened to Nirmila's application?"

"Who is Nirmila?" Mary Elizabeth asked.

"One of the ragpickers who works the garbage pile outside Laxmi's house," Kiria replied. "She's a widow, three young girls, sleeps by the old engineers' building near Loco Works bridge. Did you see her application?"

Mary Elizabeth shook her head. "No. I saw many applications, but I would remember Loco Works. And there were no applications from ragpickers."

"Yes, there was this one," Kiria insisted. "Laxmi and I talked to Nirmila this morning."

Santoshi looked over at Laxmi, who translated Kiria's words into Tamil. Santoshi's face remained expressionless as she turned her gaze back toward Kiria.

"She told me," Kiria continued, "that someone in this office told her there were no more places available in the hostel. There are only four people in this office, and I'm one of them. So which one of you spoke to Nirmila?"

Kiria folded her arms across her chest and waited. Laxmi translated for Santoshi again.

After a few seconds Santoshi removed her glasses and said hesitantly, "I talk Nirmila, Kiria Madam."

Of the three women, Santoshi, whose own circumstances should have made her sympathetic to Nirmila's situation, would have been Kiria's last choice for the culprit. "Why, Santoshi?" she asked as gently as she could manage.

Santoshi looked down at the desk and remained silent. Mary Elizabeth watched as confidence drained out of Santoshi's posture. She understood why Santoshi had told Nirmila there was no place for her but knew Kiria would not.

Laxmi, sitting tensely on the edge of the bench, was the first to break the silence. "She did it for a good reason. Tell her, Santoshi. Tell her why you had to do it."

"You knew she did it?" Kiria swiveled in her chair to face Laxmi. "While you were translating? And you said nothing?"

Laxmi held her head high and looked Kiria firmly in the eyes. "Santoshi helped me when no one else would. I won't turn on her now. You are a smart woman, Kiria, but you don't understand."

"We should all be as fortunate in our friends as you are, Santoshi," Kiria said. "Okay, I don't understand. So one of you will have to explain it to me. Santoshi?"

"She sweeper, madam. She not . . ." Santoshi's English broke down. She turned to Laxmi and spoke rapidly in Tamil.

Laxmi translated for Kiria. "Santoshi is trying to explain that ragpickers don't know how to live . . . cleanly. The other women in the hostel are not going to accept Nirmila."

"Nirmila is not clean because she has no access to water," Kiria said. "Here she can bathe."

"It's more than just that. She doesn't know how to behave. Her life is different. She won't . . . fit in," Laxmi finished lamely.

"I don't understand this." Despite her best efforts, Kiria's anger came out clearly in her words. "This is a hostel, not a social club. She doesn't have to fit in. Nirmila is a widow with no family who does honest work. She is exactly the kind of woman we are trying to help." She turned to Mary Elizabeth. "What do you think?"

"I think you are right, but Santoshi is right too. The other residents won't accept a ragpicker family. Her children will be bullied. She will be shunned. Some women will refuse to live here."

Kiria pressed her fingertips to her temples. "All children are cruel. I'm sure Nirmila is accustomed to being shunned. And I certainly won't force anyone to live somewhere they don't want to. I'm sorry, but I just don't think those are good enough reasons.

And I don't believe that excluding Nirmila is for her benefit. She gets a room."

Laxmi translated for Santoshi, who stared at her employer in shock.

"But Kiria Madam!" Santoshi exclaimed. "She Untouchable!"

The Pollution of Purity

HAVE YOU HEARD THE ONE about the dyslexic agnostic who can't decide if there really is a Dog? That's me—spiritually dyslexic.

As a teenager I read the Bible from cover to cover and Christianity lost me about halfway through the atrocities of the Old Testament. God was just too petty, a lot like my mother actually. I did not give up easily, though, and at various points over the years I shopped for a religion but found the products on offer less than impressive:

- Islam—same Old Testament God; zero appeal for a woman
- Judaism—same Old Testament God; a country-club religion
- Buddhism—a shortcut to psychosis, especially Zen Buddhism; to this day I avoid thinking about the sound of one hand clapping

- Daoism—a celebration of chaos; not a good choice for a control freak
- Wicca—a DIY religion; if I have to perform my own miracles, what's to worship?

I gave up the search and decided that if a higher power exists, it doesn't want to be found. I could understand this. I'd stay under the radar too if I'd made such a mess.

Somehow during all this shopping, I missed the Hinduism aisle of the religious store, a strange oversight considering my five-year crush on George Harrison. I knew about reincarnation and how it supported the caste system, but Santoshi's bizarre behavior over the applications made me realize there was more to be learned. I hauled out my trusty laptop and went cruising on the Internet.

After two eye-watering days of slogging through a small percentage of the over three million hits on Google for Hinduism, I emerged terminally confused. Hinduism was a complex system of beliefs that would take years to get my head around. And frankly, even if I lived long enough, I had better things to do with my time.

But I learned enough to figure out that Santoshi's objection to Nirmila had something to do with the codes of purity and pollution, a vast body of behavioral restrictions based on caste. Traditionally, Hindus believed the way to be reincarnated higher up the caste ladder was to behave purely in this life and avoid pollution. Untouchables, or Dalits, as they prefer to be called, were thought to be born polluted, and because pollution was seen as contagious, touching a Dalit, or even touching something that had been touched by a Dalit, would transfer pollution to a higher-caste person, hence the name Untouchables.

In this light, I could understand why Santoshi wanted to

avoid living with Untouchables. Although modern, forward-thinking Hindus no longer believe that pollution is transferable, Santoshi came from a village and had no formal education. All the articles I read about the caste system indicated that the uneducated and rural communities were the last strongholds of traditional values, and I knew Santoshi was a very religious person; the only time she ever spent money voluntarily was when she bought a blessing.

What I couldn't understand was why this would make a difference to her now, after living all those years in the shelters. In India, there is an almost universal belief that lighter skin equals higher caste. In practice, however, there is no way to tell a person's caste by skin color. For all Santoshi knew, she had been eating and sleeping with Untouchables for most of her life.

For the two days of my research, Santoshi and I kept up a pretense of normality. She cleaned and cooked and shopped as usual. In the evenings we continued our language classes. On the third day, we sat on the terrace in the evening and had our talk. It took all the patience I possessed to get through her long and frequently incoherent methods of storytelling. In the end, her actions boiled down to a fascinating blend of common sense and optimism.

For the inmates, life in the shelters was the last stop before the ultimate horror of pavement dwelling. Eviction from a home was the most dreaded punishment imaginable. The women did everything they could to minimize friction among themselves. Behavior was circumspect. Tasks and chores somehow devolved to those most suitable in the context of the women currently in residence, and "sweepers" (another name for Untouchables) were even appreciated, since one of their traditional roles was latrine duty, a chore that would pollute a higher-caste woman even more than touching an Untouchable.

It didn't always work; some women were too angry or too

crazy to play nice. Santoshi was well aware she'd acquired some pollution during her time in the shelters. Being a pragmatic and logical woman, she reasoned that if she lived as purely as possible for the rest of her life, she had many years left to stockpile enough purity to balance out the pollution she'd accumulated to date, which would improve her chances of promotion to a higher caste in her next reincarnation, or at least mitigate the possibility of demotion to a lower one.

Now I admired Santoshi as much as I had ever admired anyone in my life. She was hardworking and honest and a survivor. I had worked for months to create a place where she could live. In the process I'd lost a significant percentage of both my body weight and my personal savings. I really, really wanted to tell Santoshi that it was okay, we would tear up the applications she'd hidden, Nirmila was out.

But although I'd come to India primarily to improve Santoshi's life, I had to draw the line somewhere. Stomping on destitute women to make Santoshi feel better was beyond me. In the end, I made the only decision I could live with.

Santoshi's face crumpled when I told her. I couldn't bear to see her cry, and I was furious with myself for barging into a culture I didn't understand, and forcing my standards on someone who didn't want them. I left the terrace and went to bed.

The next morning I found the missing applications by my laptop. Santoshi was gone.

The Lonely Lentil

SANTOSHI HAD NO IDEA WHERE she was going. She knew only that she had to get away from Kiria Madam's anger and her own intense disappointment with herself. She should never have believed there was a place to live decently in this city. She should never have dreamed of a provisions store. How could she have been so stupid?

She walked through the night, passing people sleeping in doorways, avoiding the dog packs that trotted through the quiet streets. When the first birds began to call just before dawn, she found herself standing on Loco Works bridge and realized she had walked in a huge circle. She was very tired. Crossing the bridge, she dropped her bundle and sat down against the wall surrounding an old railway building. She was almost asleep when she heard movements to her right. She turned to see that she was sitting at the edge of a small community of pavement dwellers.

A woman crawled out from under the nearest ragged tarpaulin hanging on the wall. Santoshi recognized Nirmila, the ragpicker. What was it Banu at the home had said? The gods laugh at our sufferings? Surely they were laughing now, watching Santoshi sitting here beside the woman she had tried so hard to avoid.

Nirmila pulled a small pile of sticks from inside her shelter and lit the morning fire. She scooped the last of the water from a jar into a battered pan, added a handful of grain from a rusted tin and set it over the fire for the morning meal. A girl crawled out of the lean-to, clutching a baby. Nirmila sat down by the fire, opened her sari blouse and held the baby's head to her breast, wincing as the little mouth began to suck. The girl picked up a stick and bent over the fire to stir the thin gruel. A younger girl crawled out of the lean-to and squatted down to rest her head sleepily against her mother's arm.

A wave of loneliness and envy washed over Santoshi as she watched the destitute little family begin its day.

Nirmila heard a small gasping sound. She looked up from her baby's face and saw a woman sitting against the wall a short distance away. Under the light of a nearby streetlamp, the woman's face, with its huge dark eye sockets and sunken cheeks, looked like a skull. She seemed to be staring at the pot on the fire.

"Are you hungry, Auntie?" Nirmila asked. "Would you like some gruel?"

Santoshi snatched up her bundle and fled into the darkness. She ran until the pain in her side became unbearable, then collapsed onto the side of the road. She had run to an empty place. There were no people here. The first light of dawn showed her only the shell of a building and a strangle of bushes and grass stretching back from the road. She knew this place. She had a jar buried by the foundations of the building.

Santoshi walked to where her jar was buried and sat down with her back against the cool stones of a partially collapsed wall while she thought of what to do next. She could not get a job without references. Mary Elizabeth had told her there were no places available in the shelters, and she knew in her heart that she would be very unhappy returning to such a small life. Although she was no longer afraid of living on the streets, she did not want such an uncertain and dirty life.

What she wanted was a provisions store. But only Kiria Madam would be willing to rent space to a woman who had no man to give her status. Santoshi pried up the rock she'd buried her jar beneath, and thought about how she'd wasted all those years of working and saving money that could not buy her dreams. Money only bought the dreams of men. If her father had had so much money, he would have paid for her to attend the village school. She would never have been sent away with that man who said he was taking her to a government school.

She began digging up her jar. As she scooped up the damp earth, she tried to make a plan for starting a new life. In Chennai, she felt like a lentil in a bean pot. She did not belong in this huge city, where there were no rules and no boundaries. Perhaps it would be better to go to a smaller place, where people were decent and it cost less to live. Perhaps a village like the one she was born in. Or . . . Santoshi stopped digging and sat back on her heels.

Why not the village she was born in? She had a nice sari and some money to take home. If she lied, no one in the village would ever know she had been a slave. Santoshi knew that her father had been tricked by the man who said he was taking her to a government school, but she also knew that many of the other children she had lived with as a beggar had been sold by families too poor to feed all their children. Her father had been poor and village gossip was harsh. She would need a good lie and one that explained why she had not come home sooner.

Because she could read and do arithmetic, everyone would believe she had gone to school. But her only skills were cooking and cleaning and marketing. A housekeeper, then, for an old couple, like Venu and Geeta, who no longer needed to employ help because their son had recently married. Santoshi added details to her lie as she finished digging.

She thought about retrieving her other jars but realized, as she pulled this jar out of the ground and remembered how much money was in it, that no one would believe her story if she came home with too much money. Better to leave her other jars where they were for now. As for her suitcase? The bankbook was of no use to her unless she asked Priya or Mary Elizabeth to go to the bank. And Kiria Madam was rich and seemed too honest to steal. In a few weeks, perhaps Kiria Madam would be less angry. Santoshi would write to ask for her suitcase then.

She stood up, tucked the jar into her bundle and dusted off her hands. It was time to go home.

Bad News

RAJ STOOD IN THE DOORWAY of the hostel office and watched Mary Elizabeth working at her desk. Today her skin glowed in the light reflected by her bright yellow sari. A rope of jasmine tumbled from the heavy knot of hair at the back of her head, cascading over her shoulder and stopping just short of the swell of her left breast. Its perfume filled the office.

"Good morning, my love." Taking advantage of a few minutes alone, Raj crossed the office to stand behind Mary Elizabeth and placed his hand lightly on her left shoulder. Jasmine traced a cool trail across his wrist as she tipped her head to rest it momentarily against his arm.

"Go sit across the desk," she ordered as she lifted her head. "Kiria will be here any minute."

"She knows about us," Raj replied, but he obeyed, walking around the desk to sit across from her. "And she sees no harm in two people being in love."

"Of course she does not. Her culture is different. Here it is not right for us to be seen touching like this. It is not right for us to be in love."

"I wish it were." Raj frowned down at his knees. At first their romance had been amusing, a small flirtation once a week in a coffee shop. But over the months of working together almost daily, it had become something much stronger. More and more he found himself thinking about her dark, warm eyes, the sweet curve of her sari over her waist, the line of her neck as she bent her head. She had become like a drug and the days he did not see her were long and empty. He had no reason to be here today; he just wanted to see her. He sighed and looked up to find her watching him with sad eyes.

"I wish it too. But it is not," she said.

"Must we always do what's right?"

Mary Elizabeth frowned. "What do you mean?"

Raj took a deep breath and hesitantly broached a topic he'd been thinking about for some time. "What if I bought a place?"

"A place." Mary Elizabeth's voice dropped flatly.

"For us. A place close to my office where we could be alone."

"Alone to what?" There was no mistaking the anger in her voice now. "Alone to what, Raj?"

For all the time he had known her, Mary Elizabeth had been gentle and submissive. Raj had never met the woman he was looking at now, her eyes narrowed, her lips hard, her hand knotted into a fist on the desk. He found her anger strangely erotic.

"We are no longer young, my love. We should not waste the time we have."

"Is this why you gave money for my father's medicine? Did you think I was for sale? Did you think you bought a whore?"

"No!"

"Because I will pay you back. Every penny."

"No! That's not why I helped you. I would never . . ."

"I have been a fool. I thought you loved me." Mary Elizabeth's shoulders dropped. She lowered her face into her hands. "I am shamed."

Raj leaned back in his chair, uncertain of how to repair the damage his suggestion had done. He should have known better. He did know better. He stared at the top of Mary Elizabeth's head, wishing he could erase all that had just passed between them.

"Mary Elizabeth? Are you okay?" Kiria's voice from the doorway startled them both.

"I am fine, Kiria. I have just had bad news." Mary Elizabeth raised her head and looked at her friend. "What happened to you?"

Kiria's eyes were puffy and red in her drawn face. Her sari was poorly wrapped, the hem uneven and the pallu pulled untidily across her waist. She came into the office and sat down heavily in the chair beside Raj. "I'm fine, but I'm afraid I have more bad news. Santoshi has run away. Hello, Raj."

Raj embraced the distraction with relief. "Why did she run away?"

"Because I told her she was wrong to hide the Schedule Caste applications," Kiria told him, using the modern term for Untouchables. "This morning I found them on the table, and she was gone."

"Did she take her things?" Mary Elizabeth asked.

"Her clothes, yes. But her suitcase is still in her room. So is all her money. And her bankbook." Kiria looked hopefully over at Mary Elizabeth. "I thought she might come to you."

Mary Elizabeth shook her head. "She has not come here."

"Where else could she go?" Kiria's voice trembled with worry. "She has no money. Does she have any friends?"

"Perhaps in the shelter," Mary Elizabeth answered.

"I will drive you there," Raj offered.

"No."

Mary Elizabeth's harsh tone startled Kiria. "I'm sorry. You said you had bad news too. What happened?"

"It is not important." Mary Elizabeth rose from her chair and picked up her bag from under the desk. "I'm sorry, Raj. You will have to leave. Kiria and I must go to look for Santoshi."

Homeward Bound

SANTOSHI SAT ON A BENCH outside the Madurai bus terminal, her hands folded neatly together in her lap. Tied up in the old green sari, her possessions rested in a bundle at her feet. In three hours she would be boarding the bus that passed her father's village. She leaned back against the wall of the terminal and let the sun warm her face while she waited.

She had spent one-fourth of her life in this bus terminal. It had changed almost beyond recognition in the past fifteen years. The carts of the snack vendors had been replaced with stalls. There were more buses coming in and out, more passengers milling about in the huge, dim hall. She could remember names and faces and events from the old time, but she could not remember how she had felt then, or what she had thought about. Too much had changed, both here and in herself. Now her memories were like a story about someone else. She felt no connection to the child who had begged for Rahul all those years ago.

What had happened to Rahul? Was he still bringing children

to the terminal every morning and taking them back to the slum room at night? There were no children begging here this morning. Perhaps Rahul had died, or found some other livelihood, one more profitable than the few hundred rupees collected by a handful of child beggars.

A black van pulled up to the curb in front of her. A handsome young man, dressed in blue jeans, a black T-shirt and strange pointed boots got out and walked to the rear of the van. Santoshi knew she had seen him before. He was too young for her to have seen him when she was a child here, so she must have seen him in Chennai. It came to her suddenly: He looked like that movie star, the one whose face filled the billboards advertising Hindi movies.

The young man opened the back doors of the van. Six children in dirty clothes climbed slowly out onto the road, blinking in the sunlight. Without saying a word, the man shut the door, walked back to the front of the van, sat down in the driver's seat and drove off.

Santoshi leaned forward and studied the children with interest. They stood together for a few minutes while the tallest boy spoke. She thought the youngest might be about six, an awkward girl with long matted curls. The oldest was definitely the pretty, pale-skinned girl whose thin chest, under her T-shirt, showed the first swelling of womanhood, making her about twelve. The tall boy stopped talking and the children moved away in different directions.

One of the children, a boy with a clubfoot, limped past Santoshi and entered the terminal. She picked up her bundle and followed him. He stood just inside the entrance for a few minutes, carefully studying the travelers, then went over to where two white people, a man and a woman, were standing beside two large backpacks, studying a book.

Good choice, Santoshi thought.

The boy hunched his shoulders, tipped back his head and held out his cupped hand. The woman's face showed pity and concern when she saw him. Reaching into his pocket, the man pulled out a handful of coins and dropped them into the boy's hand. The boy folded his hands together over the coins and bowed before limping off toward his next target.

Santoshi watched the beggar boy working the crowd inside the terminal. He did well for his age, which could not have been more than eight years. Certainly the clubfoot helped, but he had a good eye for potential targets, and wasted little time when he picked a bad one. The terminal was not very crowded today. She estimated he would make no more than three hundred rupees by the end of the morning.

Watching the boy made Santoshi feel vaguely sad. She went back outside to discover her seat on the bench had been taken by a large man in a plaid shirt, so she walked a few feet farther and sat down on the pavement with her back to the wall. When the bus pulled up, she climbed on board with a sense of relief to be escaping once again from the Madurai bus terminal.

The bus rumbled along uneven roads, bouncing Santoshi up and down on the hard wooden bench. She had been lucky to get a seat by the window. On either side of the road, endless rice paddies stretched into the distance. Small clumps of coconut palms and banana trees broke up the flat fields. At this time of year, the paddies were mostly dull and brown, but in a few that were fed by underground wells, women with bent backs and their saris hiked up above their knees waded through standing water, planting rice seedlings.

Santoshi felt she was traveling backward through time. She could remember her mother and the other women of the village working like this. She found she could not remember her mother's face. She closed her eyes and searched for some memory of her family, but nothing came. Only the front step of the hut where she had played with her sisters was clear in her mind now. No matter. Soon she would see her parents and her sisters. Soon she would have a family again.

Six hours later, Santoshi stood beneath the fierce scowl of the statue that guarded her village from evil spirits. Now that she saw it, this weathered guardian was familiar. But nothing else was the same. The village had grown. Real houses made of concrete and painted in pastel colors lined paved streets where once she had run along muddy dikes between the fields. There were shops and a market. Confused by the new landmarks, she had no idea where her father's hut stood.

An old man pulling two goats on rope tethers passed by.

"Uncle," Santoshi called out, "do you know where the house of Padhu the basket maker is?"

The old man looked surprised. "Padhu the basket maker? That was a long time ago."

"Does he not live here now?"

"Oh, he lives here." The old man raised a withered arm and pointed back along the way he had come. "His hut is where it always was. In the old part of the village. Go to the center of town. There is a tea shop and a bangle shop and a paper shop. Turn right at the paper shop. Go to the end of that street. Padhu's house is there."

Following the old man's instructions, Santoshi found her father's hut. The weaving of the palm-leaf walls was uneven and the roof sagged, but the stone step was the same. She put down her bundle by the door and called into the darkness of the hut.

"Hello? Father? Mother? It is Santoshi. I have come home."

Gumshoe

❁ ❁ ❁ ❁ ❁

KIRIA SAT ON THE CHAIR offered by the young policeman and tidied the folds of her sari around her knees. She had been at the police station for over five hours now, trying to file a missing-persons complaint. She fought to hide her frustration. Across the desk, Detective Krishnamoorthy smoothed his mustache down over his lip and studied the folder in front of him. He had agreed to talk with Mrs. Langdon primarily because she was white and had impressed him with her perseverance. Now that he'd reviewed her complaint, he could see nothing that would benefit either of them in it.

"Mrs. Langdon," he began.

"Yes."

"You are reporting that your maid is missing?"

"Yes. She left five days ago."

"And she took her clothes and personal possessions?"

"Everything except her money."

"Mrs. Langdon, have you any reason to believe she left against her will?"

"No. I'm pretty sure she wanted to leave."

"Then why are you here?"

"Because I know Santoshi. She was obsessed with money. She would never leave it behind. I found her bankbook and all of her wages in her room. If someone abducted Santoshi, why would they take her clothes and not take nine thousand rupees in cash? She left her money because she was afraid she would lose it and she knew it would be safe with me. So who is she afraid of? And what is she living on?"

"Perhaps she withdrew money from the bank?"

"No. I checked. They wouldn't tell me the balance, but they did say there had never been a withdrawal from the account."

"Perhaps she has other funds?"

"When I hired her, she was living in a government shelter. She is very poor. I'm sure she has no other money."

Detective Krishnamoorthy studied the report on his desk. He placed his finger halfway down the page and asked, "Have you checked at her previous address?"

"Yes. The warden told me she has not seen Santoshi since she came to work for me."

"Could she be lying?"

"I doubt it. I offered a big reward for information. She's not the kind of woman to pass up money."

Detective Krishnamoorthy closed the folder and pressed his fingers together over his small paunch. "Mrs. Langdon, there has been no crime. A servant has terminated her employment. I agree that leaving behind her wages and bankbook is strange. But I must point out that if I thought there was foul play, you would be my primary suspect."

"Me!"

"Who else has benefited from your maid's disappearance?"

"That's what I'm asking you to find out. Look, if I'd done

anything to Santoshi, do you really think I'd be trying so hard to report her disappearance? Why would I come here at all?"

"To look innocent."

Kiria lost patience. "Detective, if it will get you to look for Santoshi, then I'd be delighted for you to charge me with something!" She rubbed her temples and continued in a lower tone. "I'm sorry. I've been here a long time. Is there anything the police can do?"

Krishnamoorthy hated to close a door, but there was just nothing to work with here. If the old woman had done something to her maid, he needed more than a missing-persons report filed by the perpetrator to justify using police resources. If the maid really had just walked out, on her own or more likely with her boyfriend, that was her right. "Mrs. Langdon, Chennai is a very large city with a high crime rate. Our resources are limited. Unless you have some evidence of a crime, I cannot take an officer from some other task for a missing maid. She will come back for her money."

Kiria heard the finality in his voice and gave up. She rose, picked up the tote bag containing the information she had hoped to give the police and held out her hand. "Thank you, Detective," she said as they shook hands. "I'll just have to hope for the best."

Krishnamoorthy rose and followed her to the door of his office. "Do not hope too much," he said softly after the door closed behind her.

Out on the street Kiria checked her watch and decided to go shopping for a microwave oven. The gas ring had not been lit since Santoshi's disappearance. She flagged down a passing auto and negotiated a price to the Rathna store in Purasavakkam. Halfway through the trip she leaned forward and told the driver to stop. He protested. They had not negotiated waiting time. She held out the full fare. He pulled over.

Kiria walked back along the auto's route and stopped in front of a short row of box stores. She looked up at a bold-lettered sign hanging from a second-story railing.

P. RAMASWAMY
PVT INVESTIGATIONS
ENGLISH SPOKEN

Lifting the front of her sari slightly, she climbed the outside stairs, walked along the narrow balcony to the door directly behind the sign and knocked sharply.

RAMASWAMY CHOSE private investigation as his life's work due to an excess of Dashiell Hammett novels read as a teenager. If his father had not died and left him the little plaza that housed his office, he would eventually have outgrown his youthful enthusiasm for American crime fiction. The income from the rents on the plaza, more than enough to support his mother, allowed him the luxury of following his dream, so Ramaswamy became a private detective. After two years and a total of six very dull cases, he was starting to wonder if Chennai had anything to offer a man of his talents.

Recently, his mother had begun introducing him to a number of nice girls. He had no interest in any of them. Nice, homely girls made little impression on a man whose sexual fantasies were filled with tall, cool blondes. He was in the middle of a particularly steamy one involving a Hollywood starlet and a bucket of ice cubes when the knock came on his office door.

Ramaswamy quickly zipped up his fly and went to unlock the door. He opened it to an older white woman wearing an elegantly wrapped silver gray sari and carrying a large tote bag. She stepped past him into the office and looked around.

"Where is the investigator?" she asked.

"I am the investigator," he replied. "Please have a seat. How can I help you?"

Kiria studied the bespectacled young man as he walked around the desk and sat behind it. This was probably a waste of time, but she had nothing better to do. She sat down in front of the desk, where a disintegrating copy of *The Maltese Falcon* lay open facedown. On a hunch, she decided to play up to the novel.

"You can help me, Mr. Ramaswamy, by finding my housekeeper." Kiria clipped her words with precision.

"You've lost your maid?"

"No, I have lost one of these." She opened her purse and extracted a pen drive, which she placed on the desk beside the novel. "This one is blank. You can keep it for identification purposes. The one I am missing has the same logo on the side. It contains information that could be worth up to a billion dollars."

His body tensed slightly. Extortion? "Well, perhaps I can help you, Mrs. . . . ?"

"Langdon. Kiria Langdon."

"What kind of information are we talking about, Mrs. Langdon?"

"If I told you that, it would be worthless. My concern is that no one learns what is on the device."

"Well then, what can you tell me about the circumstances of the theft?" Ramaswamy opened a desk drawer and pulled out a yellowing notepad that hadn't seen daylight in almost a year and a well-chewed pencil.

Kiria proceeded to give an entirely accurate account of Santoshi's disappearance, finishing up with the theory that the housekeeper had accidentally taken the pen drive. "She is barely literate, certainly not computer literate. She cannot possibly use the information herself, or know anyone who could. I doubt she would even be able to understand why it is so valuable."

"Have you taken this to the police?"

"Yes. However"—Kiria lowered her voice and leaned forward slightly—"I'm sure you can appreciate that I could not afford to be entirely honest with the police about the nature of my true concern. I felt it prudent not to mention it at all. I reported Santoshi as a missing person."

"The police are indeed very inquisitive." He was burning with curiosity himself. "What can you tell me about your housekeeper, Mrs. Langdon?"

"A great deal, actually." Kiria reached into the tote bag and pulled out a thick manila folder. "I contacted her former caseworker. This is her complete history since she came to Chennai. I've added some notes of my own, concerning her daily routine while she worked for me. Which you will see, when you review them, gave no indication at all of duplicity. I find it impossible to believe she would do this intentionally."

Ramaswamy looked at the business card stapled to the front of the folder. His client was not a tall blonde, but she was the CEO of a company. He opened the folder and studied the two photos lying on top of the written pages. One showed his client and a short, painfully thin woman standing together against the background of a blooming bougainvillea tree. The other was a blowup of the smaller woman's face. He flipped through the pages. Physical description, list of known contacts, then what appeared to be several years' worth of a social services file.

"Who put this together?" he asked.

"I did."

"You should have been a detective, Mrs. Langdon."

"Perhaps when I retire. Will you take the case?"

"I'm sure the police have told you that Chennai is a big city and India is a big country. If your housekeeper has disappeared into the slums or left the city, there is little chance of finding her."

"So the case is too difficult?" Kiria reached across the desk to retrieve the folder.

"No! I mean yes!" Ramaswamy put his hand on the folder. "Yes, the case is difficult. I cannot guarantee total satisfaction. But I can make inquiries."

"And your fee?"

He did a quick upward revision to his fee schedule. "A thousand rupees a day plus expenses."

Kiria opened her purse, pulled out her wallet and extracted ten thousand rupees. "This will get you started." She handed over the money. "I expect daily reports, Mr. Ramaswamy, and receipts for all expenses. My number is in the file. Call me if you have questions."

Ramaswamy ushered his client to the door, then returned to his desk. He swiveled the chair to face his office computer and typed his client's name into Google. Ten minutes later, all thoughts of starlets had been replaced with thoughts of industrial espionage.

Kiria made it halfway down the stairs before starting to giggle.

Almost Family

THEO HELD THE HEAVY BRASS and glass door open for a woman with a baby stroller before passing through himself to join Rik at the top of the courthouse steps.

"Go ahead, say it." Rik slipped his sunglasses off the front of his sweater and put them on.

Theo said nothing as he reached into his suit pocket for his own sunglasses.

"Okay. I'll say it. You told me so."

Theo grinned. " 'It is our opinion,' " he quoted in the social worker's high, nasal tones, " 'that Mr. Lachapelle's domestic skills are more than adequate to cope with two young children.' " He returned to his own voice and slid his sunglasses over his eyes. "I'll bet it was the ears."

Rik quoted back, " 'Mr. Megler's even temper and calm demeanor indicate that he will be a stable and supportive influence for the family.' " He laughed. "Which basically translates to you tone down the flake. I can't believe we're almost there. We should celebrate."

"We're not there yet. But we're close. I'm hungry. Want to get a sandwich and eat in the park?"

"Sure. How about trying the new deli in the mall?"

They walked along together, elbows close, strides matched. The day was bright and warm. Office workers, out to catch the noontime sun, crowded the streets. Just inside the entrance to the mall, Rik pulled Theo to a stop in front of a toy store and pointed at the elaborately constructed LEGO display that filled the window.

"We should get those. I loved them when I was a kid. Look at the dinosaur. Mine never came out that good. Mom says she's still finding them under the furniture. Did you have them?"

When there was no reply, Rik turned to find he was standing alone in front of the toy store. "Theo?" He scanned the mall and spotted his husband, in front of an electronics store, staring at a huge flat-panel television. He walked over. "We can't afford this kind of stuff anymore, hon. Kids are expensive."

Theo registered Rik's presence, but didn't hear the words. "My God, she's lost weight. Is she sick?"

"Is who sick?"

Theo gestured toward the woman speaking on the screen. "Kiria."

"That's her? She didn't look like that before?"

"No. She was bigger."

There was no sound, but Kiria's crisp hand movements and intense expression indicated she felt passionate about her topic. She was made-up for the cameras and the heavy fringe of mascar-aed lashes gave her light gray eyes an almost mystical appeal. Rik found it hard to pull his gaze away from them to study her face.

"She looks a bit tired," Rik said, "but she seems energetic enough. She didn't say anything about being sick in her last e-mail. Maybe this is an old interview."

"She didn't look this old. I think she's sick."

Rik thought back to the six months he'd spent volunteering at a hospital in Ecuador after graduating from college. "There's a million diseases and parasites in the tropics. I guess she could be sick."

They stood together in front of the screen, shoulders almost touching, and watched until the program ended and the credits began to roll. Theo was quiet as they bought their lunch and walked to the park. Rik suppressed his own urge to talk and waited. They'd been on the Kiria roller coaster long enough for Rik to know that Theo needed time to process any new thing about her. When they came to their favorite bench, across from a flower bed now brilliant with daffodils, they sat down to eat. Rik was halfway through his bagel and lox before Theo unwrapped his own sandwich.

Theo took a bite of pastrami on rye and tilted his head toward his husband. "Do you think she would tell me if she was sick?"

"Why wouldn't she? She's told you about the hostel, and her maid and her landlord and everything else." Rik reached out to wipe a smear of mustard from the corner of Theo's mouth.

"Yes, but that's not about her. It's about what's around her. I'm doing the same thing. I only tell her surface stuff. It's like we're reading about each other between the lines."

"You're both being careful. You don't know where this is going."

"What if she dies before I find out?"

"You don't seriously think she's dying? I know as much as you do from her e-mails, but I'm sure she wouldn't hide something that big."

Theo smiled. "I'm supposed to be the stable and supportive influence here." He took another bite of his sandwich and chewed slowly before continuing. "I guess I don't really think that. But when I saw her on TV, I thought, what if she dies and I never get to know her? I mean, she'll never be my mom, but I want to know her better."

"I like her now. I'm going to see if I can find a repeat of that interview on CNN when we get home." Rik pushed the last piece of bagel into his mouth and felt around in the take-out bag for napkins. "Maybe you should think about speeding up the process. We've always wanted to see India. If everything works out with the adoption, it's going to be camping and Disneyland for the next few years."

"You mean go see her now?"

"Why not? The inoculations we got for Thailand last year are still good. Hold still." Rik wiped more mustard from Theo's chin with a napkin. "This is really good practice."

Mourning Sickness

KIRIA WOKE JUST BEFORE DAWN. The air conditioner and fans were silent. Her sweat-soaked nightdress clung to her body. Another power outage, she realized, and a long one, judging by the stifling air in her bedroom. She reached out and groped around the surface of the nightstand for the flashlight. By its feeble light, she stripped off her soggy dress and walked to the bathroom. Five full buckets of water were lined up beside the wall tap, a trick she had learned the hard way, as more frequent power outages prevented the pump from filling the roof tank. She scooped water out of one of the buckets and poured it over her head and body. Not bothering to dry herself, she pulled on a fresh nightdress and went to the kitchen.

The new electric kettle mocked her from the cement work top. She thought about trying to light the gas ring to make coffee, but discarded the idea and poured herself a glass of water. The first birdcalls started up from the branches of the bougainvillea, strange jungle shrieks and whoops that still startled her after all these months. There was no point in sitting around inside; at least outside there might be a breeze. She went back into the bedroom, wrapped on a sari by touch and left the apartment to find an auto to take her to the hostel.

Kiria arrived at work just as Nirmila pushed her cart out of the hostel gate.

Nirmila stopped and pressed her palms together in front of her chest and gave Kiria the traditional Tamil greeting. *"Vanakam."*

"Vanakam," Kiria replied, mirroring the gesture. "Good hunting today." She stood in the gateway and watched the rag-picker shuffle away along the street.

Because she ate well at the hostel, Nirmila's body was filling out, but she still pushed her cart slowly, conserving energy for the long day ahead. Kiria was amazed by the stamina of the woman, especially now when the temperature was climbing into the low hundreds by early afternoon.

Before entering the office, she stood looking over her little empire. She'd done it. It was real. Like all start-ups, it was limping badly. Almost half the available space remained unoccupied and applications were coming in slowly. But construction on the box stores was almost complete. A tea stall and a tailor were waiting to move in and more would come. Soon, even half full, the hostel would be standing on its own.

She wanted to feel proud of this achievement, but without Santoshi the hostel was a failure as far as Kiria was concerned. What made it worse was that Santoshi's fears had been groundless. Nirmila had moved in first, taking a room in the north wing. Gowrie and her daughter came next, taking a room in the south wing. Between these extremes the construction workers, basket sellers, maids and shopgirls had sorted themselves into a stratified society, north to south. Santoshi would have found her place here.

For the thousandth time Kiria wondered where Santoshi

was, or even if she was still alive. Maybe it was time to stop holding her room, but she could do nothing so final. Not yet.

Mary Elizabeth was already seated at her end of the desk when Kiria walked into the office. "Good morning. I didn't expect you to work this week. How are you doing?"

Mary Elizabeth looked up from the folder she'd been studying. "Good morning. I am fine. I am sad, but working helps me. Thank you for coming to the funeral."

"You're welcome. Did your cousin call?"

Mary Elizabeth's long mouth turned down in a rare expression of distaste. "He says I must come to live with him. He says he will sell my father's house. It is his to sell. But I do not want to live with his family. They are not like me."

Kiria had met Mary Elizabeth's cousin. He'd seemed perfectly normal, perhaps a bit pompous and, judging by the way he'd left Mary Elizabeth to cope with her father's last illness unaided, certainly selfish. Still, unless she was willing to live alone, Mary Elizabeth had no other choice. Kiria said the only thing she could think of to lighten her friend's mood. "Then you'll have to come and visit me very often."

She put her laptop bag down in Laxmi's chair, walked around the desk to her own chair and opened the expenses folder. It was the last day of the month. She could finally sort through the bills and work out the damage to her savings account.

"In the West, do women live alone?" Mary Elizabeth asked casually.

"Many of us, yes."

"And in the West, do many people not get married?"

Kiria misunderstood the question. "Some. It's not so important now that living together is accepted."

Mary Elizabeth thought about this. "I think your way may be better," she said, and turned her attention back to the folder.

Three hours later Kiria found herself staring out the office window at four young women doing laundry in the courtyard fountain. The rhythmic slapping of the clothes against the stone rim of the fountain mingled with the girls' chattering and laughter. It's like jazz, Kiria thought. She mopped her face with the pallu end of her cream and black sari and forced herself to focus on the bills again.

"This can't be right!" she exclaimed, holding up the electricity bill. "I thought we handled the squatters."

The previous month a group of pavement dwellers had attached canvas lean-tos against the outside back wall and spliced into the hostel's power lines. The electricity bill soared until Kiria hired an electrician to find the problem and cut it off. The squatters moved on the next day.

Across the desk from Kiria, Laxmi stopped frowning at the laptop screen and held out her hand for the electricity bill. Although she had begun her career in jeans, lately Laxmi had returned to wearing saris. Today she wore pink and green cotton, wrapped loosely because of the heat. "Let me see." She studied the bill for a moment. "We did. How can this be so high?"

"It is the fans," Mary Elizabeth said without looking up from the school enrollment form she was filling in for Nirmila's oldest daughter. "Everyone is sleeping with the fans on now. They are running all night and all day."

Laxmi made a face. "I should have anticipated that." She turned back to the laptop and began correcting the financial-projection spreadsheet she was working on. "This would be a lot easier if everyone would pay rent."

"How much this month?" Kiria asked.

"Almost three thousand rupees," Laxmi said.

"That's almost half the tenants!" Kiria was shocked.

"I did tell you," Mary Elizabeth said.

Laxmi tried to look on the bright side. "Some of them may still pay."

"This isn't a shelter." Kiria's pale eyes were hard. "If they don't pay, we're going to start evictions. Give me a list of the defaulters, Laxmi."

"How are you feeling?" Mary Elizabeth asked Laxmi to break the mood. Laxmi had arrived at work that morning gray-faced and dizzy. She'd insisted that she was fine; it was just the heat and traffic fumes from the auto ride in to work.

"Better," Laxmi replied.

Kiria looked down at her swollen hands. "Don't ask me how I'm feeling. I think I'm going to work from home this afternoon." She began gathering up the bills spread out in front of her. "Maybe we all should. This place is like an oven, even with the fans."

"Stay for lunch." Mary Elizabeth looked over at her friend in concern. Since Santoshi's departure, Kiria had not been eating properly. Her skin hung loosely on her arms, and the flesh beneath her jaw sagged. Mary Elizabeth had suspected a parasite, but a checkup at the Apollo Hospital turned up nothing. "You must try to eat something," she urged her friend.

Kiria looked at her watch. "Okay, call the canteen. I guess I can hold out for that long. Just rice and sambar for me. Unless Cook made beans today. She makes good beans."

Mary Elizabeth called the canteen. "They have beans," she said as she hung up. "It is coming now."

The cook's assistant delivered lunch a few minutes later. Mary Elizabeth and Kiria lifted the lids from their metal plates, but Laxmi just looked at hers.

"You're not hungry either?" Kiria asked her.

Laxmi suddenly bent over beside the desk and vomited.

"Laxmi, are you ill?" Mary Elizabeth rose and moved swiftly around the desk to support Laxmi's head.

"It's the food," Laxmi whispered, and vomited again.

Kiria picked up the plates from the desk, and took them back to the canteen. She returned to the office, and waited with Mary Elizabeth until Laxmi finally stopped retching and sat up in her chair. The smell of vomit filled the room.

"Let's get you outside." Picking up her water bottle, Kiria led the way out of the office. The three women sat on the bench beneath the Flame of the Forest tree. Kiria handed the water bottle to Laxmi.

"Is it food poisoning?" Kiria asked, memories of her own intestinal difficulties triggered by the smell in the office.

Laxmi shook her head.

"Are you pregnant?" Mary Elizabeth asked, fanning Laxmi with a manila folder.

Laxmi nodded, and managed a small smile. "But please don't tell my family," she begged Kiria.

"Of course not," Kiria assured her. "But why don't you want them to know? They'll be delighted."

"I will tell them. But not yet. They'll make me stop working. I'm enjoying this. I don't want to go back to staying in the house."

"How long before you're showing?" Kiria asked.

Laxmi rested her hand on her stomach. "Maybe two more months."

"Well, we'll work it out when the time comes. But it's just maternity leave, you know. You'll be back at work soon after the baby is born. Meanwhile, maybe we should work more from my apartment, where there's air-conditioning."

Laxmi's face brightened. "This job has maternity leave?"

"Only if you hire an assistant," Kiria replied. "Otherwise I expect you to deliver the baby here."

A Mother's Love

❁ ❁ ❁ ❁ ❁

"MA! MA! WANT PLAY TOYS."

Gowrie smiled down into the pleading face of her daughter. "Stay with me, Meeta. Play with me."

"No. Toys. Want play toys." Meeta rejected her mother's suggestion with the callous disregard of a two-year-old.

Six days a week, Gowrie left Meeta at New Beginnings Day Care and went to work. She did not want to take her daughter to day care on this, her only free day. On the other hand, the bright toys and companionship of children seemed to be bringing Meeta out of the uncharacteristic timidity that had followed her father's death. Looking down into the pleading face so like her late husband's, Gowrie could not find the heart to deny her daughter.

"Okay. But first you must put on clothes. What do you want to wear?"

"Pink," Meeta replied without hesitation.

Five minutes later Meeta, wearing a pink blouse and skirt covered in sequined daisies, pulled her mother out of their room on the ground floor of the New Beginnings Hostel and across the compound to the day care building. Unlike most of the children who came to day care, Meeta knew all about toys. She knew the blocks and the sorter and the stacker. She knew the dolls and balls. Until a few months ago she'd had toys of her own. Dropping her mother's hand as they entered the building, Meeta ran over to her current favorite, the trampoline. She flung herself onto it and squealed with happiness as it bounced her back up.

Gowrie followed her daughter into the building and walked across the room to where Banu was sitting on the floor minding three babies.

With this job as a child-care worker, Banu's self-pity and anger were fading as her sunny nature returned. She had no illusions about her prospects for a normal life. But she could still make a useful life. Babies did not know or care about their caretaker's hideous scarring. Here, Banu poured all the maternal love she would never be able to give to her own children into the children of other women and found within herself the beginnings of peace.

"Have you found me a blind man yet?" Banu joked as Gowrie sat down on the floor beside her.

"Only in one eye," Gowrie replied. "But I'm still looking." She picked up the smallest infant, a four-month-old boy, and began to thump him rhythmically on the back. "Banu? If I go away for a day or two, would you take care of Meeta for me?"

"Where are you going?"

"To get my papers. The lawyer is right. I must fight for my daughter's future."

"I will be happy to take care of Meeta for you." Banu reached out and pulled back a boy who had crawled too far into the path of the older children. "When are you going?"

"I'm not sure. Soon. Thank you. I will pay you."

"For this small thing? No payment is needed. And what would I do with money?" Banu touched the gnarled stub where her right ear had been. "Buy earrings?"

Back in her room, Gowrie decided to catch up on the laundry. Life in the hostel was better than life in the shelter and infinitely preferable to being forced into marriage with her mother's brother's retarded son. But working six days a week left little time for chores. She picked up the laundry buckets and headed out to the washing fountain. As the clothes soaked, she sat on the rim of the fountain and thought through her plan one more time.

For all her life Gowrie had ordered servants to clean and sweep and wash and cook for her. Now she took orders from salesmen at the sari shop where she worked as a tea lady, swept her own floors and scrubbed her own laundry. She did not want this for her daughter. She wanted Meeta to live the life she had been born to. More important, Meeta must never be forced into marriage. Her daughter must be able to marry the man she loved, the way Gowrie had.

Like all good lies, the story Gowrie had told to Mary Elizabeth and Raj was primarily composed of truth. Her oldest brother *was* a gambler. Her husband's family *had* objected to the marriage and disowned their youngest son. She *had* been locked in a shed. But there was no dowry of land and there were no deeds.

If her brothers had waited until her first grief for her husband had passed before pushing her to marry her retarded cousin, she probably would have agreed to the marriage. Her cousin had the mind of a ten-year-old, but he was sweet and gentle and with her husband gone, Gowrie needed a family to raise her daughter in. Instead, her older brother locked her in the shed, refusing to let her out until she agreed to the marriage. He tied Meeta to a nearby tree, saying Gowrie should think about her daughter's fate. Sitting amid the old baskets and tools, listening to her daughter crying and calling for her, Gowrie knew that Meeta was like her father. Meeta was strong and passionate. She would rebel. And one day, almost certainly, she would be locked in the shed. Gowrie could not let that happen.

So, when her sister-in-law came out with food, Gowrie pretended to surrender. Two days later, as her family began preparations for the wedding, she told her brother that she wanted to visit a school friend. Before leaving, she slipped into her brother's room and stole the family cashbox, hiding it in a bag of clothes that she said were gifts for her friend's family.

But when she broke off the lock, Gowrie found a bundle of account books and only a small amount of money, not enough to build a new life. The box was broken. It was too late to go back. She had no choice but to flee with Meeta to Chennai, where her money was soon gone.

By the end of her second month in the shelter Gowrie knew there was no way for a poor widow to make a real home for her daughter in Chennai. One evening, on her way back to the shelter after work, she stopped at a pay phone and called her family.

"It's Gowrie," she said when her brother answered the phone. "I want to come home."

"Where is the box?" her brother bellowed.

"I threw it away. I am sorry. I should not—"

"Where are the books?"

Even through the telephone, her brother's rage was terrifying. Something stopped Gowrie from replying. She'd expected to be shouted at, but not about account books. She hung up.

Back in the shelter, Gowrie locked herself in the bathing room and really looked at the account books for the first time. Each page had a strange word at the top. The first entry under the heading was a large amount of money in the first column, followed by smaller amounts, dated weekly, in the second column.

She knew nothing about business, but she did know that these were not normal account books. Her brother wanted them back very much. Enough to pay for them? Gowrie needed money. She decided to find out.

Her plan to blackmail her brothers was dangerous and Gowrie was afraid. She had done everything possible to protect herself and her child. The account books were hidden in the old well at the back of the New Beginnings Hostel. The well was boarded over and never used now that the hostel was on city water. To be sure her brothers had no opportunity to lock her up again, she would call two women friends from her married life in Tiruchchirappalli, the wives of important men, and invite them to come with her when she visited her family. Her brothers would do nothing in front of such witnesses. She would take nothing with her that could be traced back to the hostel. If her brothers knew where to find Meeta, they would use the child again.

Shrieks of children's laughter came across the courtyard from the day care building. Gowrie could easily identify Meeta's voice amid those of the other children. Love for her daughter burned away the last of her fear. "Very soon," she whispered. "Very soon."

There's No Place Like Home

❁❁❁❁❁

SANTOSHI SAT ON THE COCONUT grater in the kitchen corner of her father's hut, rhythmically passing the broken nut over the serrated teeth of the iron cutter between her knees. In the front area of the hut, her father lay on the concrete floor, snoring off the last of the whiskey. She could hear her younger sister, Kalai, splashing water in the backyard as she finished rinsing the laundry.

This was not the family Santoshi had left Chennai to find. She felt foolish now when she thought about the fantasy of loving parents and happily married sisters that had prevented her from coming home for so many years. There was no one here to shame. Her mother was long dead. Her older sister had disappeared years before. Her younger sister was the village prostitute. And her father had not yet been sober enough to recognize his middle daughter.

She finished grating and mixed the coconut into the shredded cabbage. Removing the rice from the fire, she replaced it with the pot to make sambar. Kalai came in from the yard, her bright yellow sari damp from wash water and sweat.

"Big lunch today, older sister?" she asked.

"This is not a big lunch," Santoshi said.

Kalai looked doubtfully at the cabbage and coconut. "Be careful, older sister. I cannot work right now." Then she smiled. "We can afford one special day. I like having you here. Not many people in the village talk to me."

"Once, I would not have talked to you either."

"Now?"

"Now I see that the gods like to laugh. Pass me an onion."

"What is it like in Chennai?" Kalai handed her sister a small, half-rotten onion from a pot by the door.

"Is there no better onion?"

"It's the last one."

"Then this is what I will use. Come back with me and see for yourself."

Kalai gestured toward the front room. "One of us must stay with him." Resentment edged her voice.

"Why?" Santoshi asked, carefully peeling away the rotted part of the onion.

"Are you mad? What would people think? A man with three daughters, left alone."

Santoshi put down the knife and looked up at her sister.

"What do they think of you now? Selling your body to buy his whiskey. How can they think worse?"

"What can I do in Chennai? How can I live?"

"You will live with me. You will find work." Santoshi picked up the knife and returned her attention to the onion.

"Two women alone? No man?"

Santoshi lifted her chin in the direction of the front room.

"His liver is rotted. He will die soon. Then you will be one woman alone. Wash the dal."

The two sisters finished preparing lunch and ate it squatting on the kitchen floor. In the front of the hut, Padhu continued to snore heavily throughout the afternoon. He woke just before sunset, and staggered out to relieve himself in the backyard. His hands shook fiercely. Urine splashed on the laundry hanging closest to the door. When he returned, he collapsed back down onto the floor and called out, "Daughter, bring me whiskey."

Kalai and Santoshi were sitting on the front doorstep. Kalai rose and entered the house. "There is no more whiskey, Father."

"Go buy some."

"I have no money today. Would you like some sambar rice, Father?"

"I don't want rice. I want whiskey. Go out and work."

Santoshi entered the room. "She cannot work today, Father. She is unclean."

Padhu squinted up at the strange woman. "Who are you?"

"I am your daughter. I am Santoshi."

Padhu scowled. "Santoshi is dead."

"I am here, Father. I am not dead." She turned to her sister. "Why does he keep saying I am dead?"

"When you disappeared, our mother told people you died."

Santoshi's eyes lost focus. She stared out at the street for a moment, then looked down at her father. "I will buy you whiskey, Father. But first you must eat."

Padhu would do anything for whiskey. He grunted consent. The shaking of his hands prevented him from picking up his food. Santoshi fed him like a child. He ate fretfully and complained of feeling sick after a few bites. She gave up.

"Where is the wine shop?" she asked her sister.

"By Senthil's market, on School Street. How can you buy whiskey? We have no money."

Santoshi untucked the sari pleats from her waist and showed

her sister the pocket she had sewn into one of the pleats. "I have some money."

Although her father and sister had long since given up any claim to decency, Santoshi stood in the shadows across the street from the wine shop and waited until all the male customers had left, not wishing to be seen as a woman who bought whiskey even by these drunkards. Finally, when the street was empty, she approached the counter.

"Where are you from, Auntie?" the wine shop owner asked politely.

"Chennai. I want one bottle of the cheapest whiskey."

The merchant studied his customer and thought he recognized her features. "Are you related to old Padhu?"

Santoshi thought quickly. "He is my father. I have come with a marriage proposal for my youngest sister. He is too upset to listen to me. Perhaps the whiskey will help him decide."

"Good luck there," replied the wine shop owner.

Santoshi did not know if he was talking about her sister's chances of marriage or her father's ability to think. She paid the man and took the whiskey home.

She squatted down in front of him and held up the whiskey bottle where he could see it but not reach it. "Before I give you this, Father, you must answer a question."

Eyes locked on the bottle, Padhu replied, "What question?"

"What happened to Santoshi?"

"She is dead."

"No, she is not dead. What happened to Santoshi?"

"She is gone."

"Where did she go?"

"Madurai. The man said Madurai."

"What man?"

Padhu's patience ended. "The man I sold her to. Now give me the whiskey, woman!"

Santoshi studied the old man in front of her, his bloodshot eyes, his shaking hands, his full set of yellowed teeth. Finally she stood up, lifted the bottle high over her head and smashed it down to the floor.

"Take it, old man."

A Death in the Family

❁ ❁ ❁ ❁ ❁

CARRYING THE MORNING EDITION OF the *Deccan Chronicle*, Kiria entered the office to find Mary Elizabeth seated on the visitors' bench reading through a folder of case notes.

"Good morning," Kiria said, crossing the room to sit behind the desk. "What are you doing here? I thought you were going to do interviews today."

"I will," Mary Elizabeth said. "I came to ask you for a favor."

"Sure. What?"

"Can you keep Meeta with you today?"

"No problem. Where is she now?"

"She is in the day care."

"I'll pick her up after breakfast," Kiria promised. "Why do you want me to watch her?"

"Banu came to me yesterday morning. Gowrie left Meeta with Banu four days ago, and went somewhere to get her papers. She hasn't come back. Banu is worried. Then yesterday afternoon two women came here. They said they were Gowrie's sisters. They said Gowrie had sent them to pick up Meeta."

"That doesn't sound likely."

"Banu did not think so either. She brought them to me in the office. I told them I could not legally release the child without a letter from Gowrie and they went away. But I feel something is wrong. I do not want to leave Meeta in the day care."

"Very strange. I wonder where she went." Kiria could not believe Gowrie would leave her child for so long. "I'll keep Meeta with me today. If I don't see you later, she'll come home with me. Is that okay?"

"Wonderful. Thank you."

"Had breakfast?"

"No, not yet."

"Stay. Have breakfast with me. I'll call the canteen and order an extra dhosa."

Mary Elizabeth looked at her watch. "Okay. I have time." She went back to studying her notes.

Kiria called the canteen and ordered two coffees and two rava dhosas, then unfolded the morning paper across the desk. She skimmed the lead articles and was just turning the page when a name in the lower right-hand corner caught her attention.

> **Woman's Body Found in Field—Tiruchchirappalli.** Police are investigating the brutal murder of a woman found in a field on the outskirts of the city yesterday. The woman's severely mutilated body was discovered just before dawn by Mr. T. Avaranadan, a local laborer, when he took his small herd of goats to the field to graze. Mr. Avaranadan told a local reporter that the woman had been stabbed or cut in several places, and had charred skin on her feet and hands. The corpse has

> been taken to a local mortuary for autopsy to determine the exact cause of death. The woman has been identified as T. S. Gowrie, resident of Chennai. Police are following several leads at this time.

"Oh my God! Mary Elizabeth! Look at this!"

Mary Elizabeth stood up and walked across the room. Kiria turned the paper around and pointed to the article. Mary Elizabeth read through it. Her eyes widened. When she came to the end, her face went completely blank. Her knees folded. She braced her arms against the desk to stay upright.

Kiria hurried around the desk and supported her friend to the bench. Mary Elizabeth sat down and lowered her head into her lap.

"Look at me!" Kiria put her hand under Mary Elizabeth's chin and forced her head up. "Look at me. Focus. That's how they found Meeta."

Mary Elizabeth looked blankly back at Kiria.

"Gowrie was tortured," Kiria spelled it out. "That's how her sisters knew the hostel address. They are looking for the deeds."

Mary Elizabeth began to shake. Kiria recognized the signs of shock, but there were more important things to be done. She went to the door and saw Nirmila's oldest daughter in her school uniform heading out the gate.

"Shankari!" she called out. "Go find Meeta. Bring to me."

"I am going to school, Kiria Madam," Shankari protested.

"Now, Shankari! Go now. Hurry."

Shankari turned and ran back toward the main building. Kiria went back into the office, pulled her cell phone out of her purse and called Raj.

"Hello?"

"Raj, this is Kiria, have you got today's *Deccan Chronicle*?"

"Yes."

"Page one. Lower right-hand corner."

Responding to the urgency in Kiria's voice, Raj walked to his front hall where the papers were lying on a table. Kiria heard the rustle of the pages as Raj unfolded them. She put her arm around Mary Elizabeth's shoulders and waited.

"Has Mary Elizabeth seen this?" he asked when he finished reading.

"Yes, and she's not taking it well."

"I am coming."

"Wait. Listen. Mary just told me that Gowrie's sisters tried to take Meeta away yesterday."

"How did they . . . ? No, wait. . . . Yesterday? After?"

"Yes."

"I must talk with the police."

"I'm taking Mary Elizabeth and Meeta back to my place. Meet us there as soon as you can."

"I'll call you. And Kiria? Take care of Mary Elizabeth."

"I will, Raj."

After hanging up, Kiria poured a glass of water and sat down beside Mary Elizabeth. "You're in shock. Drink."

BY TWO O'CLOCK, Kiria, Raj and Mary Elizabeth sat in Kiria's living room, while Meeta squatted in front of the television watching cartoons and chewing on a stick of sugarcane. Kiria sat on a garden chair from the terrace. Across from her, Raj sat on the sofa with his arm around Mary Elizabeth's shoulders. Mary Elizabeth, her anger washed away by guilt, leaned into the safety of his shoulder, crying uncontrollably.

"This would never have happened if she had stayed in the shelter," Mary Elizabeth wailed. "This is my fault. I should never have encouraged her to live in the hostel."

"It wouldn't have happened if she'd stayed in the hostel either," Kiria said.

"Kiria is right. Gowrie chose to go to her family. This is not your fault." Raj tightened his arm around Mary Elizabeth's shoulder and tried not to show his joy at being able to hold her again.

"But she was locked up in the shelter!" Mary Elizabeth wailed.

Kiria pressed her lips together but said nothing.

Raj tried again. "Gowrie made a mistake by going to her family. It was her mistake. Not yours. Would you be this upset if her family had welcomed her back?"

Mary Elizabeth sniffed loudly and felt around for the end of her sari to wipe her face.

"Here." Kiria picked up a roll of bathroom tissue from the coffee table and handed it to Mary Elizabeth. "Raj, did you learn anything from the police?"

This was not the first time Raj had been grateful for Kiria's practicality. While Mary Elizabeth blew her nose, Raj began his report.

"The autopsy showed Gowrie died of heart failure. The police in Tiruchchirappalli do not think the death was intentional. She was abducted from a car two days ago by four men. They took Gowrie but left the driver and two women unconscious in the car. The driver went to the police the next morning and was able to describe the kidnapping and identify Gowrie's sari. When the police questioned Gowrie's family yesterday, they appeared horrified to learn of her death. They said she had come to them asking for money and they gave it to her."

"How much?" Kiria asked.

"Ten lakhs, cash," Raj answered.

"A million rupees in cash? So much for the gambling-debts story," Kiria said.

"The police say there was no money with her," Raj pointed out.

"And the abductors?" Kiria asked.

"Not known. But now that the police know the sisters came to Chennai to get Meeta before they were notified of Gowrie's death, it is suspected that her family was involved. Her brothers are being questioned by the police now. Their wives have disappeared. Mary Elizabeth must come with me to give a statement to the police today."

"Does she have to get involved?" Kiria had heard enough stories from the hostel residents by now to know how foolish her original idea that Gowrie should go to the police had been. "You said Gowrie's family was powerful. Doesn't that put her in danger?"

"Not when I'm involved. The police will investigate this by the book."

Raj spoke without pride or humility. It was just another fact. The raw power of his statement raised the hair on the back of Kiria's neck.

"What about the land deeds?" she asked.

"Not found yet. The Chennai Police are going through Gowrie's possessions from the hostel."

Meeta stood up and walked over to a corner, where she squatted and defecated.

"Lovely," Kiria said, rising from her chair.

"I will clean it!" Mary Elizabeth sprang up from the couch.

"No, sit. It's okay." Kiria picked up the roll of bathroom tissue and intercepted Meeta on her way back to the television. "Meeta, bend," she said gently in Tamil.

The girl bent over obediently and allowed her bottom to be wiped. Then she sat down in front of the television. Kiria went to the corner and scooped up the excrement.

"Back home we do this for dogs," she said, and went into the bathroom. Returning with a bucket of water, she squatted down and began washing the floor in the corner. "So what happens to Meeta now?"

"I don't know. Normally a child goes back to her family, but in this case . . ." Mary Elizabeth's voice faded away.

"Certainly not her mother's family. But what about her father's family?" Kiria suggested.

"They showed very little interest while her mother was alive," Raj said.

"Still, I will contact them." Mary Elizabeth was determined to do her best for the child. "Perhaps they will reconsider, now that Meeta is an orphan."

"And if they don't?" Kiria asked.

Mary Elizabeth sighed. "It will have to be an orphanage. But I no longer work for the government. I may have to look for a private one." Her shoulders drooped.

Raj looked at his watch. "We should go to the police soon."

Mary Elizabeth rose from the sofa and walked over to the television. "Come, Meeta."

"No!" Meeta, in love with the cartoons, had no intention of leaving.

"We must go, Meeta." Mary Elizabeth reached down and pulled Meeta to her feet.

"Noooo!" Meeta screamed. "No, no, no, no." She writhed in Mary Elizabeth's grasp.

"Meeta, stop this. Stop right now." Mary Elizabeth, drained by guilt and exhausted from crying, had no reserves left to deal with a temper tantrum. She struck Meeta sharply on the arm. "Stop this right now!"

In the corner Kiria rolled her eyes in exasperation. "Leave her with me. You have enough to deal with right now."

Mary Elizabeth let go of Meeta, who promptly stopped screaming and plopped herself back down in front of the wonderful cartoons.

No One Wins a Pissing Contest

❁ ❁ ❁ ❁ ❁

DID YOU KNOW THAT IF you are reading this book in the bus on your way to work, surrounded by strangers, you are statistically safer than if you are reading it lying in bed beside the love of your life? It's true. The number of people violently attacked by a total stranger on public transportation is quite small. On the other hand, the minimum number of domestic violence crimes per year in the United States alone is over one million, and that's just the attacks that are reported. Given the most recent estimate of the U.S. population, this means that one out of every three hundred people is a domestic criminal. Makes you wonder about the person snoring beside you there, doesn't it?

Remember Gowrie, the woman whose case gave Raj and Mary Elizabeth an excuse to meet clandestinely? Gowrie became one of the hostel tenants. Shortly after moving in, she was tortured and killed by—you guessed it—her family. We all assumed she was tortured to reveal the location of the land deeds. But during the police investigation it became obvious that Gowrie's story about her brother wanting to sell land to pay for gambling debts was a total fabrication. Her family didn't need the money. They were rolling in the stuff. They could afford to give her a million rupees in cash.

There weren't any deeds either. What the police eventually found, tied under the cover of an unused well behind the hostel, were two account ledgers, documenting the profits from a very exclusive brothel in Bangalore offering young white women to the nouveau riche outsourcing moguls. This is how Gowrie's older brother funded his gambling addiction. Presumably Gowrie wanted in on the action. It was quite a surprise. She seemed like such a nice, quiet person. But everyone says that about serial killers too.

Until Gowrie's brothers were taken into custody, Mary Elizabeth was in a certain amount of danger because it was her testimony that proved Gowrie's family knew about her death before being informed of it. During this period I got a brief glimpse of the real Raj and it was pretty damn spine tingling, I can tell you.

Raj's family fortune was small compared with Gowrie's, but he had connections. Through his relatives, through his work, Raj stood in the center of a vast web of status and influence. He had real power. He knew this. He knew it at a cellular level, the way he knew the shape of his own hand. He didn't abuse his power; Raj was a decent, moral man. He didn't flaunt his power; I'd never have known about it if he hadn't thought Mary Elizabeth was in danger.

What chilled me was the casual way he used his power. Just before Raj and Mary Elizabeth left my apartment on the day we learned about Gowrie's murder, Raj made a call on his cell phone. He spoke one sentence, like he was talking to a friend, and hung up without waiting for a reply. A few minutes later three police cars pulled up outside the house. Five armed policemen escorted

Raj and Mary Elizabeth down the stairs and into the middle car. Now, Mary Elizabeth could not possibly have been in that much danger. It was, as the Chinese say, like shooting a mosquito with cannon. No one should be able to wield that much power that frivolously.

Gowrie's death left me in temporary possession of a two-year-old. Babies cry a lot, but they can be sweet. Five-year-olds are annoying, but they can be funny. Toddlers, unless they're your own, have no redeeming qualities. Meeta was well into the tantrum stage and too young to understand that her mother was dead. She went through shrieking phases, beating her heels on the floor and calling for her mother. Meeta had a will of iron and the lungs to prove it. I spent more than one sleepless night trying to comfort her. Eventually, she calmed down and got used to me. I think it helped that we both spoke Tamil at the same level.

By far the worst part of having a toddler was the waste products. Babies in India generally do not wear diapers; disposables are too expensive for most families, and the bacteria remaining in cloth diapers washed in a bucket of cold water would result in life-threatening diaper rash. I bought a package of disposables, but Meeta would not tolerate them. She pulled them off as soon as I put them on and continued to squat wherever she happened to be when the need arose. Having gone to considerable effort to create a sanitary refuge from the worst of India, I came very close to committing murder myself. I could handle the droppings. Shit washes off, as Erma Bombeck so wisely pointed out. But the smell drove me crazy. I did some research on the Internet, bought a potty and started toilet training.

Modern theory holds that potty training is best accomplished through example. Meeta, who was extremely competitive, turned this into a game. She scored points primarily on sound and was not above throwing her toys into the potty to ensure victory.

We were in the bathroom one day having a pissing contest. Gowrie had shaved her daughter's head, probably in an attempt to keep the lice to a minimum. Sitting on the potty with her knees touching and her little face scrunched up with the effort of forcing out urine, Meeta looked exactly like a constipated billiard ball.

I found myself trying to picture what life would be like for this unwanted little girl. She could not be returned to the family who had killed her mother. Her father's family flatly refused to take her. The only option for Meeta was an orphanage. She would grow up lost in a harsh, uncaring environment. Although some children might be tempered by this, I felt Meeta, with her rigid personality, would be one of the broken ones. My heart contracted.

Meeta's urine trickled to a halt. She looked up at me, her little face given artificial dignity by the absence of hair. "You not pee. I win," she announced solemnly. "Wash me."

I pulled the sprayer off the wall, handed it to her and turned on the tap. "Wash yourself."

I got very wet.

Alone at Last

❁ ❁ ❁ ❁ ❁

"IT HURTS!" THE OLD MAN shouted, pushing Santoshi's hands away. "I need whiskey."

Santoshi gave up trying to wash her father's wounds. The cuts on his arms and knees were swollen and suppurating, despite her attempts to keep them clean. No amount of water would help him now.

Kalai twisted around on the front step of the hut. "You should buy him whiskey."

"No." Santoshi picked up the pan of water and rose to her feet. "I will not waste my money."

Kalai rose as well. "Then I will work."

"He is dying, sister. If not today, then next week or next month. Whiskey will make his fever worse. You will only kill him sooner." Santoshi walked to the back of the hut and threw the water from the pan onto the ground. When she returned to the front of the hut, Kalai had reseated herself on the front step.

"You must think about what will happen when he dies," Santoshi told her sister. "You cannot stay here alone. Come back to Chennai with me. You are pretty. Perhaps you will find a husband there."

"A husband?" Kalai laughed shortly. "Another man to serve? Another man to drink my wages?"

"What about children? Do you not want children?"

Kalai's head drooped. "That is no longer possible." She stared at her bare, dusty feet.

Santoshi did not ask why this was so. She did not want to know. "Then we can stay together. You can work as I do, as a maid."

Kalai looked out into the street. "I am not like you."

FOR THE three weeks preceding old Padhu's death, the village of Pachur got very little sleep. The old man screamed almost constantly, first for whiskey, then in fear of imaginary insects and finally in pain as tetanus from the deep cuts on his hands and knees locked his muscles in increasingly vicious spasms.

Even the meanest-spirited village women had to give credit to Kalai, who stopped working and joined her sister, recently returned after many years in the city, in the struggle to care for their father. Of course, as they had no money to take him to the hospital, everyone agreed old Padhu would soon be dead. One or two of the more curious village women brought leftover rice to the girls occasionally as an excuse to see old Padhu and report on his condition to the rest of the villagers. When they came, the sisters did nothing to correct their assumption that Santoshi was Padhu's oldest daughter. There was no need for the villagers to know her true story.

AS THE sun rose on the morning after the burning of her father's body, Santoshi sat on the floor of the hut wearing her good navy sari. The rest of her possessions, tied up in her old green sari, rested by the front door. Today, she would return to Chennai. But she could not leave without trying one more time to convince her sister to come with her.

Kalai entered the hut, her pink sari bundled clumsily around her waist and her hair trailing in oily strands down her back.

Santoshi stood up. "I am leaving. You should not stay here. Come to Chennai with me."

Kalai sat down. "In Chennai there are too many women like me."

"You do not have to sell your body in Chennai. You can be different there."

"Scrubbing floors for five hundred rupees a month? I made six hundred rupees last night, sister. You should stay here with me. We can both live well." Kalai lay down on the floor. "I am tired. I must sleep."

Santoshi stood above her sister, not knowing what else she could say. "I cannot," she whispered finally. She picked up her bundle and turned to say good-bye, but Kalai was already asleep. Santoshi set her bundle on her head and walked out the door.

Giant Steps

From: meglertheodore@rogers.net
To: kiria@novio.com
Subject: Big News!

Hi Kiria

We made it! The adoption has been approved. We got the news yesterday.

The boys are coming to us at the end of the school year. Now that we know for sure, I feel like I can tell people about them. I didn't want to make it too real before.

Eddie is four years old. He's been in foster care for two years. Before that he lived with his mother and her other two children. She couldn't manage with three so had to put Eddie in foster care. We've met her. She's a good person and Eddie's sisters seem to be turning out well. We think we can make a kind of extended family with them.

Jason is about seven. No one knows exactly how old he is because he was abandoned in a supermarket parking lot when he was a toddler. He's small and he has a short leg. His current foster parents say he is quiet and good in school. Rik thinks the leg may be repairable when he stops growing.

Next to meeting Rik this is the most exciting thing that has ever happened to me. I feel—I don't know what I feel. Mostly nervous. We don't know how to be parents. What if we screw up?

Rik says Hi. He also says we're going to be limited to camping and Disneyland for years to come after the boys arrive and we're thinking of taking one last big vacation at the end of the month. We'd like to come see you in India. But only if you're okay with it. It's really no problem if now is not a good time.

Theo

From: kiria@novio.com
To: meglertheodore@rogers.net
Subject: Congratulations, Papa!

Hi Theo

This is fantastic news. I'm very happy for you and Rik. Even happier for Eddie and Jason. I think you will be good parents. You had excellent role models and from what you've told me about Rik, so did he.

And I'm more than okay with you and Rik coming out for a visit. I'd love for you to come. Just tell me when your plane gets in and I'll come pick you up at the airport. If you're up for it, I'd like you to stay at my place.

Sorry I didn't write sooner, but I had to get a new laptop.

You're never going to believe this, but I have, quite unintentionally, beaten you and Rik in the acquisition of a child. I am temporarily caring for a two-year-old girl. Her mother was one of the hostel residents, who died last week. Mary Elizabeth has not been able to find Meeta a placement in an orphanage yet.

Be thankful yours are out of the terrible twos. When she's not screaming her head off, Meeta likes to do things like test gravitational theory by throwing laptops off the terrace. . . .

Pickups

❁ ❁ ❁ ❁ ❁

"THE MALARIA HAS RETURNED." THE doctor poured water from the pitcher on his desk into a basin and rinsed his hands. "Do you want the drugs again?"

Rahul studied the girl slumped on the examination table. "Yes."

The decision was not motivated by kindness or even pity. He was a businessman. The girl was a valuable commodity. She was a good beggar and with her light skin and Persian features she would make even more when she was old enough to move into one of the brothels. A few hundred rupees for medicine was a small price to protect his investment.

The doctor walked over to a cupboard and took out six foil-wrapped packages of pills. "One every day for thirty days. Be sure she takes all of them. Keep her warm. She should not work for at least a week."

Rahul took the foil packets and turned to the young man

leaning against the far wall of the doctor's office. "Sekar, take her out to the van. I will be out soon."

Sekar looked up from admiring his new cowboy boots. "Yes, Uncle."

He picked up the girl and carried her out the back door. She weighed almost nothing. Her skin was hot. Her muscles were flaccid. He laid her on the floor in the back of the van, then got in behind the wheel, started the engine and turned on the air-conditioning. The girl moaned as the chilled air blew across her body. Sekar flipped down the visor to check his hair. A few minutes later Rahul came out of the doctor's office and climbed into the passenger seat.

"Turn off the air-conditioning," Rahul snapped. "Weren't you listening? The doctor said to keep her warm."

"Sorry, Uncle." Sekar switched off the air-conditioning. "Where now?"

Rahul looked at his watch. "It's getting late. Let's go pick up the kids."

SANTOSHI STOOD in the women's ticket line at the Madurai bus station watching the clubfooted boy working the lines for the ticket windows. She had spotted two of the other children: the tall boy working the entrance and a lively girl at the city bus stand on the far side of the building. They were well trained, moving deftly through the crowds, selecting the right people to approach.

There were few women buying tickets today and Santoshi soon found herself at the front of the line. She placed her bundle on the floor at her feet and bought a one-way ticket on the night bus to Chennai. Holding her ticket, she turned to pick up her bundle and saw Rahul entering the terminal.

He stared right at her, eyes narrowed, brows drawn together.

He recognized her. Her heart stopped beating for an instant, then began to slam painfully against her ribs. Without thinking, she picked up the skirt of her sari and fled through the crowds toward the back entrance.

IN ALL his years of business Rahul had bought many children, and sold them when they became too old to control. To him they were like apples sold by a street vendor, forgotten, as though they had never existed. But he recognized Santoshi the instant he stepped into the station. The smart one. The one who ran away. The one who stole the thirty thousand rupees she was worth right out of his pocket. He watched her flee and considered chasing after her. But she was worthless now, and obviously still afraid of him. She had said nothing for fifteen years. She would say nothing now.

Rahul signaled to the boy working the entrance. "Get them into the van," he ordered when the boy trotted up. "And go pick up that." He pointed to a bundled green sari lying by the ticket window.

RAMASWAMY HAD taken the day off from private investigation to take his mother to the Koyambedu bus terminal because his aunt from Madurai was arriving for her annual visit. He felt a rising sense of doom as the bus pulled in and his aunt waddled down the steps. She gave him the first of the thousand and one cheek pinches that would leave him bruised and twitching by the end of her two-week stay.

"Look at you, so tall and handsome," his aunt teased. "Oh, big sister, I have had the most terrible trip!"

Both women being too large to do more than wrap their arms halfway around the other's body, they embraced like elephants at the bottom of the bus steps, effectively blocking other passengers from descending. Ramaswamy pulled his mother and aunt gently off to one side. From years of pickups he knew there was no chance of getting them into an auto before the greeting rituals were completed. He allowed his aunt's catalog of the horrors endured on her journey to wash over him unheard and gazed at the other passengers descending from the bus.

The last passenger, a small woman, stepped onto the pavement and walked off into the terminal. He stared at the empty bus door for a second, then swiveled around in a jerky double take. It was her!

For three weeks Ramaswamy had carried her picture through hutments and pavement-dwelling communities, to hospitals, police stations, shelters, hostels and transportation hubs. Along with the promise of a reward, he had pasted her picture on corporation water tanks, stapled it to tree trunks and published it in both Tamil and English newspapers. Aside from a few crackpot leads that took him nowhere, there had been no trace of Mrs. Langdon's maid anywhere in Chennai. He had finally given up a month ago and advised Mrs. Langdon that he was unable to find Santoshi. And now she'd just walked by under his nose!

"Where is he going?" Ramaswamy's aunt broke off her graphic description of midnight motion sickness to watch her nephew galloping off into the bus terminal.

"Ramaswamy!" his mother shouted after him. "You come back here right now!"

SANTOSHI STOOD at the entrance to the Koyembedu bus terminal, staring in shock at a picture of herself pasted to a pillar.

Wanted in connection with an investigation into the loss of a valuable item.

Information leading to the whereabouts of P. Santoshi.

Reward.

Contact P. Ramaswamy, 934 555 5555.

A valuable item? A reward? Santoshi tried hard to make sense of this.

A man's voice called out. "Santoshi! Santoshi!"

She looked up and saw a tall young man, elbows out and knees pumping as he ran toward her. She looked around but realized there was no place to hide in the open area between the bus terminal and the road. She turned to face the man.

He stopped in front of her. "Mrs. Langdon is looking for you, Auntie."

"Kiria Madam is looking for me?"

"Yes. She needs her pen drive."

"What is a pin drive?"

"Pen drive. She said you wouldn't know." Ramaswamy reached into his pocket, then remembered he'd returned the pen drive. He pulled out his cell phone instead. "We can call her and then I will take you to her."

"No." Santoshi had no intention of going anywhere with this man, however young and innocent he looked. "I know where she is. Is she angry with me?"

He shook his head. "I don't think so, Auntie. She said if you took it, it was an accident." The little woman's face was so concerned that he decided to tell her what he thought. "She said she wanted the pen drive, but we talked every day and I think she was really more worried about you."

It had never occurred to Santoshi that Kiria Madam would worry. "I will go to her. Will you call her and tell her I am coming? What is your good name? I will tell her you found me, so that you will have the reward." She pointed to the poster on the pillar.

He nodded. "Of course. My name is Ramaswamy. There is no reward for me. But I am happy I found you."

MEETA SAT on the floor of the living room, trying to push a blue block through the triangular hole in the yellow wooden box. She liked this toy very much, though she rarely managed to get anything through the holes. She liked the colors and the heavy weight of the pieces and she knew that when she did push a piece into the box, it made Kiria happy. Kiria was sitting on the sofa speaking the strange language.

"Thank you, Ramaswamy. Thank you very much." Kiria closed the cell phone and placed it carefully on the coffee table. She drew in a deep breath, then suddenly leaned over as though her stomach hurt and began to cry.

Meeta knew exactly what to do when people cried. She had learned this when she first came to stay with the white woman. She even remembered the special word. She got up from the floor and stood in front of Kiria. Wrapping both arms around Kiria's head, Meeta pulled it to her chest and began to chant.

"Okay," she whispered. "Okay. Okay."

War Stories

❁❁❁❁❁

YOU'D THINK THAT BY MY age, I'd have learned to stop making assumptions, wouldn't you? You'd be wrong. Age is no defense against stupidity.

Santoshi's return was easily the most shocking event of my entire stay in India because she came back with a small fortune, mostly in coins and very low-denomination bills. I had turned my life upside down for a fake poor person.

The idea that Santoshi had money, real money, just blew me away. I'd looked at her living conditions, her wardrobe, her lack of teeth, and seen what I wanted to see. And then she came sashaying back to Chennai, wanting to live in the room she'd rejected two months before and planning to open a provisions store on my property. I studied the other hostel residents with suspicion and wondered just how much of a fool I had been.

Unlike me, Mary Elizabeth was not upset by Santoshi's wealth, but she was curious. She sat Santoshi down and got the full, sad story about the years of running errands for two-rupee tips, and hiding them from avaricious wardens in jars buried all over the city. Mary Elizabeth asked Santoshi why she'd never spent any money on herself, and Santoshi replied that until recently she liked the money better than anything else. Now she liked a provisions store better.

Laxmi was remarkably pragmatic about Santoshi's money. She pointed out that Santoshi could not be held responsible for my erroneous assumption, and if I really came to India to improve Santoshi's living conditions, I should be happy with the plan to open a provisions store. And eventually I was. I even came to appreciate the humor of the situation. Those of us who have learned to laugh at ourselves have an endless supply of entertainment.

Laxmi repaid Santoshi for all those housekeeping lessons by helping to set up the store. Not only did she teach Santoshi how to keep books and make financial projections; she convinced her to put her money in the bank and earn interest on it. You just can't overestimate the benefits of a good deed. Mary Elizabeth gave Santoshi a cashbox as a start-up present for the business. I gave her a large sign to hang on the front of the store. Laxmi got the Brahmans in to puja the heck out of it with incense and chanting. Within three weeks of returning to Chennai, Santoshi rolled up the metal shutter at the front of her store, hung a garland of chrysanthemums and jasmine over the counter and began her career as a businesswoman.

About this time my patience with defaulting tenants came to an end, and Operation Back Rent swung into action. It was an uphill battle. After going to so much effort to find women who had no relatives to fall back on, I could hardly just shove the defaulters out onto the street. At the end of the first week of empty threats on my part and lame excuses on theirs, the score was tenants twelve, Kiria zero. At this rate they'd all stop paying rent.

A more aggressive strategy was required. I revoked their canteen privileges, kicked their kids out of day care and cut off water and power to their rooms. At the height of summer in Chennai, this made the rooms practically uninhabitable. Two previous shelter residents made up on the arrears. The rest of the defaulters began cooking over fires behind the main building, leaving their kids alone, carrying water from the laundry fountain and sleeping on the roof. Week two ended with a score of tenants ten, Kiria two.

The first few days of week three were spent in a time-out. Mary Elizabeth felt I'd crossed the line by turning off the power and talked me out of initiating further offensives until we'd seen the fallout from the previous week. Lack of power didn't really bother the defaulters. By then the city had begun daily power outages as a means of stretching the city's dwindling hydroelectric power, an annual highlight of the summer drought. But untended children ran me ragged. After a few days of trying to keep an eye on the kids myself, I relented on the day care ruling.

I didn't really have any more weapons in my arsenal, or at least any I was willing to deploy. I was about ten minutes away from surrendering to the inevitable when one of those freak events that historians describe as turning the tide of battle occurred. Old Viji's father's younger brother's oldest son's wife showed up. There's probably a special word for this relationship in Tamil, but for the sake of intelligibility we'll call her the cousin-in-law.

Sally's efforts to locate a relative had not unearthed this branch of the family because they had moved to Hyderabad many years before. However, on a trip back to Chennai to visit her aunt, cousin-in-law had checked in with a childhood friend who was still living in the house where she grew up, which happened to be across the street from Old Viji's father's house. Falling into conversation on the street with the current owner of the house, cousin-in-law learned that an investigator had shown up a few months before, looking for Old Viji's relatives. Cousin-in-law had never heard anything about Old Viji. She called her husband, who asked his father, who said yes, my brother had a daughter, but she died. Cousin-in-law decided to check it out anyway. She got the investigator's card from the current homeowner and eventually found her way to the hostel.

She was horrified. She gave me a strongly worded piece of her mind about the irresponsibility of housing a disabled patient under such conditions and insisted on relocating Old Viji to a more suitable facility at once. Despite the blatant injustice of being accused of maltreating a mental patient by a woman whose own family had created the neglect, it was a relief to be rid of the responsibility. I called Sally in San Francisco with the news and went back to planning my dignified surrender in the rent wars, only to learn that I had won them.

After we transferred Old Viji, I had the hostel possessions from her room packed up and locked in a storeroom. The tenant grapevine erroneously reported that I'd confiscated her possessions for nonpayment of rent and evicted her. By the end of the third week everyone had paid up. Final score: Kiria twelve, tenants zero.

Once the rent situation had been sorted out, I had very little to do. Under Laxmi's guidance, the hostel was running smoothly and the financial situation improved rapidly as the box stores began to generate income and Mary Elizabeth continued to find tenants. With Santoshi firmly established on the path to prosperity and independence, I'd accomplished what I set out to do, admittedly due more to her efforts than mine. The only responsibility I had left in India was Meeta.

I'd become quite attached to Meeta. With the flexibility of the very young, she had adapted quickly to her new situation.

She still had tantrums and called for her mother some nights, but as her natural exuberance and curiosity returned, we'd developed a bond of sorts. Not anything as strong as mother and daughter, but a definite preference for each other's company. I began to dread the day when Mary Elizabeth finally found an orphanage.

Commitment

❁ ❁ ❁ ❁ ❁

THE MARRIAGE HALL WAS LARGE and air-conditioned, but the air was stale and heavy with the exhalations of more than three thousand wedding guests. A thousand conversations drowned out the efforts of the musicians seated in the balcony at the back of the room. On the stage at the front of the hall, the exhausted bride and groom struggled to smile. It was their second day onstage. A long line of well-wishers still waited to climb up, present their gifts and be photographed with the new couple.

Raj felt sorry for them. He remembered his own much larger wedding forty years before. Standing beside a woman he barely knew, cheeks aching from endless hours of smiling, knees trembling with fatigue, heart filled with misery. Was the boy on the stage hiding despair as well? Was the girl hiding dread? He wanted to go up and tell them it would get better, that lust died and caring grew in its place.

Raj and his wife had each put aside romantic attachments and dutifully married for family. At the time he'd thought it was the end of the world, but his parents had chosen well. Over thirty-four years of marriage, Raj had grown a deep, true bond with his wife, and now, seven years after her death, he still missed the comfort of her presence and the sound of her quiet breathing beside him at night.

Spotting an empty chair on the men's side of the room, Raj walked over to claim it. "Is anyone sitting here?" he asked the man in the next chair over.

"No, please sit. Are you a relative of the bride or the groom?" the man asked politely.

"Neither. I work with the groom's father. And you?"

"My brother's daughter went to school with the bride. We came down from Mysore for the wedding. A nice hall, is it not?"

"Yes, one of the best in Chennai, I believe. Is there a problem?" Raj asked as the man's polite face shifted into an expression of dread.

"What is *she* doing here?" the man whispered. He slumped down and moved his head to hide his face behind Raj's shoulder.

"Who?" Raj turned to look at the women's side of the room.

"That woman in the gold sari by the fountain. The Angry Widow."

Raj spotted her instantly, a plump scowling woman standing with her hands on her hips.

"The Angry Widow?"

"She is our neighbor. A dreadful woman. Her husband died last year, probably from nagging. She's looking for a replacement."

"And you are . . . ?"

"The leading candidate. Have you eaten? Would you like to join me in the banqueting hall?"

Raj was careful to keep his body between the man and the woman's line of sight as they walked up the staircase leading to the banqueting hall. At the top of the stairs a young man stepped away from a group leaning against the wall and ushered them to two empty seats at the end of a long table.

"Veg or nonveg, Uncle?" the young man asked.

Raj and his companion both chose the vegetarian meal. The young man gestured to the small army of waiters by the kitchen and within minutes two banana leaves were laid down and artistically filled with an aromatic selection of sweets, spiced vegetables and biryani.

As they ate, the two men traded war stories about their families' attempts to marry them off. Raj, who thought he'd been subjected to every trick in the book, experienced a profound sense of relief that he'd never been pursued by anyone as tenacious as the Angry Widow.

"She must really like you," he said as they washed their hands after the meal.

"Oh, it's not just me. Every bachelor in the neighborhood is terrified of her. Personally, I think she'd rather go live with her son, but his wife would never allow it." At the top of the steps the man suddenly whirled around. "Is there another staircase?" he demanded of the young men still leaning against the wall waiting to seat the guests.

One of them gestured at the kitchen area. "At the back, Uncle."

Without saying good-bye, Raj's dinner companion fled toward the back stairs. Raj watched him run off, then turned to see the reason coming up the main staircase. The Angry Widow was hungry. He smiled to himself as he started down the stairs. "Good luck, my friend," he said softly. As he approached the woman, Raj realized she was talking to his second son's wife.

"Father!" his daughter-in-law called up. "I am glad to see you. There is someone I'd like you to meet."

The Angry Widow turned and slapped the younger woman

playfully on the arm. "You never told me your father was so handsome," she cooed.

Raj's jaw bulged with the effort of keeping the smile on his face.

LATER IN THE DAY, as he drove through the gates of the New Beginnings Hostel, Raj was still shaken by his encounter with the Angry Widow. He'd had much practice in discouraging matrimonial advances over the past few years, but this one had been surrealistic, with Mary Elizabeth's elegant face flashing over the Angry Widow's broad features. In the end he had clumsily excused himself and given in to the overwhelming desire to be with the woman he loved.

He sat for a moment after parking the car in front of the office. He was nervous, a novel sensation these days, but he was even more determined. He'd made a foolish mistake suggesting an affair to Mary Elizabeth. It wasn't until Gowrie's death brought them back together that she'd finally been willing to listen to his apologies. Although it was a joy to be seeing her again, after today, just seeing her would never be enough. Long ago, he'd sacrificed love for duty and known he made the right choice. He had done his duty to his family, and although they would not be pleased with his decision, Raj intended to make a different choice this time.

He took two deep breaths, got out of the car and went into the office to ask Mary Elizabeth to marry him.

The office was empty. The desk was littered with papers. He could see Mary Elizabeth's bag on the floor under a chair. The sound of a woman wailing came from the courtyard. Raj went to the doorway and saw Mary Elizabeth and Kiria coming out of the day care building. The scarred woman followed behind them, the pallu of her sari pulled over her head. Raj could hear the women talking as he strode across the courtyard.

"I will look, madam. I will find her," Banu wailed.

"This is not your fault, Banu." Mary Elizabeth tried to comfort the wailing woman.

"Tell her to stay in the day care and make sure we don't lose any more," Kiria snapped at Mary Elizabeth. "You and I will look."

"What is this?" Raj asked.

"Raj! Just in time. Meeta is missing," Kiria explained. "We don't know how long she has been gone."

"Not more than an hour," Mary Elizabeth said. "I'm sure she is fine."

Kiria stood with her hands on her hips looking around the hostel grounds, reminding Raj of his first sight of the Angry Widow.

"Well, let's make sure of that. I'll take the hostel. Raj, Mary Elizabeth, you two search the grounds." Kiria switched to Tamil. "Banu, watch children." She strode off toward the main building without waiting to see if her orders were followed.

"She is upset. She did not mean to be rude. You do not have to search," Mary Elizabeth apologized for her friend as she tucked the floating end of her sari in at the waist, preparing to search.

"I'm accustomed to her." Raj decided this was not the best time to propose. He looked around the grounds. "Not too many places to hide out here. If she is anywhere, she'll be in the bushes. Let's start over there by the office."

At this time of year the ground was dry and dusty. Thousands of little bare footprints circled the bushes. Mary Elizabeth and Raj made their way around the plantings, bending and peering through the dry foliage.

"Aiee!"

Raj looked up to see that Mary Elizabeth had caught her hair on a branch while backing out from under a bush. She was bent at the waist with a large lock of hair pulled halfway out of her knotted bun. He admired the view as he walked over to help.

"Stand still. I'll get it." He knelt and fumbled with the heavy hair for a moment. "There's too much caught. I'll have to pull out the bun."

"Just hurry," Mary Elizabeth told him.

Raj loosened the knot. Warm, silky hair cascaded over his forearms. This was the first time he had ever seen Mary Elizabeth with her hair down. He gently pulled the snagged strands out of the bush, then slid his fingers through her hair and turned her face toward his.

"My love," he whispered hoarsely, "please marry me."

KIRIA HAD finished searching the ground floor of the main building and was just starting up the central staircase when she heard Meeta screaming. She raced through the building and out the back door to see Raj and Mary Elizabeth walking toward the hostel from the back of the grounds. Raj carried Meeta, his head leaned as far as possible away from the child's enraged fists.

Kiria ran toward them. "Where was she? Is she all right?"

At the sound of Kiria's voice Meeta twisted around in Raj's arms and stretched out little starfish hands. "Keera! Keera!" she wailed.

"She's fine. We found her trying to climb into the well." Raj handed over the child with relief.

Kiria hugged Meeta fiercely. Meeta buried her face in Kiria's neck, her small body heaving with sobs.

"Okay, it's okay," Kiria whispered, patting the girl's back. "She must still be looking for Gowrie. I'm going to take her home. Can you find us an auto, Raj?"

"I'll drive you. I'm taking Mary Elizabeth home. I'll drop you on the way."

Meeta calmed down in the car and fell asleep in Kiria's arms. Kiria stroked the stubble on the child's head. "Raj, I'm going to adopt Meeta. Can you recommend anyone to help me?"

"I'm sure it can be arranged. It may take time, though. Adoption is not common." He met Kiria's eyes in the rearview mirror. "Are you sure you want to do this?"

"Very," she said simply.

When they pulled up outside the apartment, Kiria climbed awkwardly out of the backseat with the sleeping child in her arms. She leaned down beside the driver's window. "Thank you again. Both of you." She looked past Raj at Mary Elizabeth in the passenger seat. "You look lovely with your hair down, Mary Elizabeth." She turned and carried the sleeping child through the gate to Venu's house.

"I agree with her." Raj reached out and coiled a lock of his fiancée's hair around his fingers. "But perhaps it would be best to tidy up before you introduce me to your family."

Old News

❁ ❁ ❁ ❁ ❁

RAHUL AND SEKAR EMERGED FROM the Madurai Silk Emporium into the noon sun. Putting on their sunglasses, they walked down the stairs to the street, where Rahul lit a cigarette.

"How long does it take to choose a sari?" Sekar complained.

"This is your sister's wedding sari," Rahul said. "Be grateful the boy's father didn't insist we go to the weavers in Kanchipuram."

Sekar's lips pushed out in a childish pout. "But I want my lunch."

Rahul pulled a ten-rupee note out of his shirt pocket and pointed to a boiled-peanut vendor's cart a few yards away. "Get yourself some peanuts. We will eat lunch as soon as they have finished."

Watching Sekar strut off to the vendor's cart, Rahul reflected with annoyance that if the boy had the brains of a mango, they wouldn't be standing here at all. Half of the family's money was now being thrown away to buy security for Sekar's sister. It took a large amount of dowry to convince even a corrupt policeman that the illegitimate daughter of a brothel owner would make a suitable bride for his grandson.

For Sekar himself, the future was less certain. Limited intelligence made him an excellent enforcer. He lacked the imagination to empathize with his victims. But he had no other skills and he certainly did not have the ability to run the family business.

The fact that Sekar was not related to Rahul in any way did not change his sense of obligation. Everything he had he owed to Sekar's mother. They had started out with less than nothing, two orphaned children scrambling to survive on the streets. It was Vanaja's cleverness and ambition that had created their little empire of beggars and, later on, the more profitable brothels. Rahul's contribution had been as the front man, the enactor of her ideas in a male-dominated world. If she was determined that her children would have a better life than hers, who could blame her?

Sekar returned, carrying a newspaper cone filled with boiled nuts. "Do you want some, Uncle?"

Rahul reached out. His hand froze just above the hot peanuts. Grabbing the paper cone out of Sekar's hand, he shook it open, flinging peanuts in a wide arc onto the street.

"Hey! My peanuts!" Sekar exclaimed as two street dogs got up and began dodging through traffic to gulp down the windfall.

Rahul smoothed the paper between his hands and stared down at Santoshi's face. He handed the paper to his nephew, who had been educated in English.

"Tell me what this says," he ordered, pointing to the line of text below Santoshi's picture.

Sekar squinted down at the stained paper. "It says, 'Wanted in connection with an investigation into.' "

"Into what?" Rahul demanded.

"I don't know, Uncle. The page is torn off." Sekar handed the paper back.

Rahul strode over to the peanut vendor, and grabbed up the newspaper lying on the cart. He matched the stained wrapper to the torn page from the newspaper. It was an old copy of the Chennai edition of the *Hindu*.

"Where is the rest of this page?" he barked at the peanut vendor.

Unimpressed, the man shrugged and flapped his hand at the crowd on the street.

For a moment Rahul considered trying to find the missing piece, but then realized that if Santoshi had been found, his tame police official would have warned him. He led Sekar back into the Silk Emporium and over to the counter where Vanaja and her daughter sat surrounded by mounds of rejected silk saris.

"Pick one," he ordered. "We are going home."

An hour later Rahul and Vanaja sat in the dining room of her lavish house, studying the contents of the bundle he had retrieved from the bus terminal: grayish undergarments, a threadbare nightdress and a white plastic purse holding a pen, a small notebook, a handkerchief and a pink plastic wallet. Vanaja flipped through the notebook, surprised that Santoshi could write. It was full of women's names, dates and cryptic notes. "Husband alcoholic." "Works in call center." "Takes money for sex." "Begging."

"I don't like this book," Vanaja said. "What is this? Blackmail?"

"If it is blackmail, why does she not approach us?" Rahul pointed to the greasy piece of newspaper with Santoshi's picture. "But perhaps that is why they are looking for her."

He opened the wallet. There was no money, but there was a folded paper. It was a partially filled-in rental application for the

New Beginnings Women's Hostel in Chennai. Santoshi had listed her profession as maid. She had applied for a single room.

"She has enough to afford this," he said, handing the page across the table.

Vanaja read the application carefully. She nodded at the meager pile of cloth on the floor. "True, but then she should have enough to afford decent clothes. Tell me again about seeing her at the bus station. You are sure she was afraid?"

"She was terrified. She ran the moment she saw me."

Although she did not understand the meaning of all this, Vanaja was inclined to be cautious. She could not afford to leave such a dangerous loose end dangling this close to the wedding. "We cannot take the risk. Even if the investigation is not about us, if they find her, she will lead them to us." Vanaja handed the paper back to Rahul. "She must never be found. Take Sekar."

Passage

❁ ❁ ❁ ❁ ❁

GEETA GAVE ONE LAST LOVING polish to the gold button in the center of her best offering plate and sat back contentedly to admire her work. She loved to polish the offering vessels. She loved to feel the weight of the solid silver in her hands and see the soft glow of it in the household shrine. This plate, simple and elegantly proportioned, had belonged to her husband's paternal grandmother. Through it, she felt like a conduit between the generations, custodian of the family's heart. One day, if Laxmi's child was a boy, this plate would be polished by his wife.

Until recently, Geeta had rarely been able to find the time to care for the family shrine properly. Now, with Laxmi's salary paying for two maids and a cook, the plates and vases glowed in the light of the scented oil lamps of the puja room, and fresh jasmine circled the bronze feet of Shiva and Ganesh and draped the pictures of Venu's parents and grandparents.

As she rose from her chair to return the vessel to its place, Geeta noticed the still-unfamiliar sense of lightness in her body.

She could not believe how quickly decades of chronic back pain had drained away following the arrival of the maids. Except for her knees, Geeta felt nearly as supple as the young bride who had come to this house so many years ago. She centered the plate in its proper position, lit the oil lamps and stood back to admire the effect. Movement in the corner of the ceiling caught her eye. Was that a cobweb?

Geeta picked up the chair and placed it in the doorway of the puja room. She grasped the back of the chair and placed her strong foot on the seat, intending to climb up and swat at the cobweb with the polishing cloth. Focused on the ceiling, she did not notice as she stepped on the hem of her sari. The shortened fabric arrested her movement when she straightened up, pulling her forward and off balance. She flung out her hand to catch herself on the doorjamb, but missed. Her head crashed into the wooden door, the chair toppled backward and Geeta landed on the floor in a crumpled heap.

FOR THE third time that day, Laxmi's ringing cell phone showed her home number. She rolled her eyes at Kiria, sitting on a chair directly under the fan and reviewing applications for office assistant.

"It's Geeta again." Laxmi checked her watch. "Almost lunchtime, she's probably calling to complain about the cook."

"Why doesn't she like the cook?" Kiria's question was prompted more by sympathy than curiosity. She knew there was nothing wrong with any of Laxmi's new house staff or Geeta would have fired them already. Geeta just needed more time to get used to being a woman of leisure.

"Probably because her meals taste better than Geeta's." Laxmi sighed and picked up the phone. She listened for a few moments, then stood up so abruptly her chair fell over behind her. "Is she awake?" Laxmi jerked open the lower desk drawer. "Where is Venu?" She pulled her purse out of the drawer and strode toward the office door. "Well, wake him up. Tell him to call an ambulance. I'll be there in fifteen minutes." At the doorway, she thumbed off the phone and looked at Kiria. "It's Geeta. She's fallen."

Still clutching the phone, Laxmi reached down, lifted the skirt of her sari and ran across the compound to the gate.

LAXMI STOOD in the doorway of the back bedroom and studied her mother-in-law. Geeta sat propped up against the headboard of the guest bed, still wearing the blood-splashed sari she had fallen in. Her calloused hands picked at the sheet covering her legs. The white bandage glowed smooth and stark against her dark, furrowed forehead. Her eyelids drooped.

"The doctor says you cannot sleep yet." Laxmi entered the room and put the tray she was carrying down on the bed. "I've brought you some tea. It will help you stay awake."

"I am fine," Geeta snapped. "It's just a bump."

"The doctor said it might be concussion." Laxmi sat down on the edge of the bed and held out the metal beaker of hot sweet tea.

"Why is it in a metal cup? Where is my china cup? Are you afraid I will drop it?"

Laxmi smiled with relief at this typical response. "I just picked up the first cup," she lied. "Would you like your china cup?"

"No." Geeta reached out for the tea. "I am a bit dizzy. I might drop it." She took two sips and rested the beaker on her thigh. "Where is Mani?"

"He went out with his friends." Laxmi pretended not to notice the downward slant of her mother-in-law's mouth. She knew exactly what Geeta was feeling.

Since she'd started work, Laxmi's life had expanded. She no longer needed her husband to escape from the drudgery of housework. Although she still felt affection for him as the father of her child, Laxmi had finally admitted to herself tonight, as she watched him climb on his motorcycle, that her husband was a very shallow man.

"I went to the hospital today too," Laxmi said, hoping to distract the older woman.

Geeta took the bait. "Is something wrong with the baby?"

"No. I went for tests. Everything is fine. Remember I told you about the sonogram? The pictures of the baby inside me? They took those pictures today."

Geeta, who had given birth eight times without going through any tests more advanced than blood pressure, snorted derisively. "Waste of money. You earn money and you think you can throw it away. You should be saving for your daughter's dowry."

Laxmi had not intended to tell her mother-in-law the results of the test. But watching Geeta's face collapse into its habitual sour wrinkles, she suddenly thought, Why not? There was nothing to gain by hiding the truth.

"I have the picture," Laxmi said. "Would you like to see the first picture of your grandchild?"

Geeta looked down into her tea. "Yes," she said, almost reluctantly.

Laxmi left the room, returning a few minutes later with a blurry black-and-white picture. She sat beside her mother-in-law and leaned against the headboard.

"This is the head." Laxmi pointed to the round curve of the baby's skull. "Those dots like little pearls are the spine."

Geeta leaned away from the picture to improve her focus and studied it carefully. "This is a foot?" she asked, her withered finger touching a strange lump beside the baby's ear.

"Yes. And this"—Laxmi indicated a small protrusion below the spine—"is how we know you have a grandson."

Geeta slowly bent her head. She sighed hugely from the bottom of her chest. "My grandson," she whispered.

A warm tear splashed down on the back of Laxmi's hand, then another. She sat very still while Geeta's tears rained like blessings on her skin. When they stopped, Geeta picked up a corner of the bedsheet.

"You are the mother of a son now," she said in a matter-of-fact tone as she carefully dried first the picture and then Laxmi's hand. "It is time you took some responsibility in this family. It is difficult for me to read the numbers in the account books. From now on, you will be responsible for the house money."

Laxmi hid her surprise. "Yes, Mother."

"And I am too old to be chasing after servants all day. You must deal with them."

"Yes, Mother," Laxmi repeated. "I promise you I will take good care of our home," she added to show that she understood Geeta's meaning.

Geeta grasped Laxmi's long delicate fingers and looked up. For a long minute the two women stared into each other's eyes. Then, still holding hands, they leaned back against the headboard together and looked down at the tiny perfection of their common hope while power in the family passed silently to the next generation.

Making New Friends

RIK SLAPPED AT A MOSQUITO on the back of Theo's neck. "Should have packed some insect repellent in the carry-on."

"Good thing we started the antimalarials," Theo scratched absently at a swelling mosquito bite on his forearm while keeping his eyes fixed on the entry chute for the baggage carousel assigned to their flight.

At three a.m., the baggage claim area of the Chennai airport was a heaving mass of travelers, shouting and grunting as they pulled ancient suitcases and oversized boxes from overflowing conveyor belts. Theo and Rik, tall and pale as two lighthouses in a sea of dark heads, stood slightly back from the press of sweating bodies around the belts. Beside them, an exhausted woman in a wrinkled sari clutched an infant to her chest with one hand and the arm of a shrieking toddler with the other.

Rik nodded down at the screaming child. "I know exactly how that kid feels." After twenty-six hours of traveling, more than half of it spent crammed into economy seats, both men were tired and stiff.

"Doesn't anyone in this country travel light?" Theo asked as a huge suitcase held together with fraying ropes slid down the entry chute and knocked an equally large box off the conveyor belt.

"They probably paid more for excess baggage than they did for their seats." Rik pointed to a small hunter green suitcase emerging from the chute. "There's yours."

Theo pushed through the crowds. As he reached the carousel, a chubby, elderly man in a sweat-soaked shirt reached out to tug ineffectually at a battered metal trunk. Beside him, a young man caught Theo's eye and tipped his head in a silent question. Theo nodded. Together they each grabbed one end of the trunk, heaved it off the belt and set it down on the baggage cart behind the old man, who said something in Tamil. Assuming he'd been thanked, Theo turned his attention back to the carousel.

"Sir," the young man said, "Uncle has invited you to his house for dinner tonight."

Theo tried to refuse gracefully. "That's very kind, but I'm afraid it's not . . ." He broke off and leaned over to snag his suitcase. By the time he straightened up, the two Indian men were engaged in a lively discussion.

"There is no need to be afraid," the young man translated for Theo. "Uncle says his wife is a very good cook."

"I'm sure she is. . . ."

"Theo!" Rik's voice carried over the crowd. Theo turned to see Rik pointing at the chute, then turned back just in time to see Rik's small gray suitcase disappear under an enormous canvas duffel bag.

"Fantastic," Theo muttered.

He watched the bag glide slowly along the belt, hoping someone would claim it before it reached him. No one did. He'd just decided it was better to let the suitcase pass than try to excavate it, when the young man broke off his discussion with the old man, reached out and heaved the duffel bag off the belt. Theo snatched up Rik's suitcase, picked up his own and headed back to where Rik was standing. The old man followed him, chattering away in Tamil as he pushed his baggage cart.

"Who's this?" Rik asked as he took his suitcase from Theo and extended the handle.

"No idea. He invited us to dinner."

"Invited us to dysentery more like it. You didn't accept, right?"

"Can't. I don't speak the language." Theo pulled out the handle of his suitcase. "Let's go over there and dig out the mosquito repellent before I'm sucked dry."

They moved to a less crowded corner of the room. The old man followed along behind them. Rik crouched down to open his suitcase while Theo shrugged and shook his head at the old man, who smiled broadly and continued talking.

Rik held up a bottle of repellent. "Tenacious, isn't he?"

When sufficient insect protection had been applied, Rik and Theo made their way to the exit, followed by their self-appointed, one-man entourage. They walked out of the airport into a wall of humid heat. In front of them a horde of people pressed against a waist-high metal barrier, shouting and waving greetings to the travelers. The barrier extended along the side of the building, creating a narrow walkway. Blazing white smiles lit up the darkness as Rik and Theo shuffled along in the slow conga line making its way toward the end of the metal partition. Heads turned to follow their progress.

"Kind of makes you feel like a zoo exhibit, doesn't it?" Rik said.

"Or a freak. I assume it's because we're so much taller than they are." Theo scanned the crowd. "Do you see her?"

"Not yet," Rick replied.

Behind them, the old man called out to an immense woman in a flowered sari on the other side of the barrier. Theo and Rik ignored him and kept scanning the crowd, but by the time they arrived at the end of the barrier, there was still no sign of Kiria. Around them, returning travelers were fanning out to be welcomed home by greeting committees of crying women and shouting men. They walked out into the parking lot to get away from the press of bodies behind them. The old man stayed with them.

"Where do you suppose she is?" Theo asked, looking out over the dark parking lot.

"She's right behind you," Kiria answered.

The two men turned and stared at her in surprise.

"I was up by the exit doors," Kiria continued, "but I guess you didn't recognize me. I've lost a little weight."

This was an understatement. She looked nothing like the sleek, plump woman Theo had seen in Toronto. She wore a sari, wrapped tightly around her slender body. The face that had once been soft and pink was now tanned and angular, the pale gray eyes set deeper into their sockets. Theo suddenly realized he had no idea how to greet her. A handshake seemed too formal, a hug too personal. His mind went blank. He had no idea what to say.

Kiria also seemed to be at a loss as she looked up into her son's face. Then she smiled and held out both hands toward him. He took them in his much larger ones and smiled back at her. They stood motionless for a time, while their smiles widened into grins.

"Welcome to India, Theo," Kiria said finally. "I'm so glad you came."

Theo felt the tension in his shoulders dissipate. "I am too."

She squeezed his hands slightly before letting go. "And you must be Rik." She turned to Rik and extended her hand.

He clasped it in both of his. "A handshake will do for now, but eventually I'll want a hug."

"Rik!" Theo exclaimed.

"What?" Rik replied. "She's family."

"He's affectionate," Theo told Kiria. "You'll just have to get used to him."

Kiria laughed. "I don't think it will be difficult." She gestured toward the old man, who had been joined by four other people, one of them the woman in the flowered sari he had called to across the barrier. "Do you know these people?"

Annoyance briefly replaced fatigue on Theo's face. "I helped lift his trunk onto his baggage cart. Apparently that makes us best friends. I'm told he invited me to dinner."

"I'll handle it." Kiria smiled politely at the old man and began speaking in Tamil. They conversed for several minutes; then the old man reached out to shake Theo's hand before pushing his cart off into the parking lot with his entourage trailing behind him.

"That was Mr. Subhramanian and his family," Kiria said as she led them in the opposite direction. "He wants to thank you for helping him and hopes that you enjoy your visit to India."

"And dinner?" Theo asked.

Kiria sighed in a pretense of regret. "Unfortunately you have recently been ill and will require a special diet while you are here."

Rik laughed. "He bought that?"

"Who knows?" Kiria shrugged. "It's better than telling him his wife's cooking could make you ill."

"So does this happen often? Total strangers inviting you to dinner?" Theo asked.

"Surprisingly often. I accepted a few, once I figured out how to eat safely. I was always the only one eating and the entire neighborhood came in to watch me. I think having a white person to dinner gives them status with the neighbors." Kiria scanned the parking lot and made a slight course correction. "I hired a car to get us back to the apartment. It's just over there." She pointed to a large white vehicle with a high domed roof and rounded fenders.

"That car!" Theo exclaimed. "It must be sixty years old!"

"Could be; they're remarkably durable. But the design hasn't changed in fifty years, so it's just as likely to be brand-new. It's called an Ambassador. They're made here."

As they approached the car, the passenger door opened and the driver, a short man in a white uniform, got out. The roof light came on inside the car, revealing a bald child in a yellow dress standing on the driver's seat, pretending to steer the car.

Kiria sighed. "Oh dear. I couldn't find a babysitter. I was hoping Meeta would stay asleep. Now she'll be up for the rest of the night."

While the driver helped Rik and Theo store their suitcases in the trunk, Kiria retrieved Meeta from behind the wheel. The child wrapped her arms around Kiria's neck and babbled away in Tamil as Kiria carried her over to make introductions.

"This is Meeta." Kiria switched languages to introduce Theo and Rik.

Theo and Rik both smiled. Rik wiggled his fingers.

Meeta stared solemnly at the two men for a few moments, then hid her face in Kiria's neck and whispered something that made Kiria chuckle before she whispered something back.

"Is she shy?" Theo asked.

"Not really," Kiria told him. "She thinks Rik looks like the god Krishna in her picture book. She wanted to know why his skin isn't blue like it is in the book."

Kiria sat with Meeta in the front seat beside the driver, while Rik and Theo climbed into the backseat. Before the driver could turn the key in the ignition, Meeta wriggled out of Kiria's arms, scrambled over the back of the front seat and climbed up to stand between Theo and Rik. She reached out and gently touched the blond stubble on Theo's cheek. She did the same to Rik, then leaned against him and spoke. Kiria and the driver laughed.

"She wants to know if it's prickly on the inside as well," Kiria translated.

Meeta's relentless interrogation kept everyone amused on the trip back to Perambur and by the time the car pulled up outside the gates of Venu's house, Theo and Kiria had somehow passed through the awkwardness of their first real meeting. As soon as they were out of the car, Meeta took Rik's hand in both of hers and tugged him toward the staircase that led to Kiria's apartment.

"Well, I think Rik's made a conquest there," Kiria said to Theo as she paid the driver.

"So has Meeta. She's adorable." Theo picked up the suitcases and followed Kiria up the uneven stairs. He didn't know what the next three weeks would be like, but with Meeta around, they certainly wouldn't be dull.

Hostage

❁ ❁ ❁ ❁ ❁

WHERE DO YOU DRAW THE line between brave and reckless? Having, as I do, a defective little voice, I tend to draw my line well inside the safe zone. Unless I get angry. When I'm angry . . . well, judge for yourself.

After a few months of trading e-mail with my son, he and his partner, Rik, had decided to come to India on vacation. I'd picked them up at the airport a few hours earlier and brought Meeta over to the hostel day care to give them a chance to rest up after the trip. Despite having lived in the city for over six months, I'd never done any sightseeing, so Laxmi was giving me a crash course in Chennai's tourist attractions while we sat on the rim of the fountain, watching the children in the playground. In the middle of describing the shore temple at Mahabalipuram, she suddenly shrieked out, "Aiee! It's Shah Rukh Khan."

Six months before, this would have meant nothing to me. But during construction there were endless debates among the women laborers to determine the sexiest Bollywood movie star.

The two front-runners were Hrithik Roshan and Shah Rukh Khan. I Googled them both. It was close, but after extensive study, Hrithik won the eye candy contest by Shah Rukh's nose.

When Laxmi exclaimed, I looked around and saw a young man standing just inside the compound gate. She was right—he could have been Shah Rukh's baby brother, and he obviously knew it. Now, I know all about not judging a book by its cover, but this guy was a comic book. He wore a tight sleeveless T-shirt to show off his delts and abs, tight jeans to show off his glutes and quads, and shitkicker cowboy boots to show off his intellect. Only an idiot or a masochist wears cowboy boots in a tropical country.

He saw us by the fountain and sauntered over, hips shot forward and shoulders pumping, presumably for Laxmi's benefit. Stopping in front of us, just close enough to push his pelvis gently into my personal space, he asked in heavily accented English if Santoshi lived here. Even if I'd liked him, which I didn't, I wasn't about to let him run loose in a women's hostel. I asked for his name and sent one of the children off to tell Santoshi that Sekar was here to see her.

I invited him into the office to wait. He balked at the invitation, as though he couldn't decide if it was a good thing or a bad thing. Inside the office he slouched in a chair and pretended to look around. But he overdid the slouch, swiveled his head too fast and kept his sunglasses on. He was nervous about something.

Partly because I thought a little conversation might help him relax and partly because I really wanted to know, I asked him why he wanted to see Santoshi. Now, I'd already figured out he wasn't the sharpest tool in the shed, but the length of time between my question and his response put him in the blunt-object category. When it finally came, his answer raised the hair all over my body.

"I am coming from her father. I am taking her home."

In my best dithery old-lady voice I asked if there was a problem.

"He being sick. Needs daughter."

That did it. I took two steps through the door, swung it shut, shot the outside dead bolt, hooked in the padlock and snapped it closed. Whatever reason Wonder Boy had for lying, he could tell it to the police.

As I walked back toward the main building to find a phone, mine being locked in the office, Santoshi came out the front door of the main building with Mary Elizabeth. We met at the fountain, where Laxmi was still sitting with her mouth open.

I told them what Sekar had told me. We all knew Santoshi's father was dead. She said she didn't know anyone named Sekar. As I described him to her, Santoshi's eyes expanded in an expression that looked inexplicably like fear, but before I could ask her about it, a child's shrill scream ripped across the compound.

We all turned and looked back at the office. With his arms protruding between the iron bars covering the office window, Sekar was holding Meeta by the shoulder. He had a small handgun pressed to her temple.

Isaac Asimov, a personal hero of mine, once wrote that violence is the last refuge of the incompetent. In Sekar's case, it was more like a first option. Releasing a hostage requires considerable planning if the hostage is going to survive. Sekar hadn't planned to take a hostage in the first place and he certainly wasn't going to come up with some genius plan to release one. He'd taken Meeta in front of eyewitnesses and although he hadn't figured it out yet, he had nothing to negotiate for.

You'd never guess it to look at me now, but I have personal experience with violence. In my opinion, once threats are on the table, injury is unavoidable. The trick is to make sure most of the damage is done to the other person. This is less difficult than it sounds, because Isaac was right. With the exception of serial killers, people who use violence are fairly easy to manipulate. They are either abysmally stupid or, at least temporarily, mentally incapacitated.

If he'd just sat still, Sekar would have walked out of that office. Now he was going to be carried out, preferably dead, but I was willing to settle for severely injured. Fortunately he had a gun. That made taking him down much easier.

Bad Advice

❁ ❁ ❁ ❁ ❁

IT TOOK SEKAR A FEW seconds to translate the *slam-thunk-snap* sounds into the realization that he was locked in the office. He was confused but not really concerned. How did that old woman know? She looked like she was buying the story, and then she locked him in.

He pulled up the right leg of his jeans and pulled his small revolver out of the boot holster. As he rose from the chair, he noticed the old woman's purse sitting on the desk. Might as well make a profit, he thought, opening her purse and extracting the cash and credit cards from her wallet. Then he went to the window to look for someone to threaten into letting him out.

When the little girl walked by under the window, Sekar saw his opportunity. He grabbed the girl's shoulder with his left hand and pushed the gun against her temple with his right. The girl screamed once. She was small, forcing him to hold his arms bent awkwardly through the window bars.

Four women and a cluster of children stood still and silent in the compound, staring at Sekar and his hostage. The old white woman slowly raised her hands palms out.

"Okay! Okay!" the old woman called out. "What do you want?"

Sekar didn't know. This was supposed to be an easy job, just take the Santoshi woman away. He thought it through. These were just women. The white woman seemed to be the one in charge and she wasn't much of a threat. No one was going to do anything to him. All he had to do was get the door unlocked and keep them covered with the gun while he walked out the gate. He'd handle Santoshi later. Pick her up on the street or something.

"Open door!" he yelled at the white woman.

She nodded. "Okay."

She took two slow steps toward him, then stopped. "Too many people here. Too many to watch. Let these women and children go back into the building."

Sekar considered it. She was right. It would be easier to keep an eye on just one person.

"Okay," he called back.

Keeping her hands elevated, the old woman turned and said something to the group in a low voice. The tall woman said something back. The small woman said something. They seemed to argue for a minute; then the old woman said loudly, "Shut up. Just go!"

The tall woman put her arm around the pretty woman and led her to the main building. The small woman stood her ground, staring up into the old woman's face as though to continue the argument. Sekar was just about to shout at them when the small woman nodded once, folded her hands at her waist and trotted off after the other two women.

The old woman waited until they had all disappeared into the main building before she turned, hands still raised, and walked toward the gatehouse. She stopped a few feet in front of the window, looked down at the child and back up at Sekar.

"How do we do this?" she asked.

Her strange light eyes held his. Her face was expressionless. He noticed that without a smile her jaw had deep lines curving down from the corners of her mouth.

"Open door," Sekar said. "Or I am killing child."

"That's not what I mean. Look at your arms." She illustrated her next words with gestures. "When I unlock the door, you must pull your arms through the bars and cross the room. You won't be able to see anything. The door opens outward. I can shut it while you cross the room."

She spoke slowly and clearly. Her voice was totally uninflected and her colorless eyes remained fixed on Sekar's while she spoke. For the first time it occurred to him that this woman could be a minor threat. After a moment's consideration he decided the child was a better hostage at a distance.

"Go stand over there," he said in Tamil and released the girl's shoulder. The child collapsed to the ground under the window, out of range of the gun. Sekar instantly trained the gun on the woman.

"Pick up," he ordered.

"She's fainted." The old woman's eyes lost focus for a second; then she nodded slightly. "Can you see the doorway from there?" She waved her hand to keep his attention focused. He leaned his head against the bars. He could just make out the handle of the door. "Yes."

Continuing to gesture as she talked, the woman said: "You

watch me unlock the door. I pull it open. You watch me walk over there." She pointed to a coconut palm fifty feet to the right of the gatehouse. "You cross the room and go out the door and go out the gate. I'm far away. I can't stop you."

Sekar considered the plan. The compound was now empty. He had only a few yards to go to the gate. The door was too far from the window for her to leap in and cross the room before he could pull his arm back in. There was no way anyone could be standing behind the door. He couldn't see anything wrong with the plan.

"Why you help?"

"Because the longer we stand here, the more chance of me getting hurt. You have a better idea, we'll do that."

He didn't have a better idea. He pressed his head against the window bars, pointing the gun at her chest.

"Okay. Open door."

"Good. Now, the key is hanging on a hook behind this shutter." She touched the shutter on his left. "You point the gun at my body, below the shutter. I'll pull the shutter toward me and lean in to get the key. Okay?"

Sekar pictured it in his head. The bottom of the shutter would be just above her waist. Plenty of target still available. He lowered the muzzle of the gun slightly. "Okay."

She pulled the shutter slowly away from the wall. "I'm leaning in now. Got it!" she said loudly.

Despite his lack of mental acuity, Sekar had excellent reflexes. In the split second between his brain registering the shutter flying toward him and both shutters slamming closed on his arm, he managed to get off a shot.

He heard the double crack of the bones in his forearm. When the pain came, he screamed. Then he fainted. His body hung limply from the broken arm caught between the shutters and the iron grillwork.

RAHUL WAS standing in front of the coffee stall just outside the hostel gate sipping his third coffee. What was taking Sekar so long? He should have come out with Santoshi long ago.

The sharp sound of a gunshot came from the compound, immediately followed by a man's scream. Rahul casually joined the people clustering to peer into the compound through the gate. He saw a white woman lying facedown on the ground in front of the gatehouse. Blood covered her lower body, obviously the result of the gunshot. He recognized Santoshi, crouched over the woman crying "Kiria Madam! Kiria Madam!" over and over. A small child slumped unconscious against the wall under the gatehouse window. Rahul could see no sign of Sekar; then the arm dangling from the closed shutters caught his attention. Below the limp fingers, Sekar's handgun lay in the dirt. Although he could not quite figure out what had happened, Rahul strongly suspected Vanaja's idiot son had just shot a tourist.

There was no possible good outcome from being found with Sekar when the police came to investigate the murder of a white woman. There was little hope that the boy would be able to keep his mouth shut, and Rahul had no contacts with the police in Chennai. He could see no way to avoid at least a short time in prison if he stayed. The best thing to do was run.

By now the crowd around the gate had grown, pushing in for a better view. As Rahul turned to shove through the crowd, he heard a second high-pitched scream from the compound. He glanced back and saw Santoshi, sari skirt held high in her bloody hands, face contorted in a rictus of rage, running directly toward him.

"You sent him!" Santoshi screamed. "You sent him to kill me!"

Rahul panicked. He pushed hard against the crowd, hitting out with his fists and elbows. The people reacted sluggishly at first, then parted suddenly in front of him. He stumbled out of the crowd and directly into the path of the 179B bus.

Drugs, Good

THE FIRST TIME KIRIA WOKE up in the hospital, Rik was sitting in the chair beside her bed. Meeta lay asleep on his lap, her bald head cradled in the crook of his arm.

"Meeta," Kiria croaked, and collapsed back into unconsciousness.

THE SECOND time Kiria woke up in the hospital, Santoshi was sitting in the chair, glasses perched at the end of her nose, a book open on her lap. This time Kiria managed to stay awake.

"Santoshi?"

"Kiria Madam!"

The book fell to the floor as Santoshi rose. Relief surged through her little body. Tears flooded her eyes. She reached out and took Kiria's right hand.

"Santoshi? Are you okay? What's wrong?"

"I happy." Santoshi sniffed loudly and wiped her face with the pallu of her sari.

"Fooled me. Why am I lying on my stomach?"

"Bottom shot, Kiria Madam."

"Bottom what?" Kiria freed her hand, placed it palm down on the bed and started to lever herself up. "Holy shit!" she screamed, and flopped back down on her face.

"I get doctor." Santoshi trotted from the room.

Kiria's pelvis felt like someone had driven a spike through it. Waves of pain spasmed down her left leg. Her pulse hammered into the back of her skull. Sweat soaked her body. As she lay panting and fighting nausea, memory started to come back. The man, the gun. "Meeta!" she cried out, then finally understanding Santoshi's words, "Oh my God, I've been shot in the ass!"

"Yes, you were shot." The paunch of a man in a white coat entered Kiria's line of sight. He lifted her right eyelid with his thumb and peered into her eye. "How are you feeling?"

"Horrible. Who are you?"

"My name is Dr. Mohan. I'm your surgeon." He checked her left eye, then looked up at something over the bed. "You are feeling postoperative traumatic pain. It should pass in a few days." He sat in the chair beside the bed, bringing his plump face to Kiria's level. "Your vital signs are good. I have ordered a PCA. The nurse will be here with it shortly."

"What's a PCA?" Kiria struggled to stay focused in spite of the pain.

"Patient-controlled analgesic," the doctor replied.

"Drugs. Good," Kiria gasped. "How is Meeta?"

"Meeta good, Kiria Madam." Santoshi moved from her position by the door to stand behind the surgeon. "She with you son."

Kiria squeezed her eyes shut and waited for the spasm of pain to pass. "This is worse than childbirth. How long have I been here?"

"You were brought in two days ago," Dr. Mohan said. "You were in surgery most of yesterday. We kept you sedated last night to minimize movement."

A nurse entered the room carrying a rectangular metal tray. She moved to the other side of the bed. Kiria tried to turn her head, but a dark wave passed over her vision and she gave it up.

"What's she doing?" she asked.

"She is attaching the PCA device to your shunt." Dr. Mohan reached across Kiria and picked up a short white cylinder with a blue button on one end. He held it directly in front of Kiria's face. "This is the PCA control. Pressing this button will release a small dose of opiate into your system." He looked over at the nurse, nodded, then pressed the button. "That was your primer dose. When you feel pain again, press the button." He put the cylinder into Kiria's hand and wrapped her fingers around it.

After a few seconds Kiria's eyes closed. "Oh thank God. Oh that's good. What is it?"

"Morphine," Dr. Mohan replied.

KIRIA HAD been awake for four hours. Detective Krishnamoorthy now occupied the chair beside her bed, trying to extract a statement. His notebook was filled with cross-outs, and his hair stood on end from the number of times he'd passed his fingers through it in frustration.

"Mrs. Langdon. You say you heard the girl scream. You saw the man holding the girl."

"Meeta? She's very smart, you know." Kiria beamed at the policeman.

"How was he holding her?"

"Meeta?"

"Yes, how was he holding Meeta?"

Kiria waved her fist, still clutching the PCA cylinder. "With his hand." She peered at him intently. "Did you know your mustache is crooked?"

Krishnamoorthy reflexively stroked his mustache. "Which hand?"

"That's your right hand."

"No. His hand."

"Whose hand?"

"The man with the gun. Where was it on the girl's body?"

"Meeta? She's very—"

"Yes, Meeta." Detective Krishnamoorthy cut her off. "Where was it on Meeta's body?"

"It was pushed against her head."

"His hand was pushed against her head?"

"No, the gun was."

Suddenly, Kiria raised her head. "Mee-eee-taaa!" she warbled. "He just grabbed a girl named Mee-eee-taaa! And suddenly he found . . . he shouldn't mess around"—she spread her arms wide—"with MEEEEE!" Kiria flopped her face back into the pillow. "Ouch." She giggled and pressed the blue button.

Detective Krishnamoorthy, who had no acquaintance with Broadway musicals and if he had would not have recognized the tune of "Maria" from Kiria's off-key adaptation, pinched at the pain between his eyebrows. This could not be the same woman he had interviewed about the missing maid.

Attracted by the noise, Dr. Mohan entered the room.

"Doc!" Kiria shouted, waving the cylinder. "Baby! You were sooo right! This thing is awesome!"

Dr. Mohan crossed to Kiria's bedside in three quick strides.

"What's wrong with her?" the detective asked.

"I have to adjust her medication." Dr. Mohan jerked the PCA switch out of Kiria's hand. "Perhaps you should come back in a day or two," he advised, and began to check her vital signs.

NOT MUCH later Kiria was alone, loosely flapping her arms over the sides of the bed and mumbling new lyrics she'd just made up to a Queen tune.

"Got blood on my butt . . . Won't give up . . . Got to lock that"—she yawned and closed her eyes—"ba-a-a-stard up . . . We will . . . we will . . . kill you! . . . Yeah! . . . Kill you! . . . Yeah!"

She heard the door hinges squeak and raised an eyelid to see who had come in. "Meeta," she whispered, and fell asleep.

Rik shifted Meeta to his other shoulder and peered into her little face. "You have a very odd effect on her, sweetie."

In the Prone Position

AND ONCE YOU'VE DRAWN THIS imaginary line between brave and reckless, how do you know when you've crossed it? One really good indicator is finding yourself lying facedown on a hospital bed with hamburger where your rear end used to be.

My plan had been for Santoshi to sneak around the back of the office while I negotiated Meeta out of Sekar's hands. Then Santoshi and I would push the shutters closed to trap his arm, and I would pick up the gun, go into the office and "accidentally" shoot him in "self-defense." I had a bad moment when Meeta fainted, but she fell out of his range of fire.

Unfortunately, Sekar managed to get off one shot before the shutters trapped his arm. I'd flattened my body against the office wall as I pushed my shutter closed. If Santoshi hadn't been so strong, the two shutters would have hit his arm simultaneously and I'd have completed my plan to kill him. But Santoshi's shutter, traveling faster, hit his arm a fraction of a second before mine, deflecting the gun toward me, just enough to put a bullet through my left buttock.

The angle of entry was acute. A normal bullet would have passed through cleanly about an inch below the skin, barely a flesh wound. Sekar's soft-point bullet encountered enough resistance from my droopy flab to partially fragment, resulting in a twelve-hour operation to remove eight shards of lead from my gluteus maximus. Dr. Mohan, the serious young surgeon who patched me up, considered it a miracle that none of the fragments had severed a nerve, fractured a bone, nicked a major artery or punctured an intestine.

The police showed up to question me a few hours after I woke up. This would have gone a lot better if I hadn't been testing the limits of the morphine-on-demand button just before they arrived. Between Detective Krishnamoorthy's deficient sense of humor and my sudden compulsion to rewrite the lyrics of *West Side Story*, I was lucky not to be charged with attempted murder. Fortunately, or perhaps unfortunately—I can't really decide on this point—the doctor came in and took away my beautiful button, so I was able to give a judiciously edited account of events when the detective returned two days later. Raj's earlier intervention on our behalf with the Chennai Police probably didn't do me any damage either.

A week spent in an Indian hospital may be infinitely preferable to a life sentence in an Indian jail, which is probably where I'd have ended up if my plan to kill Sekar had succeeded, but that didn't make it any fun. There are very few entertainments suitable for a person whose face is planted in a pillow. Aside from my short-lived possession of the PCA, I'd have been terminally bored if it hadn't been for Theo, Rik and Meeta.

Poor Meeta. First her mother disappeared; then, just as she was starting to trust me, she got scared out of her wits by Sekar and I disappeared. At least she was unconscious when I got shot; I suppose that counts as a blessing. Theo and Rik took care of her while I was in the hospital. She developed an instant bond with Rik, who carried her around constantly. Mostly he carried her to the hospital, since she was much calmer when she could see me.

Rik is one of those well-adjusted people with a genuine "I'm okay, you're okay" attitude. He's warmhearted and broad-minded and more in touch with his feminine side than I'll ever be. It's impossible not to like him. He kept me amused with stories of his and Theo's life together and convinced the doctors that his nursing skills were more than up to the task of caring for me when I was released from hospital, so I didn't have to return for physiotherapy every couple of days.

Theo is a bit of a fusspot. He sat by my bed most afternoons and ranted about the traffic and the auto drivers, the dogs and the dung, the heat, the smell, the poverty and the beggars. He sounded just like I did when I first came to Chennai. He even tried to put Meeta in diapers with essentially the same results. Griping about India gave us a vast arena of common ground to begin our bonding.

Now, here's an interesting little tidbit. I was transported to the hospital in the same ambulance as a man who was hit by a bus just outside the compound gate shortly after the shooting. The side of his head was crushed. I could see fragments of his skull sticking into his brain. His breathing was irregular and I held my own breath every time he went into apnea. He was a prosperous-looking man. I remember studying his face, wondering about his family, what he did for a living. His breathing became gargling as fluid accumulated in his air passages. He died just as the ambulance pulled up at the hospital.

I told this story to Santoshi when she was visiting me one day in the hospital. Her eyes lost focus as I talked. I thought she was disturbed by my description of his death, and stopped speaking. She sat motionless and far away for a few seconds, then reached out for my hand.

"Kiria Madam," she said seriously, "I must go and come."

She got up and left the room. I thought she'd just remembered something she needed to do and would be back in a few minutes. I should have known better by then. She didn't come back for three days.

Instant Family

SANTOSHI SAT ACROSS FROM THE familiar staircase with her back to the wall. She had been sitting here since before dawn. No one had come for the children. She knew they were still in the room; she could hear them talking through the window above her head. It was almost noon now. No one would come today. It was time to go up.

As she climbed the crumbling concrete staircase, Santoshi reached out and touched the dense black band on the wall beside her, created by the handprints of many, many children. Underneath the sticky surface she knew her own handprints still remained. She felt almost as though they were welcoming her home.

At the top of the steps she placed the bags she carried on the landing and studied the padlocked door, wondering how she could ever have thought this door was meant to keep people out. She pulled a hammer and chisel from one of the bags and began knocking the pins out of the external hinges. As she worked, she thought about what she would find inside and how to deal with it.

The two older children would most likely be facing the door, each of them holding something as a weapon, probably the water jug and the slop bucket. The younger children would be standing behind. After days of abandonment they were hungry and thirsty. They would not attack her if they knew she had water and food.

When an inch of the pin remained in the bottom hinge, Santoshi stopped and took a large tin with a tight-fitting lid out of her other bag. She opened it to expose the lemon rice inside, then picked up the hammer and chisel again and struck the heavy metal of the hasp to weaken it before returning to knock the pin all the way out of the bottom hinge. She inserted the claw of the hammer into the crack of the door and began to pull.

Santoshi gagged at the smell of the hot air escaping from the room: sewage, overlaid by the sharp chemical smell of fasting remembered from her own childhood and, unexpectedly, the sweet tang of corruption.

"I have food," she called out, and slid the tin of lemon rice in front of the opening so the children could see it. She peered around the door.

The younger children were huddled in the corner of the room farthest from the door. There was only one defender, the tall boy. He held the slop bucket, one hand on the rim, the other under the base, ready to throw it. Flies swarmed around the bucket so thickly it was hard to see his arms.

"I have water too." Santoshi grunted as she pulled the door open wider.

"Who are you?" The tall boy stared at the tiffin tin but did not put down the bucket.

"I am Santoshi. I have come for you." The door was open wide enough now. She stood in the opening where they could see her.

"Did you buy us?" the boy asked.

"No. I do not own you. Rahul is dead. Is there anyone else?"

"Only Sekar."

"He is in jail."

The younger children pressed closer together. The boy narrowed his eyes to hide his fear. Santoshi knew they all were terrified of what would happen now that they had no protection.

"Eat," she said, sliding the tin into the room and placing a two-liter bottle of water beside it. "Eat slowly."

"We know." The boy put down the bucket and came forward cautiously. Santoshi backed away from the door. He picked up the food and water and walked backward to set it on the floor by the children. They each took a drink from the bottle and pulled a handful of rice from the tin. They put only a small amount in their mouths and chewed long and carefully before swallowing, pouring a trickle of water down their throats after each bite.

"Are you the father?" Santoshi asked the oldest boy.

He nodded.

She looked at the children squatting around the tin. "Who is your mother?"

The boy tilted his head toward the wall beside the broken door where a small bundle lay, covered in flies. Santoshi entered the room and waved off the flies. The light-skinned girl had been dead for at least two days. Her lower body was distended with gases. Santoshi could see no marks on the body.

"How did she die?" Santoshi asked.

"She had fever. Then her head hurt very badly. Then she died," the boy said flatly.

"What was her name?"

"Fatima," one of the girls said. "She was pretty."

"How did you know about us?" the tall boy asked.

"I lived here too. It was very long ago." Santoshi squatted

down near the children. This close she could see the lice in their eyebrows and hair. They probably had worms and fleas too. She sighed. Could she do this? Or should she go to the police?

Although they had taken only a handful of food each, the children soon stopped eating. A girl got up from the group to retrieve the lid of the tin and set it firmly in place before returning to huddle with the others on the floor. Looking at them as they leaned together for comfort, Santoshi realized they had been together a long time. They were a family.

"I must return to Chennai," she said. "If you want, you can come with me."

"Are the people in Chennai generous?" the boy with a clubfoot asked.

"If you come with me, you will not beg. You will go to school."

The children looked at one another but said nothing. How could they know if they could trust her?

Santoshi adjusted herself to sit tailor fashion on the floor. "Let me tell you about the time I was here. I was seven when I came to this room. I did not know how to beg. The father then was a boy named Ganesh. The mother was a girl named Revathy. They hid rice for me in their fists on days when I had no coins to give to Rahul."

Santoshi talked for a long time. She told them things they already knew: the best ways to make people give money; where the best hiding places were when the police came; how to pick a careless pocket. She showed them the games she'd played at night with her own family after Rahul had locked them in. She talked to them about the time when she was the mother, and gentle Nambi was the father. She pointed to the wall where the smudged drawing of a child's face with huge, beautiful eyes could still be made out. "That was me. Nambi drew it."

The old grief washed through her, surprisingly fierce in this room, where she and Nambi had once explored love. For just a moment she allowed herself to remember the feel of his lips on hers and his breath tickling her ear as they whispered together after the younger children had fallen asleep. Then she put it firmly out of her mind. Nambi was lost to her forever. Now these children needed her help.

"What is your good name?" she asked the tall boy.

"I am Manoj."

"That is a good name. If you stay here, Manoj, they all will stay. If you come with me, they will follow you. You must decide."

"Where will we live in Chennai? Will you give us to the police?"

"No. You will live with me. I have a room in a nice place, with good food every day. I have a provisions store. You will go to school."

"I am twelve. I am too old to go to school."

"Then I will teach you myself and you will go to school when you are ready."

The younger children watched the exchange in silence, knowing their lives were being decided here. Manoj looked at his family, then over to where Fatima's body lay against the wall. He wished she had not died. She would know what to do.

"I don't want to beg," the girl who had put the lid on the tiffin tin said suddenly. "I want a dress and a doll."

"I want a ball," a small boy piped up.

"I want to read," the boy with the clubfoot contributed. "If we go with her, maybe something bad will happen. But if we stay here, there is no one to protect us now. We should go with her."

Manoj looked at each child in turn and saw in their faces the hope he felt himself. "We will all come with you," he said.

Santoshi rose. "Then we must get you better clothes and clean you up. You cannot get on the bus to Chennai like this."

The children rose to follow her. The girl picked up the tiffin tin.

"Leave that," Santoshi ordered, remembering the filthy hands that had scooped through the rice. Perhaps Kiria Madam's obsession with soap and water was contagious. "I will buy you parottas and korma."

The children followed Santoshi out the door. Manoj stayed behind. Santoshi sent the children down to the alley and went back into the room where the boy squatted beside Fatima's body, his chest expanding and contracting with the effort not to cry.

"It is good to say good-bye," Santoshi said. "We will wait for you on the street."

A few minutes later, he came down the steps. Looking at the boy's bleak face and puffy eyes, Santoshi thought that he was still young. She had never found another, but perhaps, in time, he would.

She turned her back on the past and led Rahul's last family out into the bright sunlight of the street.

Sanctuary

❁ ❁ ❁ ❁ ❁

"GET OFF ME! I CAN do it myself."

"Kiria, you can't do it at all. Lie down." Rik pushed Kiria firmly back down on the bed. "You are just about the grumpiest patient I've ever had."

Lying on her side, with the flesh of her face sagging into the pillow, Kiria tried to reason with her son-in-law. "I can't lie here forever, Rik. I have to be on a plane next week."

"You'll have a gurney."

"I'm not being rolled onto the plane like a corpse!"

"I think that's enough melodrama for today." Rik's tone was friendly but final. He sat down on the edge of the bed. "What's really wrong here?"

Kiria squeezed her eyes shut to push back the tears. When she was certain she could speak normally, she said, "I want to pee. I want to sit on my own toilet, by myself, and pee. Alone," she finished redundantly just to be sure he got the point.

Rik smoothed down her short gray hair. "You will, dear. But

not today." He retrieved the bedpan from the bathroom and helped Kiria relieve herself.

Meeta, sitting on the floor of the bedroom, still trying to figure out how to get the shaped blocks into her sorter toy, stood up and said something.

"What did she say?" Rik asked.

"She wants to use the bedpan too," Kiria translated, hanging on to Rik's shoulders.

"Really?" Rik sounded hopeful. Like Kiria, he was tired of following Meeta around the apartment with a bucket. Unlike Kiria, he'd had no success at getting Meeta to use her potty.

"We've just started toilet training," Kiria said as Rik eased her back onto the bed. "I'm not sure if she's got the idea of independent elimination yet. We've only ever done it together." She settled back down on her right side while Rik took Meeta and the bedpan into the bathroom. Despite her bad mood, Kiria was grateful to Rik. Having a registered nurse as a houseguest was a decided advantage to a woman with half an ass.

"That was different." Rik came back into the bedroom, dripping wet.

"Oh, sorry. I forgot. Don't let her get her hands on the sprayer."

"I figured it out." Rik took a towel off the wall hook and began drying his hair.

"Where's Theo?" Kiria asked.

"He went over to Raj's office with Mary Elizabeth to pick up the adoption papers. Those two will use any excuse to see each other." Rik had quickly caught on to the big romance between Mary Elizabeth and Raj.

"This is nothing. They're out of the closet now."

"This is out of the closet?"

"You should have seen them a few months ago when we were looking for the hostel property."

"So, are they getting married?"

"They're engaged. It's complicated, though. Wrong religions, wrong castes. He's higher caste—that makes it a little easier. Her cousin is fighting it."

"You sound so . . . accepting of all this."

"It's the culture. They have to live in it. You probably got a few choice words from some people when you got married."

"More than a few." Rik suddenly remembered something. "Speaking of culture, why did Santoshi shave her head?"

"Hindus bargain for their blessings," Kiria explained. "She offered her hair to the gods for my health and gave it to them when she figured they'd kept up their end of the bargain."

Rik looked pointedly at Kiria's hip. "Pretty low standards."

Kiria shrugged. "For much of her life she probably defined healthy as still breathing. Did you see her or the kids when you were at the hostel yesterday?"

"Oh my God, those kids." Rik's dark eyes reflected his distress. "It's hard to believe we live on the same planet. How could anyone treat children that way? How can anyone let it happen?"

Kiria studied his appalled expression and decided it was time for some tough love of her own. "This is India, Rik. It's strange and exotic to you, and that makes it a little bit frightening. But if you look past the fear, you know this happens everywhere. You're adopting an abandoned child yourself. We don't know what would have happened to those children if Rahul hadn't bought them, or what would be happening to them now if Santoshi hadn't known how to find them. We can't judge."

"How did she find them?"

"She was one of Rahul's children herself."

"You're kidding. And she just . . ." Rik fell silent, too confused to know what he wanted to say.

"You mean, why didn't she tell the police about him?" Kiria asked. "I don't know. Mary Elizabeth thinks she was afraid of him, but my guess would be something like Stockholm syndrome. For years he was the only protection she had. Something like a father."

"A pretty abusive father."

"Not as bad as the one who sold her," Kiria pointed out.

"Well, she doesn't seem terribly broken up about his death either."

After talking with Santoshi the day before, Kiria felt that the tiny woman was far from objective about Rahul's death. Santoshi had sat by the bed, ears sticking out like fans from her skull, huge eyes hard, and spoke in cold, dry sentences about how she had found the children locked in the room where she had slept as a child. It was the same way she had looked and spoken about her time in her father's village. Closed. Secretive. Somehow satisfied.

"Santoshi doesn't show her emotions much," Kiria said, and left it at that.

After two weeks of caring for this woman, Rik knew she was hiding something. But he also knew it was none of his business and he could see she was tiring.

"How about a little physio, then a nap before lunch?" he suggested.

Kiria made a face of annoyance. "I hate physio. It hurts."

Rik knew better than to show sympathy. "Well, get used to it if you ever want to walk again."

He pulled the sheets off Kiria and began gently flexing her left leg. Kiria clenched her teeth and told herself that pain was her friend. Watching her face, Rik searched for something to distract her.

"Theo and I have been talking," he said, "and we were wondering if you and Meeta would like to stay with us for a while when we get back. We'll have the boys soon. One more kid won't even be noticed. You'd have to hire a nurse for yourself, though. We can't handle you and new kids. But you'd have had to do that anyway."

Unable to care for Meeta, Kiria had planned to hire a nanny until she could walk again, although she hated the idea of turning the toddler over to yet another stranger. A sense of warmth filled her chest. "Is your house carpeted?" she asked hoarsely.

Rik froze halfway through flexing Kiria's knee. "We hadn't thought of that." He straightened her leg, and put it down. "Tell you what. You can pay for the reflooring. I've always wanted hardwood."

"Deal," Kiria said quickly, before he could change his mind.

What Ever Happened To . . . ?

DO YOU EVER WONDER WHAT your obituary will say? I don't have to. I know what's in mine. The year I turned fifty, newspapers tactlessly started sending their file copies to NOVIO for pre-approval. Eva tells me they call every once in a while to see if I've done anything noteworthy. Until I went to India, I hadn't. But now I have something truly remarkable to tell the next reporter who calls.

The New Beginnings Hostel staggered to its financial feet a year after it opened, primarily thanks to Laxmi's ruthless budgeting. It is now fully occupied and, with the box stores, surprisingly profitable. Forty women and twenty-seven children have found freedom from the indignity of the shelters, and safety inside its gates from the dangers of the streets.

But Santoshi isn't one of them.

After she took on responsibility for Rahul's beggars, there was a time when it looked like Santoshi, struggling to establish her business and control six wild children, would lose everything.

Faced with the choice of raising the children or running the business, she chose the children. She became the warden of a small orphanage run by an American NGO.

Of course I was upset by this. All that work to build her a home and Santoshi just threw it away and went back to the shelters. When I asked her why she gave up her independence and ability to make choices, Santoshi looked confused. "But, Kiria Madam," she said, "this my choice. You teach. Best thing people helping." I didn't know whether to laugh or cry.

Although Santoshi and I will never be friends in the Western sense, we have a bond, based on mutual respect and trust and concern for each other's well-being, that is, in many ways, stronger than friendship. Santoshi came up with what I think is the best definition of our relationship. On one of my visits to the orphanage, she told me she had recently rejected an offer of marriage from the widower who owned the tailor's shop down the road. I asked if she didn't like him. She said she thought he was a good man, but did not want to leave her family.

"What family?" I asked.

She pointed toward the children playing outside her office window and said: "This family, Kiria Madam. Family of my heart."

Despite Santoshi's best efforts, Laxmi never acquired an aptitude for the domestic. Within six months of giving birth to little Venu, she was back in the office, saying there was no point in staying home any longer since her mother-in-law never let go of the baby. Geeta transferred all her affections from her narcoleptic husband and her disappointing son to her new grandson. She says she is determined that this time she will not make the same mistake she made raising Mani. There is hope that little Venu will not suffer from Center-of-the-Universe Syndrome when he grows up.

Laxmi fell out of love with her handsome husband. I think,

for a time, she considered leaving him. But in her heart she knows that the best place to raise her son is in the strength of her family. As the hostel finally began to make enough profit to pay decent bonuses, she bought Mani the car he always wanted. At first I thought she was trying to kill him, but as he continues to miraculously avoid the consequences of drinking and driving, I've concluded she did it mostly to get him out of the house. Big Venu is now down to less than ten waking hours a day, which he spends ordering the maids to make him tea and playing with his grandson.

Mary Elizabeth and Raj married three months after I left Chennai. I wanted to go back for the wedding, a Hindu temple ceremony, but walking was still a distant dream at the time. I sent them a nice silver platter. Mary Elizabeth's family protested vigorously at her conversion to Hinduism and cut her off. She took it philosophically, saying she hadn't expected them to behave any differently. Raj did not try to move his new bride in with his extended family. After parading wealthy Brahman spinsters in front of him for years with no success, they were even less supportive of the marriage than Mary Elizabeth's family. Raj bought a fine house for his lovely bride in Mylapore and eventually his family learned to tolerate her if not to accept her wholeheartedly.

Mary Elizabeth continues to help the women in the hostel. She has no need of money now and works as a volunteer. Although the fireworks of illicit romance soon died down in the realities of marriage, she seems to be happy with her choice, if uncontrollable smiling and constant references to "my husband" are anything to go by.

Meeta, although technically my adopted daughter, is being raised by Theo and Rik, who took care of her when I was in no shape to handle a two-year-old. By the time I felt ready to take her on, Meeta had worked the same magic on her brothers and nephews that enchanted me into adopting her in the first place, occupying the center of their family dynamic like a bossy little sun. I demoted myself to granny status and left her where she could do the most good.

Theo and I have built a relationship of sorts. It's tragically crippled, but as with all great art, it's the flaws that give it beauty. Credit for this goes primarily to Rik, whose endless ability to laugh at us kept Theo and me honest while we grew the scar tissue over our past. Rik moved out of ER and into geriatrics, where the hours are more predictable. He says I'll be grateful for this someday. I tell him I'll throw myself under a bus before subjecting myself to any more of his physiotherapy skills.

And me? It took a second operation and eight months of physiotherapy, but I finally got out of the wheelchair and off the crutches. I walk with a cane now. The doctors tell me this is as far as I'm going to get, given the amount of muscle tissue I lost. It slows me down a bit. Eva tells me this is a good thing.

While I was cursing my physiotherapist, Piet and Eva ran NOVIO and did a pretty good job of it, once they stopped trying to avoid each other and started dating. As soon as I was on my feet, I tried to go back to work, but I had lost my enthusiasm for games, electronic or otherwise. I made Piet and Eva managing directors and turned the day-to-day stuff over to them when I went back to India.

They say home is where the heart is, and I am in love. Here in India, amid the color and the contrast and the chaos, anything seems possible; any dream can come true. I'm working on mine. The New Beginnings II opens in three months—assuming I can find a reliable electrician.

People are always asking me why I came to India. I hate this. What am I supposed to say? I came to India to save a woman I felt sorry for? That's a laugh. It's pretty obvious who saved who.

Acknowledgments

When I completed the first draft of *Sisters of the Sari*, I knew it still had flaws but had no idea what they were or how to fix them. Fortunately, I am blessed with generous and supportive friends who volunteered to read the manuscript and share their thoughts. Without the insights and enthusiastic encouragement of Donna Gorgas, Rita Pogue, Shelley Kott, Inez Schmidt, Catriona Campbell, Ann Davies, Brigitta Mohlin, Clair Aghassipour, Sarah McElhone, Tanja Michelle, Dejan Djuric and Christopher Miller, this novel would never have found its way into the world. Special mention goes to my lifelong friend Wendy Djuric, who valiantly read through the manuscript several times, both as a beta reader and a copy editor, while I struggled through two more drafts.

At this point, I thought the novel was perfect. It wasn't. Luckily, one of the first agents I approached, the optimistic and charming April Eberhardt, of Kimberley Cameron and Associates, took it under her wing. With her tactful guidance, I produced yet another draft. With her enthusiastic support, this new, improved version of the manuscript found a home with Danielle Perez, executive editor at NAL. Danielle's brilliant editorial skills and dedication to quality helped me polish off the remaining rough edges and gave *Sisters of the Sari* its final form.

So although there is only one name on the cover of the book, inside are the ideas and expertise of many people. I am extremely grateful to them all.

Photo © 2010 Miranda Studios, Peterborough, Ontario

After thirty-five years working as a computer programmer in Canada, the U.S. and the Netherlands, **Brenda L. Baker** moved to India, where she volunteered, writing funding proposals and teaching English to women residing in two shelters. She now lives in Ontario, Canada. When she's not working on her second novel, she does volunteer work. Visit her Web site at www.brendalbaker.com.

CONVERSATION GUIDE

Sisters *of the* Sari

Brenda L. Baker

This Conversation Guide is intended to enrich the individual reading experience, as well as encourage us to explore these topics together—because books, and life, are meant for sharing.

AUTHOR'S NOTE

My initial impressions of India were formed when the Beatles brought sitars and transcendental meditation back from Rishikesh in 1968—a naive picture of a spiritual and enlightened country filled with revered cows and flowers. This idea stayed with me until 1980, when I briefly dated a Hindu man whose Punjabi parents had immigrated to Canada in the sixties. He was caught between the rigid traditionalism of his family and the self-focused "Me Decade" that dominated North American culture in the 1970s. Our relationship, which ended when he acquiesced to his family's insistence on an arranged marriage, caused me to modify my image of India. I kept the cows, flowers and spiritualism, but replaced enlightenment with reverence for tradition—a no less naive picture that lasted right up until I stepped off the plane at Annadurai International Airport in Chennai to attend the wedding of a friend in 2003.

I don't remember much about my first week in India. What I can recall is limited to a few surreal flashback images of chaotic traffic, ornate temples, encounters of the nasty kind with the ubiquitous cowpats and an overwhelming sense of relief when I collapsed into the safety of my air-conditioned hotel room every night.

By the beginning of my second week, I'd replaced my jeans

and T-shirts with the much more comfortable long dresses and baggy pants of churidars, learned to walk in traffic like any other self-respecting pedestrian and bought a bottle of bleach to cope with my sandals' uncanny attraction for manure. I abandoned organized tours to famous temples in favor of random rides in auto rickshaws and, once off the tour buses, I began to meet people. They approached me on trains, buses and street corners, initiating conversations with stilted phrases learned in school: "What is your good name, madam?" Or "Madam, how do you do today?" Our brands of English were usually too different to permit real communication, and most encounters ended when my new acquaintance would hand me a scrap of paper with an e-mail address or phone number, as though lack of a common language was no barrier to forming a lifelong friendship.

By the end of my third week, I was utterly enchanted by India. This was no country filled with stodgy traditionalists and spiritual ascetics. This was a gaudy, noisy, smelly, chaotic, exuberant celebration of life; a country where the bumper sticker most often seen on the back of vehicles as diverse as ox carts and city buses read PLEASE HONK HORN. The scent of incense, sandalwood, jasmine and spices permeated my clothes, which were now as sequin drenched and brightly colored as those of every other woman I passed on the streets. My last few days in India were spent, along with two thousand other guests, in glorious, glittering celebration of my friend's marriage.

My body returned to the West, but my heart never did. I talked a friend into a three-week luxury tour of south India in 2005, a fabulous adventure that was nothing like my first and far-less-opulent visit. After that, longing for India took over my life. So in 2007, I quit my job, sold my house and went back to Chennai with the intention of living there until I got India out of my system. To facilitate meeting people, I signed on for six months as a volunteer with a social services organization. Working with their women's empowerment programs, I saw a completely different India, terrible and beautiful and more compelling than anything I'd ever experienced.

The social workers gave me the task of teaching English to the residents of two shelters they ran for homeless women. Armed with a cracked blackboard and the translation services of a shelter resident who spoke an interesting variant of English, I gave it my best shot. Unfortunately, my translator was heavily medicated and kept falling asleep in class. When the novelty of English lessons degenerated into vocabulary lists and stilted conversation practice, most of my students lost interest in acquiring a language they would never have an opportunity to speak. I gave up teaching and went to work in the office, writing funding proposals and transcribing case histories for the social workers.

The lives of my ex-students were fascinating. Some came from impoverished backgrounds, others from wealth. Some had been rejected by their families; others were fleeing abusive families. They ran the gamut from illiterate to university educated and came from all castes and religions. A number of them had physical deformities. A few had been victims of human trafficking. What they all had in common, though, was a kind of rebellious courage, a determination to survive, to make a place for themselves in a society that had no place for them. I grew to admire my ex-students as much for their obstinacy as for their optimism. With the help of the social workers, I came to see my Western ideal of education and careers for women as a simplistic approach to a very complex problem. Whatever paths these women took in life would have to follow the contours of a social and economic landscape dominated by extended family, the one thing they did not have.

My six-month volunteering obligation was almost over but I wasn't ready to leave India. I'd made friends among the social workers and shelter residents. I'd also "gone native," trading in my churidars for more sensible and flattering saris, enjoying evening walks through my neighborhood, where I chatted with shopkeepers and bought ropes of heavenly night jasmine from little table stalls set up outside the gates of the local temple. I'd lost my fear of the feral dog packs that roamed the streets and the herd of tanklike water buffalo whose evening grazing route happened to be along the road to the Internet café. Best of all, I'd developed a sixth sense about cowpats and hadn't had to disinfect my sandals for weeks.

When a chance encounter in the grocery store led to an apartment located not far from the shelters, I decided to renew my visa for another six months and make myself a home. I wouldn't have lasted a week on my own without my landlady, the resourceful and generous Lalitha. She bullied the electricity board into upgrading service to the house so I could install an air conditioner. She found the carpenter who put screens on my windows and the maid who came by every second day to do my laundry. It was Lalitha who hooked me up with the Internet provider, the drinking-water man and the cable guy. She also fed me frequently, and over delicious home-cooked lunches at Lalitha's table I learned about the strength and stability of the traditional Indian extended family.

I was still putting in a few days a week with the social services organization. One of the problems they faced at the time was the impending loss of funding for one of the shelters. No one wanted to turn the residents out onto the street. The social workers attempted to find alternate housing for those women who had steady, low-paying jobs while I wrote proposals to various organizations, hoping to obtain subsidies that would allow the unfunded shelter to be converted into an inexpensive hostel for poor working women.

The idea for *Sisters of the Sari* grew out of the hostel proposals and some if-I-won-the-lottery fantasies I had while writing them. Many elements of the book are based on my own experiences; others are composites of stories told to me by friends and colleagues. Any errors in the portrayal of Indian culture are the result of my inability to correctly interpret these stories and in no way reflect upon the many wonderful people I worked and lived with during my stay in India.

My Western friends who reviewed the first draft of the novel had many questions about India. I incorporated the answers to most of them in subsequent drafts. Answers to a few of the questions didn't fit naturally into the story, so I will attempt to answer them here.

Cuisine

Nearly everyone wanted to know more about south Indian food. I considered testing some recipes to include in this section but my local Asian grocer doesn't carry all the ingredients and my Western kitchen is ill-equipped for tasks such as grinding lentils into paste. Well, that's the official excuse. The truth is I just dislike cooking.

CONVERSATION GUIDE

South Indian cuisine is nothing like the north Indian foods on offer in the West. The most noticeable differences are the delicacy of the spices and the generous use of coconut. Chipped or shredded or ground into a paste, coconut shows up in just about everything. Most gardens have a coconut palm or two, and most kitchens have a special device to grate coconut meat from the inside of the shell, and a flat stone and roller to mash coconut meat into a paste. Curry leaves are the dominant spice in nearly every dish. They have a pungent, slightly bitter taste and are said to aid digestion.

Breakfast is generally a small meal of dhosa (imagine a crepe) or idli (imagine a dumpling) or vadai (imagine a salty donut filled with peppercorns) which are all made from ground lentils and rice. They are served with creamy coconut sauce and thick, tangy tomato sauce called chutney. For a really fancy breakfast, dhosa is wrapped around spiced fried potatoes, which is then called rava dhosa.

The main meal of the day is lunch, which includes: rice, sambar (see next page), rassam (searingly hot pepper soup), curd (thin yogurt) and a small amount of spiced fried vegetables. Special-occasion lunches will have two or more types of spiced fried vegetables, a banana, apadam (paper-thin, crispy-fried crackers) and barfi (a delicious but unfortunately named sweet made from solidified condensed milk). Nonvegetarians add a chicken, fish or meat dish, also cooked in spicy sauce.

The evening meal is a much simpler affair: dhosa, idli, chapati (similar to a Mexican tortilla except made with wheat flour), parotta (the Indian answer to croissants), and puri (a deep-fried relative of the chapati) are served with vegetables in a variety of sauces.